To Diane

Obey

PROTOCOL: BOOK TWO

LASAIRIONA LEWIS

Stay kinky!
Love Lasairiona

DRAMA LLAMA PUBLISHING

Also by

LASAIRIONA LEWIS

PROTOCOL

Book One: Control

Book Two: Obey

Book Three: Resist

Lasairiona also writes contemporary sports romance under

LASAIRIONA MCMASTER

Minnesota Snow Pirates

Two for Interference

Two for Holding

Two for Roughing

Two for Boarding

Two for Tripping

Two for Charging

Cedar Rapids Raccoons

Freezing the Puck

Pulling the Goalie

Crashing the Net

Lighting the Lamp

Dropping the Mitts

Riding the Pine

Splitting the D

Novellas

Two for Tacos

obey
LASAIRIONA LEWIS

Cover: Lori Jackson

Editor: Jess Snyder at HEA Author Services

Photographer: Jane Ashley Converse

Cover Model: Kail Walker

For all the good girls; the ones who went to school every day, followed all the rules, listened to their parents; the ones who waited to have sex, who stayed in unhappy relationships because they felt they 'should,' when all they really wanted to do was get on their knees and ttdlagg...

Dear Reader,

This book isn't going to be for everyone. If it's not for you, that's totally fine. Maybe next time. I'm also the first to admit that not all kink experiences are the same. This in my interpretation of how these characters experienced these kinks. If this hasn't been your experience, that doesn't make either experience wrong, just different. The beauty of kink is that it's not a one-size-fits-all model, and that's one of the things I love most about it.

I truly hope you enjoy Jagger and Talia's story, it was a joy to write, and I am so excited to share it with you.

Sincerely,
Lasairiona x

Content Warning

This book contains certain subjects some readers may be sensitive to, including but not limited to:

- Daddy kink (DD/LG)
- Religious trauma
- Death of a spouse from cancer (off page/in the past)
- Bangziety imminent – they don't DO IT for a long time in this book. YES, it's a slow burn, but NO, you're definitely not reading a clean/sweet romance. (Yeah, I'm putting it in the content warning so you can't 'at' me for them not boning off the bat, or for a while for that matter.)
- Snowballing (one partner ejaculates into the mouth of the other during oral sex, after which that partner transfers the semen back into the mouth of the ejaculator)

As with every book with content warnings or potentially sensitive subjects, please be cautious when undertaking this story and take care of your mental health.

CHAPTER 1
Talia

We all know how it goes.

When the tall, dark, built like a brick house man gets on the plane to Chicago and there's an empty, extra leg-room seat next to the bright-haired, bubbly pixie, they're destined to fall in love and get married.

I'm heading to Chi-town for the weekend before I head home to Kentucky, dragging my heels a bit because I'm not ready to face what's waiting for me.

So, when the giant brooding bastard—who looks like he should be a bronze statue in a museum—boards my plane and has to hunch his shoulders to make himself small to fit in the cabin, I'm already picking out my dress and cancelling my connecting flight.

Tipping my head back, I thank past Talia for splurging for the extra legroom. Though I kinda wish she'd have made me keep my waxing appointment. Can't sit next to the man of my dreams with prickly legs, and I certainly can't join the mile high club with an unruly bush.

My body heats as he approaches. It's not something I'd

have thought about before. But today, I'm not the Talia of old. I can be whoever I want to be.

And right now, I want to be a new-and-improved Talia who thinks words like "bastard" —even if it makes my whole body cringe—and who thinks about doing naughty things with strangers on a plane.

Though I do a quick shirt-check to make sure I don't have BBQ sauce from my lunch smeared down my chest.

All clear.

I have my bestest, peopliest smile ready to go. There's no way this cantankerous hulk of a man will be able to resist me. This is it, the moment I meet the man of my dreams. Harry-the-cheater will be nothing but a blip on my rearview mirror once this man starts talking to me and falls head-over-heels for the tiny bundle of joy from Louisville. There's snow coming down out the window. The setting is perfect. I'm ready.

Sucking in a breath, I prepare my greeting, but the giant keeps walking.

Huh? Maybe he doesn't like my brightly colored hair after all.

Don't be so silly, Tali, that's not what it is. There's assigned seating on this flight, so he isn't fated to sit next to me. It's nothing personal. It's not at all that he doesn't like my new do.

Though in truth, I'm not really sure I like it yet myself.

It's a new thing. As in, freshly done this morning. When my formerly honey-blonde, waist length locks tumbled onto the floor of the hairdresser's as she worked her magic giving me an undercut and colored it teal, I admit, I questioned my sanity.

But, having just found out my fiancé, my high school sweetheart, the boy I lost my virginity to, had grown up into a lying cheating scumbag... Well, it's not Weird Barbie by any means, but let's just say it wasn't a carefully calculated haircut.

I'm not generally impulsive, so as I reach a tentative hand to the underside of what remains of my hair, I shudder at the fuzzy feeling that meets my fingertips. Thankfully, she shaved it into a funky 'V,' so when my hair is tied into a ponytail, it doesn't look too weird.

I smother a giggle. My parents are going to absolutely poop their pants when they see it. Their rule abiding, Sunday school attending, straight A-student girl has never as much as colored outside the lines. And now she has a bright blue-green, Mohawk thing. I'm feeling Scarlett Johannsson right now. I imagine when I look in the mirror, though, it'll be quick to correct me.

This is... oh fudge. This is bad. This is really, really bad.

A tightness blooms in my chest, and my breath stutters as it tries to fill my lungs. Maybe he didn't mean to cheat? Maybe he tripped over something and his... his... boy thing accidentally slipped into her?

A low rumble rattles inside me as I try to rationalize his infidelity. Aside from the first time, the fateful time when I lost my V-card to him in high school, we haven't done it again since. "It's just as well considering he's a slimy snake."

When our parents sat us down and told us our act of sin, our "crime against God" had earned us an eternity together, I almost laughed. But they were deadly serious.

Then, after returning from our "True Love Waits" church camp weekend, they insisted our punishment, our penance to our maker, should be no more s-e-x before marriage. And my "beloved" fiancé nodded like one of those bobble head toys you can get.

He just agreed. Ha! I guess he agreed to their faces. Because from how acquainted he seemed with a woman I've never seen before, in what was supposed to become our marital home once I graduated college and moved home to Kentucky, it wasn't their first time.

Oh geez, maybe it *was* their first time, and he's a little... *deviant.*

My face and chest are hot and undoubtedly turning a dark shade of red as the scandalous memory replays in my mind.

I'm not completely clueless. I have a growing collection of spicy books on my Kindle app that I read when I'm alone. I wanted to try to learn how to do things, and anticipate my future husband's needs in the bedroom. I even made a bucket list of things we could try together once we're married that's tucked inside my journal.

Turns out, he was already trying them with someone else behind my back.

Unease shifts the contents of my stomach. Deep down, it's not really a surprise.

Harold Winslow the Third.

Right? Even his name makes him sound like a complete butt face. He's every bit as pretentious as he sounds, too.

The signs were all there. I glossed them over to appease my parents. I caused them great shame by sleeping with Harry. I confided in my older brother, Isaac, who squealed to our parents, and as my penance to *them,* never mind God, I followed their rules to the letter, as my way of saying sorry.

I hate being unkind about the boy I gave my heart to, but all things considered, he's lucky. It's been a couple weeks since I learned of his betrayal, but I haven't managed to calm down enough to talk to him, or my parents about any of it. In fact, the bubbling under my skin has intensified with time, not abated.

Oof. I need liquor. And I don't even drink all that much.

"This is your seat right here, sir. And again, thank you for swapping with that family so they could all sit together." The flight attendant touches her chest, with dreamy love hearts popping out of the side of her head, as Mr. Tall, Dark, and gruffly Handsome tosses a bag into the compartment above my head and drops onto the seat next to me.

Huh. There may be hope for my airplane romance after all.

I flash him a warm smile, but he doesn't even look my direction. Instead, his brow creases as he stares at his phone. I swallow down the sarcastic comment brewing in the back of my throat. As a southern woman, I've mastered the art of internally saying "bless your heart," with a wide smile pasted on my face. If my beautiful travel companion, who smells of the forest with an undertone of something I can't place, doesn't want to chit chat on the flight, then I'll leave him be.

But he's missing out. I'm a delightful conversationalist. In fact, I'm going to prove it to him.

"Hi." My warm smile returns, but he continues to ignore me.

Something about him holds my attention, he's wearing a simple button-down shirt with the top buttons popped open, and a pair of jeans.

"Business or pleasure?"

More silence. He has no jewelry on his hands, but the longer I stare at his golden-brown hands, the more I realize he has dirt in the grooves of his knuckles and under his nails which makes me cringe.

Is he a farmer? Does he like playing in dirt?

On closer inspection, he has smears of black across the thighs of his jeans as well.

Why would he travel covered in grime? Didn't he have time for a shower before he got on the plane?

Shifting as far away from him in my seat as I can, I turn my attention out the window while my row buddy pulls out a book.

"Wow." Holy moly! It's really coming down out there.

As much as I enjoy the fresh smells of spring, the warmth

of summer, and the crunch of leaves underfoot in Minnesota, I love the winters. Oversized sweaters, hot cocoa, open fires, and snow so deep you can make snow angels in. A dreamy sigh escapes me. "I could really go for some hot chocolate about now."

My seatmate doesn't respond, but he's probably not even a hot chocolate kinda guy. Which is saying something because, isn't everyone?

Winter is my idea of heaven. I tried to convince Harry to move up here, to Minnesota, permanently when we were both done with college, but it fell on deaf ears.

We don't have snow like this in Louisville, and I'm going to miss it when I move back home in a few months. My chest constricts again. Despite it being home, Kentucky isn't where I yearn to be, and it isn't where I want to return to. I'm not sure why. There's something about experiencing each season in all its intended glory that sets my soul on fire here in Minnesota.

The Captain comes over the intercom to announce a delay that's met by groans and a fairly loud F-bomb from further back in the plane.

I most definitely need a drink. Considering the fact I stepped out of the hairdressers this morning and fell on my face on the sidewalk, then got stuck in traffic due to an accident and had to run through the airport in a wholly undignified manner, I feel like I've earned myself a special treat. Maybe it'll distract me from my skinned and still pulsing palms.

When the flight attendants start their first pass with the drinks cart, I know we're going to be here a while. Either the pilot undersold the level of delay, or it's grown since his last announcement. Considering how much snow is already on the ground outside, I'd be surprised if we get to take off at all. But the professionals think they can do it, right? Or they wouldn't have let us board the plane.

I don't have payment options on my phone, so I need to stand up to get my bag down. "Excuse me, sir..." Letting my sentence trail off, I point to the aisle on the other side of his spread-wide knees. When his molten eyes meet mine, my lungs stop working. There's something so intense in them that holds me captive.

He cants his head as though he's waiting for me to say something. I mean, I stood up, I said excuse me, I pointed, can't he figure the rest out?

"I need to grab my bag." I point again to the overhead bin, like he might not know where I'm getting it from. The door to the plane is closed, so I'm hardly going to get it from the luggage hold.

"Okay." But he doesn't move. His face is unreadable. He has a strong nose and jaw, dark facial hair that's turning into a full-on beard, and if I'm not mistaken, tattoos peek out from under his shirt.

He sighs under his breath, bracing his hands on the arm rests either side of him.

"You know what? It's fine. I've got it." Steeling my spine, I drop my shoulders. If this imposing, greasy, rude man isn't going to move his sticky-outy knees for me to pass, then I'll just climb over him. I did gymnastics in high school, and I do yoga every morning. I've got this.

Picking my leg up with the grace of a gazelle, I step widely over him, half expecting applause from the surrounding passengers when my other foot makes it safely across into the aisle, too. Mildly surprised I didn't fall into his lap, I reach above his head to pop the handle of the luggage bin. He's put his bag in front of mine, and when I try to move it, well, let's just say I'm barely over five feet tall and not wearing heels.

"Uh... sir?"

His head barely moves to acknowledge I've spoken to him.

"Your bag is... uh..." Some days I hate being short.

Smoothing down the front of my shirt, I bite my lip. You know what? Nope. I'm not asking the grouchy guy next to me for his help. I can do it myself. My stomach is practically smashed into his face as I lean up into the bin, grasping blindly for some purchase on my bag.

"Ma'am?" The flight attendant's voice startles me from behind, I shriek, lean forward a smidge too far, and before I know what's hit me, I'm falling for the second time today.

Only this time, it's right into Mr. Crankypants's lap.

Strong, warm arms wrap around me, picking me up like I weigh nothing, and plop me back onto my feet between his legs.

"Thank you." My voice is barely a whisper. Heat consumes my entire body, and I don't know where to look. I can't look at my seat buddy. The vibes rolling off of him are less 'hey, no problem, it's all good, these things happen,' and more 'why did I give up my seat for that family?'

I can't look at the cabin crew either, so I return back to my mission to retrieve my bag. Because if I didn't need a drink before, I definitely need one now.

As I reach my arm up, I'm picked up off my feet again. Burly Guy—who has now rolled up his shirt sleeves revealing inked forearms that could probably rip the door to the plane open without unlocking it—moves me out of his space.

Reaching into the overhead locker with ease, he tugs my bag free and hands it to me, still scowling. When was the last time he smiled?

He sits down again with a grunt. I've never been so tempted to run through an airplane wall before. Prickles of humiliation cover every square inch of my body, and by now I'm sure even the cabin crew are experiencing second hand embarrassment on my behalf.

Peachy.

Staring up at the open lid of the luggage bin, I shake my

head. I know before reaching for it I can't close the stupid thing. Tossing a pleading look to the flight attendant and hoping they take pity on me, I scooch back into my seat, muscles heavy and a light coating of sweat sprouting up across my skin.

I order chardonnay, hand over my card, and accept the drink with no additional drama, politely thanking the cabin crew as they pass. The seatback tray table comes down without any fuss, and I make the decision to turn this day around.

Sure, I fell on my face, twice. Sure, I have sore hands and hurt pride. And sure, I'm seated next to a man who could probably snap me in half if he chose to.

But I have a mini bottle of wine, blue hair, and I'm heading home to Louisville.

Huh. There's that twinge again.

Putting the small bottle into my palm, I try twisting the top off but end up hissing in pain. Oh, no. I try the other one, same result. It's cruel and unusual to be holding a bottle of wine in my still-throbbing hands and be unable to open it.

I have two options, I can use my teeth—which I'd really prefer not to, last thing I need right now is a cracked tooth—or I can try again with The Grump.

Swallowing down the sour lump at the back of my throat, I spin in my chair, presenting him with the bottle. "Could you help me, please?"

CHAPTER 2
Jagger

SHE'S GOT TO BE FUCKING KIDDING ME, RIGHT?

When the blue-haired pain in my ass repeats her question, I wonder which part of my *fuck off and leave me alone* face let me down. Usually my R.B.F doesn't let me down with strangers. Resting bastard face. Works every time.

Usually.

Except right now.

Right now, the bubbly Half-Pint in the seat to my left stares up at me with wide eyes and up-turned palms covered in scratches and scrapes, holding out the bottle of liquor. Her pale, white skin is accentuated by various shades of blue, her bright blue hair, her sea-blue eyes, even her fingernails are painted blue.

She's giggling, nervousness making her voice shake. "I'm not normally so clumsy. I fell..." Her sentence trails off as though she sees something on my face that tells her I'm not in the mood to chat.

Heaving out a sigh, I roll my eyes.

It's like sitting next to a goddamn child.

Without another sound, I open the bottle and hand it back to her. The striking difference between her tiny, pale hand compared to my tawny bear-sized-paw is almost laughable. I want to say her blinding grin and sheepish thanks don't affect me, but the warmth behind the softly spoken "thanks," is undeniable, and seeps into my skin. Just a little.

"Can you believe how heavy it's coming down out there?" She hooks a thumb at the window before turning to give a wistful look outside. "You think we'll be able to take off?" She gnaws on her thumbnail.

I don't have headphones within reach. I left them at home. Usually my gruff disposition is enough to turn people off from making small talk. But Half-Pint isn't taking the hint.

What the fuck is she prattling about? Is she expecting me to answer? If she'd take a goddamn breath I'd consider getting a word in. Maybe. Probably not. Tipping my head back onto the headrest, I close my eyes. Would she even notice if I fell asleep? Do I need to be an active participant in this conversation?

Seems not, since she's even answering herself. She's playing both parts in the discussion and doesn't seem at all phased that I've checked out.

After a beat, her high-pitched voice stops for a blissful moment. Cracking open my left eye, just a slit, I hold my breath not wanting to draw attention to myself.

"Oh! You're awake. Thought I'd lost you for a second."

Fuck.

She's relentless.

I'm regretting my decision to let that family sit together. I want my seat back. I want my peace and quiet back.

Is this woman really telling me about her grandparents? The fuck?

As a mechanic, I'm surrounded by people all day every

day. Not just by my team in the garage, but I have to interact with clients, too. I get by. I mean, people aren't my favorite, but I make it work.

Yet I've never met someone who launches into their family history at the drop of a hat. I don't even know this woman's name, but her mamaw makes the best peach cobbler in the entire world. Her brother is married to a rodeo cowgirl who just broke her leg getting bucked off a prized horse. And her family dog is named Bark Twain.

She barely slows her roll to down the chardonnay before turning to me with a second little bottle of liquor. "Would you?"

My only hope at this stage is that consuming two drinks at speed will make her fall the fuck asleep so she shuts the hell up, and I can go back to reading my book.

She's been talking at me for so long I have no idea what the hell happened on the last page. Or even in the last chapter. My watch tells me it hasn't been days or hours. In fact, this elfish hurricane has been in my life for less than an hour.

With any luck, when I hand her back the second bottle of liquor, she'll leave me alone. As I crack the seal on the bottle, she gasps so loudly the people sitting across the aisle from us turn toward us.

Heat creeps up the back of my neck. If there was a trap door under my feet, I'd yank it open and take the emergency exit straight out of this tin can. She points at my hoodie now hanging from the chair in front of me. It ended up on the ground after our tangle when she landed in my lap, I figured hanging it up was the safe bet, but apparently it only makes her want to talk even more.

"You went to the University of Minnesota?"

My stomach drops. I don't want to have anything in common with this woman, because it seems any potential shared interests will result in lengthy conversations I have no interest in pursuing.

She doesn't wait for an answer. "Oh. Em. Gee. I went there too. And so did Harry, my fiancé."

The tension in my body loosens at the announcement that she's off the market, and she's not hitting on me. If she was, she's going about it the wrong way. I love a woman who knows the value of comfortable silence. Or at least one who doesn't fill every single goddamn moment with banal chatter.

Speaking of quiet, she's been silent for longer than a heartbeat, so I risk a glance. Her face has crumpled, her shoulders curled, and her head hangs. If I focus really hard on her mouth, her chin trembles.

Oh, fuck no. Is she going to cry?

It's too late to get my seat back from the family a few rows back, but perhaps there's a chance the captain will trade seats with me so I can escape the ball of emotions sitting next to me. I'm a quick study. I'd happily fly this bird to Chicago, if he'd take Little Miss Chatterbox off my hands.

Sounds like a fair exchange to me.

She seems to have forgotten I'm sitting next to her. She's muttering about what a cheating dillweed this guy was and how she didn't expect to be single on her visit back to her grandparents. The ice wall around my heart thaws. Just a little. There's nothing worse than an asshole who steps out on his woman.

Digging into my back pocket, I pull out my handkerchief and offer it to the now sniffing bundle of palpable sadness. She stares at the piece of cloth in my hand, then my face, then the handkerchief, then my face.

I wiggle the fabric a little. If she doesn't take it soon my momentary lapse in judgment is going to expire.

Her button nose wrinkles, and her shoulders shake. Is she... laughing at me?

"You're quite the contradiction, Mr. Grumpypants, aren't you?"

Mr. Grumpypants? Shaking my head, I can't help but roll my eyes. Again. I'm a fit guy, but my eyeballs haven't had this level of workout in a long time.

I mean, she's also not wrong.

"You use handkerchiefs?" She tips her head, whatever emotional outburst that was brewing within her only moments ago having simmered down at least for the time being.

Maybe if I give her a tidbit of personal information it will feed her for the flight. "My grandfather used to carry handkerchiefs. He said it was the key to a long and successful marriage."

"That's a lot of responsibility for such a small square of material."

I offer it to her again, and she accepts it before blowing her nose. For a moment it seems like she's thinking about offering me back the now snot-covered cloth as indecision flits across her face, but instead, she scrunches it in her hand and places it on her lap.

There's a moment of blissful silence that's verging on euphoric. But I'm not naive enough to think I'm getting the quiet I need to read my fucking book. I lean my head back, and just as my eyes are drifting shut, she sniffs. "Were you close?"

"To what?" Refusing to turn my head, I let my eyes drift closed. Maybe if I start snoring she'll give up. Wouldn't count on it.

"Your grandfather."

I was. My parents worked multiple jobs to make ends meet. They were always so busy that my grandparents played a pivotal role in my childhood. I miss my gramps more than I care to admit, and the urge to press my fist into my chest, to massage away the ache his death left me as a teenager, is consuming. She doesn't need to know that, though. She's gotten her factoid about me. And unlike her, I don't share my life story with strangers on a plane.

So instead, I simply grunt in response.

"Ladies and Gentlemen, this is your captain speaking. As you can see, it's coming down pretty heavy outside. Despite our best efforts, air traffic control has reported all flights are being grounded, and the airport is closing until the storm passes."

The collective groan is so loud the captain is drowned out for a long moment. He's probably telling us to talk to our flight carriers about rescheduling our flights, but half the passengers are already on their feet grabbing their luggage from the overhead bins.

Half-Pint is praying for everyone in the storm, she's asking God to keep everyone safe and return them all to their families. She pauses, cracks the eye closest to me, and adds "even Mr. Grumpypants. Amen."

Another gasp. "Was that a...?" She points at my face. "Smile?"

Shaking my head, I cuss internally.

"I think it was." She beams like she's won the lottery and doesn't have to pay tax.

"You want out?" Jerking my thumb at the throng congregating in the aisle.

"I'll wait." She pulls out her phone and pounds the keyboard for a few moments. I should probably do the same, but I'm not sure who lives close enough to the airport to come and get me in this weather.

I left my car at Protocol—one of the local kink clubs where I work as a house dominant—and one of my colleagues brought me up to the airport. I don't like leaving my pride and joy, my car, my baby, Raquel, in the airport parking lot. She draws too much attention. At least at work, there are cameras in the parking lot and enough people around to keep an eye on her.

But I didn't have a plan for getting snowed in at Minneapolis-Saint Paul International Airport. Fuck. I should have bounded up out of my seat and hit the rental desk to grab a car. Shooting off a bunch of texts to friends in the area, I mentally cross my fingers.

My seat mate shivers, still looking out the window to her left. As though she's reading my thoughts, she turns to me, concern piercing me from her stare. "Do you have a ride?"

My phone pings with any number of laughing emojis in response to my request to get picked up. I'm fucked.

In the half-beat I hesitate with my answer, she must read something on my face.

"My car is at the airport. As long as it starts I can give you a ride home."

Another long pause from me doesn't dissuade her.

Another phone chime, more laughing emojis.

"Please? You were so nice to me on an otherwise sucky day." She flashes her cut up hands at me. "Let me do something nice for you."

She's a bullshitter. I don't do nice. And for a half second when I first moved to this seat and ignored her bubbly disposition it took her a long minute to slide her smile onto her face. Then she got pissed I wasn't chatty like she is. She was big mad I was rude to her off the bat.

She gasps again. Thankfully people are too busy trying to deplane to pay her much attention. "I've been drinking." She gestures to the empty glass on her tray table. "I can't drive after that."

Fuck. She's probably not wrong. But she's also not my

problem. She got herself into this, she can get herself out of it. She's a grown-ass woman.

When the aisle clears, I stand up and grab my bag from overhead, then, before she can ask me to pull hers down too, I sit hers on the chair I vacated.

"Thanks." She stands and shuffles into the aisle. "Hey, so, do you drive? If so, you could drive my car. It makes no sense you trying to find a ride in this weather. Unless you have some really daredevil friends, I doubt you'll find anyone to come out here and grab you."

Another check of my messages, and it seems she's right. I'm on my own. The weather is bad across the city and people are staying the fuck home where they can. I don't blame them, even if it's inconvenient for me.

Ugh. Fuck. Generally speaking, I don't do strangers. I have my people, and they're my people, and I don't need new people. But I need a ride back to Raquel and this chick needs to put some time between the alcohol and driving anywhere.

Logically, it makes sense. Even if I don't like it.

We deplane and head back into the airport. A frenzy of people and noise and movement surround us. There's no way I'm getting out of here alive by myself, and if she stays here she'll probably end up offering to drive a serial killer or two home.

She's not my responsibility, but I'd rather not be interviewed by the cops or a news crew when her dead body is found post-thaw. Why she's even offering to drive me anywhere when I could be one of the aforementioned serial killers is anyone's guess. But *I* know I'm not a serial killer, and I'd rather not feed her to one by leaving her here.

That said, if anyone could chase away a murderer it'd be this woman. She'd talk at them until they curled into a ball on the floor.

She's still talking at me. Though at this point I have no idea about what.

She grabs me by the elbow and jerks me forward so hard I almost let go of my hand luggage. She's surprisingly strong for a five-feet tall word tornado. "Come on, Mr. Grumpypants. Let's go find Bessie and get out of here."

Who the fuck is Bessie?

CHAPTER 3

Jagger

Turns out, Bessie is a two hundred year old, piece of crap Camry. There's rust on the doors, the trunk doesn't close all the way—so much so, it's tied closed with a piece of rope—and at least two of her tires are damn near bald.

I dread to think of what Bessie looks like under the hood.

Raking my hands through my hair, I'm struggling not to look a gift horse in the mouth. But this gift horse is asthmatic, on life support, and could crap out at any moment. "What the fuck is this?" Apparently, I'm not only *looking* a gift horse in the mouth, I'm giving it a verbal smack for good measure.

She leans toward the car, dusting snow off the hood. "Don't listen to the grumpy man, Bessie. You're a beautiful, strong, and capable machine, and we really need for you to dig deep and take us to safety. Okay?"

I'd laugh at her for talking to her car, but my own ride, Raquel, is probably my best friend. She doesn't talk back, doesn't let me down, and doesn't judge me for not being a bright and sunshine-y dude like a lot of humans do.

Without another word, I hold my hand out for the keys.

She looks at it, looks up at me, then slides her hand into my palm.

Oh, for fuck's sake.

Pulling my hand from hers, I shake my head before reaching across to take the keys from her other hand.

Her hands flutter to her mouth, but she doesn't speak. Her face turns crimson, jaw hanging open as she stares at the keys in my grasp, not making eye contact.

Leaving her to her feelings, I circle the car and get in. I'm not a religious man, but I consider sending up a prayer to whoever might be listening for this piece of shit car to start.

My travel buddy slips into the passenger seat, the worn and cracked leather squeaking under her ass as she settles in place. "Bessie knows you're judging her."

Good. She fucking should. This car should have been sent to car heaven years ago. It's probably older than this chick's mamaw who makes peach cobbler. Almost on cue, my stomach gives a roar. First stop, food. Otherwise neither of us will make it to where we're supposed to be.

Mercifully, Bessie doesn't need any foreplay to get her going. She starts first time, and we inch our way out of the airport.

"You good with Wendy's?"

The woman has finally fallen silent. She's not asleep, but her eyes are glazed over as she stares out the window at the growing sheet of white coating everything in sight.

When I touch her arm to get her attention, she flails, catching my face with the back of her tiny hand. If she was bigger than a fairy, that could have done some damage.

"OhmygoodnessohmygoodnessohmygoodnessI'msosorry-Ididn'tmeantohityou." She doesn't take a breath, I'm not quite sure what she said, but her hand now rests on my forearm, and I hate that I don't hate it. Especially since she's leaving my jaw alone. That actually kinda stung.

"Wendy's?"

She purses her lips like she's giving it real consideration. "Chili cheese baked potato, twenty spicy nuggets, and a large chocolate Frosty." That crimson color seeps back into her cheeks.

Given the state of the roads, she'll get what she gets.

"Please." Her voice is quieter, and her eyes are focused on something that isn't me.

If I wasn't driving I might be tempted to hook my knuckle under her chin and make her look at me. "You sure that's what you want? I'm getting a burger. If you want a burger, get your own. I don't share food."

Her head snaps back to me, eyebrows arched. "I don't either. Get your own spicy nuggets." She folds her arms, a challenging glint flickering in her eye like she's daring me to comment on the amount of food she wants me to get for her. What she wants to put in her body isn't any of my business. Unless what she wants to put in her body is attached to me.

Her face falls when I don't say anything back to her. I want to laugh, but I don't want her to take that as a sign I'm warming to her. I'm not.

It takes an extraordinarily long time to get to Wendy's. I'm not sure if it's because her car sucks, the weather's bad, or everyone's driving like it's their first time behind the wheel. Might be a combination of all three.

By the time I hand her the bag of food at the drive thru, her stomach is growling even louder than mine. I've never seen someone so gleefully happy to be given food before. Her smile is so bright I might go blind. I have to force myself to look away.

She wastes no time before diving in. Instead of tearing into her nuggets, she carefully, half unwraps my burger and folds the excess paper around it before handing it to me. She pauses before I can accept. "Do you eat fries first?"

I can't give her the look I want to because we'd end up in a snow bank. "I eat it how it comes." I'm not fussy. In fact, if I had more hands and space, I'd toss my fries into my burger. But I'm not asking her to do that for me. She's not my personal servant.

Though the thought sends a brief shudder through my spine.

She hands me the burger. "Let me know when you're ready for your fries, 'kay?"

What do I do with that? Usually, my co-pilots take their food, drop the bag with my shit on my lap, and I've got to figure it out for myself.

When one of the condiments on my burger trickles down my chin, I shove my hand in the door pocket for napkins. Except this rust bucket isn't my car, and there's something sticky inside.

Now I have a burger in one hand, something sticky on the other, something running down my chin, and a car to keep on the road with limited visibility and using my knees to steer through snow.

This wasn't my smartest plan.

A hand clutching a napkin shoots out and catches the liquid before it drops onto my shirt. She mops my face like a mother hen, pats it a couple times, then takes my burger away.

She digs into the bag at her feet and produces hand sanitizer. "Hands out." She drops a blob onto my palms, and I scrub away the gluey crap on my fingers, dry my hands on my jeans, and rescue my burger from her.

After I take a giant bite, she clicks her tongue. "You're welcome."

I can't help but laugh at her passive aggression, or rather, straight up southern aggression, which forces the food I swallowed to get lodged in my chest, making me cough-snort. Pretty sure I have lettuce in my nostrils.

This woman.

It takes a long moment to swallow down the stuck hunk of beef and wash it down with a gulp of pop. "Thank you."

Her lips twitch. "You're welcome."

We eat in silence, and to her credit, she clears every morsel of everything she ordered. I'm starting to think she's a sociopath though. Who gets a Frosty without getting fries to dip into it?

Feels like Wendy's blasphemy if you ask me. Why do they even let her eat there?

"How old are you?" She asks.

"Twenty five."

"Any siblings?"

"Nope, only child." Usually I wouldn't entertain rapid-fire question-time like this, but if she wants to poke into my life to make sure I'm not a murderer, then I'll do whatever makes her more comfortable in this situation.

"Favorite fruit?"

"Pineapple." It's not, but there's an almost in-joke in the kink community about pineapple being a safe-word. My joke falls flat.

She rolls her lips, a 'v' appearing between her brows. "Good choice. Not my favorite, but good choice."

Huh. I guess she's big into her fruit.

"If you could go anywhere in the world and cost or time wasn't an issue, where would you go?"

Away from this fucking situation I've somehow found myself stuck in. "Japan."

"Where do you live?" She's craning to look out the window, her brows scrunched in confusion as the white wonderland out the window passes by at a snail's pace.

"My car's at work." I fold the last few fries into my mouth, hoping my answer didn't crack the door to further questioning.

"Where do you work?"

"A garage." I'm not telling her I work at a sex club. Mary Poppins here would probably cry and attempt to launch herself out of the moving vehicle. Granted, we aren't going all that fast at the moment, and there's a thick blanket of snow on the ground, but I bet she'd do some damage if she ejected herself out the door.

"And a bar."

She hums. There's a quick beat of judgmental silence then the car pings. It could be the temperature alert to tell us it's getting colder outside, but the check engine light comes on.

Goddamn mother fuck. Of course I get sat beside someone who doesn't maintain their held-together-by-tape-and-rope vehicle.

"Don't panic. Bessie does this sometimes. You don't need to check the engine."

"The hell I don't." I said the quiet part out loud again.

She flinches, not sure whether it's at the language choice, the tone, or the fact I told her she's wrong.

Fire flashes in her eyes before she leans forward to poke my arm. "Listen here, Grumpasaurus. I know how to take care of my car. I can change a fuse, change a headlight bulb, check the oil and the battery connections, *and* fill up the wiper fluid." She huffs. "Technically I can change a tire too, but I'm usually not strong enough to loosen the nuts."

Her indignation is adorable, like a storm in a teacup. There's something hot as hell about that spark of life. Also about the fact she claims she can maintain her car to that extent. She's probably right about loosening the nuts to change a tire, she looks like I could pick her up and put her in my pocket.

"I'm still going to check." It's the responsible thing to do, especially in inclement weather. I wouldn't bet on her having an emergency kit in the trunk. And even if she did, I'm not sure she could untangle the knot holding the damn thing shut.

I pull over and pop the hood. To her credit, it's pretty clean and well maintained. She could do with a washer fluid top up, especially in a fucking snow storm, but nothing seems out of place.

"Told you so." She doesn't sound smug or patronizing when she speaks, more defeated. Whatever her damage, it isn't my problem.

By the time we pull into the Protocol parking lot, it's really coming down, and an emergency weather alert comes through on our phones saying that the city is shutting down. I'm not sure we're going to get very far beyond the club.

With a heavy sigh, I cut the engine and turn to my Half-Pint co-pilot. "You should come inside."

Her brows bounce up her forehead. "Wh-what?" She's got a "He's most definitely a serial killer" look on her face.

I gesture out the window.

She blinks.

Sighing again, I pull out my cell and find the weather report and radar. I don't know where she lives, but the whole city is getting worse by the second. Her face pales as she eyes the map on the screen. Then silently slow blinks yet again.

"I can't get home." Her breathing skips faster. She stares at her own phone, back out the window, then back at me. Her jaw trembles. "I can't get home." She whispers it this time.

"You can't get home." It seems like she needs confirmation there's no hope either of us are leaving this parking lot any time soon. I'm not responsible for this woman or what she chooses to do, but she'd be fucking stupid if she tries to leave right now. And she'll freeze to death if I leave her here in the parking lot in *Bessie*, the car that seems close to taking her last breath.

She texts someone, then hangs her head in her hands with

a groan. "I could stay out here." Her body's already shivering from the cold, there's no way she can sit out here. She'd harden into an ice cube before long.

"Get out of the car, Half-Pint."

"Excuse me?"

With a shrug, I pull the door open. "You called me Grumpasaurus. Turnabout is fair play. Come on, before we both freeze."

Reluctantly, she opens the car door and grabs her bag. I've got the door to the club open before she's even circled the vehicle. This woman has no self-preservation. She needs to hustle or I'll reconsider letting her stay outside with her friend Bessie and the fucking weather.

She's got a thin dusting of snow on her when she steps into the building. The heat is off, but the space isn't frigid. Yet.

"I'll go and turn the heat on."

She shudders, brushing the snow off her. "I'll be here." She's looking around the space. From this position, Protocol looks like a regular old bar. As long as she doesn't wander down to the dungeon, we should be fine.

I'm reluctant to leave her by herself, but I don't want to take her with me. "There's bottled water in the fridge behind the bar."

Her cautious glance tells me she's a rule follower, and the idea of going behind the bar where only employees should go makes her uncomfortable, which, of what little I know of her, tracks.

An edgy haircut does not an edgy person make. She's a Miss Goodie two shoes. She glides her hand up the back of her neck. I'm not sure whether it's a nervous thing, or an adjusting to her new haircut thing, but either way it's cute as hell.

"Can't I come with you?"

Fuck no.

At least I kept that inside my brain.

"It's downstairs." I almost said "In the dungeon," but caught myself at the last minute.

She shivers again, looking over both shoulders. If I had to guess, something about the building is ringing her fight-or-flight, and she can't figure out why. Neither can I. My money says once she gets to the bottom of the dungeon stairs and sees the St. Andrew's Cross she's going to bolt like a racehorse out of the gate.

"There's no one else here. You'll be okay."

She doesn't look convinced, hugging her arms around her. "Please?" Her small, uncertain voice speaks to something inside my chest.

"Fine. But you're going to need to brace yourself for what's at the bottom of those stairs."

Her shoes squeak as she slams on the brakes. "Wh-what's at the bottom of the stairs?"

Just gotta pull off the Band-Aid in one quick tear. "Half-Pint, you're standing above a sex club."

A semi-hysterical laugh squeaks out from between her lips. The way she's tilting her head and squinting at me suggests she's waiting for the punchline. But when it doesn't come, she swallows. Hard.

Here it comes.

After a long moment where she looks like she might puke up her spicy nuggets, she nods. "Oh. Okay."

That's all she says before she strides toward the stairs. I don't know her enough to read how she's really feeling, but I can tell she's shitting her pants under her vaguely calm exterior. Her face is pale, beyond white, she's tinged with green. She's picking at the cuticles on one of her fingernails, and she keeps glancing around like a murderer may jump out from the shadows at any second.

There's vanilla, and then there's Half-Pint.

To her credit, yet again, she's steeled her spine, and she's not been dissuaded by the fact that at the bottom of the stairs is a den of debauchery and fuckery. I should probably stay close behind her in case she passes out at the sight of the sex apparatuses when she hits the dungeon.

"You could stay up here if you wanted to."

She's stopped at the top of the stairs, staring down into the darkness, clutching the handrail next to the staircase. She sweeps her free hand. "In for a penny..." Her nervous laugh is back as she sweeps her hand toward the darkness. "Mr. Grumpasaurus, lead the way to your dungeon of depravity."

CHAPTER 4
Talia

I GET TWO STEPS DOWN AND CHANGE MY MIND. THIS is beyond sensible. So I double back on myself. "I'll stay up here." There's a note of hysteria to my voice, that's contrasted by his silence as he continues his descent into the quiet.

The silence is creeping me out, but I'm in a sex club that this stranger coincidentally has the keys to, and I'm supposed to just willingly going down the stairs with him where he could do anything to me? I think not.

I don't know how long I stare into the darkness, but the hairs on the back of my neck are standing to attention. I'm bouncing on the balls of my feet, and the throbbing in my palms is back. I can hear my heart beating, my heavy breathing, and... Oh my goodness. What was that?

A noise behind me sends a chill through my whole body, and suddenly I'm halfway down the stairs, choosing time with the guy from the plane in a sex dungeon over whatever made the noise up above.

With each step I take down the staircase, my chest tightens, and the air thins. I have no idea what I've gotten myself into. If Dad saw me now, he'd probably take his belt to me.

Not that he's ever been physically abusive to me before, but this would give him pause.

It was foolish to get into Bessie with a stranger. I still don't know his name! It was worse to let him drive me to a building I didn't know the address of, or even what it was, without more information. And I absolutely, positively had no business walking into a s-e-x dungeon with the man who's currently looking at me with a glint in his eye.

If he thinks he's getting near my person at the bottom of these stairs, he has another think coming.

He knows I'm single, but that doesn't mean I'm open for anyone to come by and do business. That's not how I work.

In hindsight, staying upstairs by myself was probably the more sensible plan. But I've spent my whole life being sensible. New Talia is pushing herself out of her comfort zone, facing new things like getting her hair shaved and coloring it blue. And apparently going to deserted sex clubs with strangers in snow storms.

And now he's staring at me with a raised eyebrow. Is there something on my face telling him I've barely lost my... eh... v-card?

My face heats. I read dirty books. I know what happens in the type of dungeon I'm walking down into, but I can't make my skin cool down, even with the bite in the air. I've almost made it all the way to the bottom, but my foot slips as I approach the last step, and I miss the landing.

He doesn't even grunt when he catches me. He picks me up and dumps me back on my feet.

"Sorry." I smooth down my shirt. I guess I didn't wait as long as I thought I did to bolt down the stairs behind him.

"It's fine. Happens more than you'd think."

To me that suggests someone should probably look at the step and make sure it's not something bigger than being overwhelmed by a dungeon full of sexy times, but that might be wishful thinking.

When I find my balance, he steps around me to flip on a light. After a beat of adjusting to the shift, I blink a couple times. Shapes start forming, and I take a step back, apologizing to the handrail as I bump into the staircase.

The giant man chuckles. I try to tell my body it's not supposed to react to the grumpy man, but it's not listening. There's something about the timbre of his laugh that warms my insides. Does he... participate in the activities this place is designed for?

I swallow, but my mouth is dry. There's a giant cross in the space I find myself in. The temptation to bless myself is overwhelming as my feet remain glued to the cold floor. This is a St. Andrew's cross. I know this from the select few books I've read that passed the exit for steamy-ville and took me straight to kink-city.

I don't know what most of these other things do, benches, tables, rooms branching out from dark corridors. Drawing in a long, slow breath, I'm surprised when I don't smell anything but the vaguely lemon tinged scent of cleaning products.

I guess when s-e-x is your business, you make sure people clean up after themselves. Or you employ someone to do the cleaning for the whole building.

Either way, the smell isn't offensive. If I concentrate, there's a musky edge to the air, patchouli? Or some incense? It's not bad.

Mr. Grump chuckles again. "Searching for the scent of the debauchery and depravity?"

My cheeks burn as I fold my arms across my body to protect myself from this man's judgment. "I figured there'd be... I don't know." The wind has left my sails, and I'm kind of standing here, rolling onto the balls of my feet. Waiting. For what, I'm not sure. I'd say for the ground to open up and swallow me, but given my surroundings, I wouldn't put it past the place to have a trap door. And who knows where that would lead?

"We do wipe down the equipment you know. We aren't completely feral." From the wolfish smirk on his face, he's baiting me, like a predator toying with his food.

Trying to fight a reaction showing on my face, I shelve that nugget of information away in my chest. Mr. Still-don't-know-his-name might be one of the single most beautiful people on the planet, but he's probably into things I couldn't ever be into.

Though the idea of those kinds of *things* coming to life off the pages makes my soul burn. The books I read weren't born from ignorance. I mean, I *was* clueless for the longest while. All it took was a bestie with a penchant for Mafia romance novels, curiosity, and an eReader, and I got lost down the rabbit hole.

A piece of my brain knew people did a lot of the things in my books in real life, but I guess I'd never really put the two together until now, when I'm standing in front of a kinky man who looks like he might want to eat me. Whole.

Dad has told me many times I never know when to back down, and it seems this grumpy, deviant butt-face brings out the worst in me. Planting my hands on my hips, I flare my nostrils. "I'm aware. Though for a place of this size I'd have expected..." I give him a one-shouldered shrug. "More."

His brow twitches, but the eye roll suggests he doesn't believe me. I don't blame him, I don't belong in a place like this. I stick out like a sore thumb. I'm an anomaly. Nothing about this space makes me comfortable. Not the colors, the furniture, not the fact we're here alone—and I bet I'd feel even worse if there were more people here.

It's one thing reading it between the covers of a book on my eReader where I can dip my toes into the dirty underbelly of sexy things without jumping in with both feet. But standing in a real-life club like this reaffirms this space is absolutely not my jam.

"Sure. I bet you go to places like this all the time." He pauses, rolling his lips between his teeth like he might laugh, but schools his face just in time. He doesn't crack a smile. "For research." There's a challenge in his voice.

I'm being baited again, toyed with, teased, and while part of me wants to shrink away from the conversation, another, much smaller and unhinged piece of me wants to whip off my shirt, or go lie on one of the benches to show him I know exactly what to do with the equipment I'm surrounded by.

Except I don't. I'd most definitely do it wrong.

And if I were to take my shirt off he'd get a Birdseye view of my plain, white cotton bra. Guys like him don't do plain Jane underwear. It's not wild enough, or lacy enough, or adventurous enough, or full enough for that matter.

A shiver rolls through my bones, it has little to do with the cooler temperature down here and all to do with the way his stare bores through my clothing. This man is dangerous. Not in the I-gave-a-psychopath-a-ride kind of way, but from the heat blazing in his eyes, the tattoos curling up his neck and peeking out from the cuffs of his sleeves, and the way he carries himself as he walks and speaks, this man screams danger.

Which would be fine if I could hear my parent's warnings in my head right now. All I can hear is a voice whispering to move toward the fire, to reach out and touch the glow, despite knowing I'd undoubtedly get scorched.

His pull is strong, like planets caught in the sun's orbit. But unlike earth as she circles the sun, I'm not sure I can hold my line and stay at a safe distance.

I need to get back outside into the snow. That'll send the arctic chill to my core and put out the fire raging in my loins, right? It'll wake me up from this caught-in-a-snowstorm-with-a-beautiful-stranger moment, and remind me of the danger being in a sex dungeon with someone I don't know could bring.

I'm a smart woman. I have a business degree—no intention of using the darn thing mind you. My ex is setting up the practice we talked about Mr—and—Mrs—ing once we graduated. But my heart's not in it now that I know he's not prone to using his superpowers for good.

Part of me also knows I'm drawn to the grumpy stranger because he's the exact opposite of everything Harry is. Or rather, what I thought he was. Tall, dark, bad boy vibes ooze from him as he regards me. Is he assessing me? Do I get points for different things? Where do I fall on his scale?

Tiny, munchkin sized woman.

Perfectly average in every aspect.

Green around the gills with zero experience.

My face heats. Why am I even thinking about him thinking about me? He's probably staring at me wondering how his favorite sports team will do over the weekend. Who knows?

He hooks a thumb over his shoulder. "Are you going to be okay here for a sec while I go turn the heat on?" He shivers. "It's chilly."

Nodding slowly, I take in my surroundings all over again. "Sure. Go ahead." I wave him off like it's no big deal. Like the wrought iron fixtures, dark velvet drapes, low lighting and plush leather sofas people have done who knows what on don't intimidate me.

There's not a single surface in this place I want to sit down on. Even though he says he cleans up after himself. As I trip over my feet, catching myself on an unlit standalone sconce, my mind wanders. What has he done down here? And with whom?

Is he one of the dominants I read about? Or would he surprise me and be a submissive?

A laugh catches at the back of my throat. His presence is too imposing, too intense, too bossy and protective for him to be submissive, right?

I can't come right out and ask him, but the question burns my tongue. The urge to investigate is too strong to ignore. I need to look around, and since no one's here to stop me, I do. The corridor I've chosen has rooms branching off on each side, they've got numbers on the doors, and despite knowing no one's inside, I still knock.

My giggle echoes around the hall as I twist the handle and push the door. As soon as I take a step into the room, my lungs expel every ounce of breath in a microsecond. I feel like I'm in an old castle. There's a commanding, ornate, dark wood with gold accent throne sitting in the room on the far side of a giant window. The floor is bare wood, dark, with a plush cream rug sitting underneath the throne.

On a plush blue velvet cushion lies an equally lavish crown. There's no way it can be authentic, but it also doesn't look fake. It looks like if it rested on my head I'd feel it's presence in all of my muscles.

Money drips from every piece of the space. Even the walls and the various toys and implements hanging from hooks scream opulence. This isn't a seedy establishment. I might not know much about much, but I know that. The mix of textures, the furry rug, the smooth satin, the intricate golden work on the chair makes me want to enter the room and trail my fingers over all of it, just to see how it all feels on my skin.

The window suggests whatever happens on the throne is destined to be viewed by whoever stands over there. I'm guessing it's some kind of voyeur room. I'm not sure if the idea horrifies me, or intrigues.

The walls look like castle walls, giant concrete blocks

exposed, but perhaps if I were to touch over them I'd discover it was extravagant wallpaper. It couldn't possibly be real brick, could it?

How do the people feel who sit on the throne? What do they wear? What things do they do?

I've read a few BDSM books but none of them have a throne. What's the goal of the chair? To make people feel strong, empowered, beautiful? I have to admit, I'm surprised at the royal vibes the room is giving off. If I had to guess before coming down the stairs I'd say these rooms would have been used to degrade people, make them subjects, not queens.

And yet.

"Want to sit in it?" Grumpy Smurf's voice is so close to my ear it skates across my skin leaving gooseflesh blooming in its wake. I can't fight the shiver, or the sharp intake of breath, I can't fight the tilt of my head to the side as my bones ache for him to do it again.

"No." My breathy voice communicates my lie. Curiosity burns my insides. It wouldn't do any harm, would it? To sit on the throne wearing a crown? I can't see how it would, as long as this man understands it wasn't an invitation to do anything. Maybe just for a moment?

"Liar." The single word falls from his lips caressing the sensitive skin at the nape of my neck.

I don't move. But every time I breathe, my back grazes his chest. The rise-and-fall of my body gliding against his rock-hard chest makes me feel things I'm not qualified to feel.

"What's it going to be, Half-Pint?" That challenge in his voice might be my undoing. I'm deciding right here right now I don't want to know his name, it makes him mysterious and even more intense, and if I know his name, it might ruin whatever this experience could be for me.

His words skim my skin again, making me shiver, and the

rest of my higher brain function and ability to rationalize, falls away.

Maybe it's being snowed in a s-e-x dungeon with a beautiful devil man that provokes the next words threatening to fall from my lips. Or it could be the fact I can be whoever I want to be in this moment. I don't have to be heartbroken Talia whose boyfriend cheated on her. I can be this new blue haired, punk-esque spitfire who sits on thrones in dungeons while wearing a crown.

"Okay."

CHAPTER 5
Jagger

I DIDN'T THINK SHE'D DO IT.

I have no idea what I thought would happen when I challenged the sunshiny tigress into sitting on the throne in one of my favorite rooms in the damn building. But here we are.

Well, she hasn't actually sat on the thing yet, she's staring it down like it might bite her in the ass. It's okay, though, we have time. We aren't going anywhere fast. I'm glad we stopped for food on the way here. This place is well stocked with high energy snacks for after intense sessions in the rooms, but there's nothing like a greasy burger in a snow storm, with a gorgeous woman, even if she's probably terrified of you.

Or something.

Half-Pint tentatively reaches a hand toward the dark, ornate wooden chair. Her fingers flinch. I expect her arm to recoil, but a shiver rolls through her when she skims the wooden finish. She steps to the side so she can walk around the seat. Eyes closed, she explores with her fingers as she moves around the throne.

Is this how she always is? Or is she internally freaking out at the idea of sitting on a sex seat in front of me, and she needs an out?

The gruff clearing of my throat in the otherwise silent room makes her start. "You don't have to, you know."

Consent can always be revoked. That's one of the cornerstones of kink, and while some people get off on non-consensual sexual activities, I'm not one of them. If the woman doesn't want to sit on the throne, she doesn't have to. No skin off my nose.

And nothing she should be ashamed about either. I'm not going to gloat or be smug that she didn't rise to my challenge. Disappointed, maybe, but only because I know there's fire in that tiny belly of hers.

I'm not sure if my declaration helped or hindered Half-Pint's decision. She's rounded the chair and now faces me, her fingers still on the shiny wooden arm, blue eyes wide open. I can't read her, and something about that bothers me.

I shouldn't be surprised when she plops down on the purple velvet seat, but I am. And a deep satisfaction claws through my chest and into my veins. Now that *is* surprising.

Now, what?

Your move, shortcake.

She closes her eyes again as she tips her head back against the cushioned headrest. I can't tell if she's closing her eyes to enjoy the experience, or to avoid having to look at me. No reason it can't be both.

Her feet don't touch the floor, which is probably to be expected. She swings her legs a little, and my hand twitches. The restraints around the legs are adjustable. If she was my woman, she'd already be cuffed.

Turning away from her, I shake my head. The close quarters are getting to me. I'm not used to having people in my space, especially balls of bright, bubbly energy like this one.

The fact she's a blank canvas calls to my inner educator. A stunning piece of clay to be shaped into a timeless piece of art.

Ugh.

Just because she's new in the club doesn't mean she doesn't know who she is and what she's about. *Not everyone has to become part of your deviant world, Jagger.* The barb from an old girlfriend settles under my skin like an intruder. I need to pull myself together.

Being in a confined space with a stranger is often my idea of a good time. But not this stranger. Especially when she looks at me like one second she's afraid I'm going to growl at her, and the next she's judging my jeans and tattoos.

"It's more comfortable than it looks."

When I turn back to the Mighty Mite, her eyes are open, and she's staring straight at me, head tilted to one side. Her hands move back and forth on the armrests like she's appraising the furniture before deciding to buy. I can't help smiling.

"Why is that amusing to you?" Her brows crunch, and I'll be damned if she isn't the most adorable disgruntled person I've ever seen. "Well?" She's barely given me a breath to answer, and her impatience is like a rag to a bull.

"Just is."

Something flares in her eyes at my dismissal. She should be damn near swallowed up by the imposing stature of the throne, but something about how she's holding herself makes her seem tall, royal, like she belongs there. It's a contradiction I wasn't expecting.

"You shouldn't make fun of people." She folds her arms.

"You shouldn't assume what's going on in someone else's mind."

She points at me. "If you don't tell me when I ask, assumptions are all I've got."

"Sounds like a you problem." My half shrug makes a muscle in her cheek twitch. I kind of like it.

After a long, stretched out moment of glaring at me, her shoulders soften. "Dare I ask what happens on this chair?" Her eyes search mine for a moment before she glances down at the seat, wiggling her butt. "They clean it afterwards, right?" She cringes but doesn't stand up. I kind of like that, too.

"They do. And what happens depends on who's sitting on it and what they want."

She purses her lips like she's thinking about the kinds of things people want to do on the chair. I'd be lying if I said I didn't have to silently convince my dick to stay soft. Last thing I need is for this woman to believe I'm a predator and have her feeling unsafe and try to brave the elements outside to escape from me.

I can see the headlines now, *"Local woman flees sexual predator at seedy sex club."* It's almost laughable. Nothing about Protocol is seedy, it's one of the best clubs I've ever been to. And considering I travel the length and width of the country for conventions, that's saying a lot.

"Like what?"

I'm a good six feet away from her, not wanting to crowd or intimidate her. But the urge to hit the handle to tip her back is strong. A demonstration is often far more effective than an explanation.

I don't move, though, jerking my chin at the legs of the chair and the leather restraints dangling from the arms. "Some people like to be tied to it." I point to the lever at the side. "This particular chair reclines."

Gesturing at the shelf of crowns sitting over the top of a second shelf of toys and a coat rack full of paddles and crops, I swallow down my smirk. "Some people want to feel strong, regal, they wear crowns, hold scepters, play with their partner, or are played with."

Something flickers in her eyes as she processes my words. "You mean submissives?"

Huh. I wasn't expecting that, but I'm also not going to shut her down. "I do, yes. Some dommes and dominants bring their subs in here to play with. There's something about the throne that brings an air of power, status."

She wiggles again on the seat. Is it from being aroused, or from discomfort? How does someone like her know about doms and subs? Have I misjudged her? Perhaps she's not the vanilla, Goody Two-Shoes I thought she was.

"Can you show me?"

Blood rushes to my dick at the invitation, but I hold back. There's no way this tiny woman is ready for me to *show her*. That much I know, regardless of who she is or what she's into.

"I'm going to need you to be more specific about that request, Half-Pint."

She goes quiet, casting her eyes down to the straps dangling from the chair. It's like she has no sense of self-preservation. What if I was a psychopath?

She swallows hard. "I'd like to know what it feels like to be tied to the chair, and reclined." She holds out her hand like she expects me to pounce, but I keep my distance. "Maybe only arms, or legs."

The implication she could still punch or kick me with half of her limbs untied hangs heavily in the air. She has no reason to believe me, or trust me and my motives, but I try to reassure her all the same.

"My name is Jagger Coleman."

She blinks, flinching.

"I work at this club as one of the house dominants. If I am in any way inappropriate with you, my boss is Slade and I can give you both of our cards if it'd make you feel better. I can also hand you your phone in case you feel a need to call the cops."

I've never had to be so overt with anyone to this extent before. I tend to negotiate terms of play, boundaries, aftercare, and part ways. She was very trusting to come down to the basement with me. Probably a stupid move on my part, but if we're stuck here, it's better to be downstairs than trying to find a comfortable place to sleep on the bar upstairs.

"Thank you." Her voice is small. She places her wrists on the arms of the chair, looking up at me expectantly.

I'm a giant compared to her, and this space is comfortable to me. For her to capitulate in this moment takes some fucking balls.

I don't know how I restrain myself from physically touching her as I strap her into the seat, other than to position her legs where I need them to be. When she's secure, I tilt the seat back. Even though she's expecting it, she gasps at the movement.

Her cheeks are pink, from the cold, or arousal, I'm not sure. The more I stare at her, the more beautiful she is to me. The intensity of her eyes, the slight wave to her hair I'd love to tangle my fingers in, the delicate Cupid's bow lips. She's exquisite.

"What would you do next if we were... uh... what did you call it? Playing?"

Endless possibilities flash through my head at her question. If we were playing, she'd be naked, and not bundled in layers of warm weather clothing, first and foremost.

I still haven't touched her. I'm a good foot away from the chair, ready to intervene if she panics, but far enough away I hope she doesn't feel crowded.

"It depends on who I'm with, and what they enjoy. For a brand new playmate..." My brain whirrs with ideas, short circuiting with the list of things I'd like to do to a woman like this. "Well, you'd be naked."

Her cheeks darken as her eyes flicker away from mine. Part

of me wants to get filthy with my words, see how red I can make her face, how uncomfortable I can make her, how much I can make her squirm on the chair. The other part wants to kiss every inch of pinking skin to see what makes her tick.

This isn't a good idea. Listing things I want to do to the annoying woman from the plane isn't going to end with anything other than a case of blue balls, though it does put me in mind of using a gag.

She's been quieter in the dungeon, but her chatter and oversharing from the plane and the car still ring in my ears. I can't stop the smile spreading from my face as I turn to the shelves of toys.

Presenting a ball-gag to her has the shock impact I'm going for. Her eyes widen, her breath stops dead, and the pinkness in her cheeks quickly recedes as she pales. "Where does that go?"

I chuckle. She scowls. "Stop laughing at me. It's a valid question."

Since her arms are still free, for the moment. She flaps them out in annoyance. The crinkles between her eyebrows are cute as hell, but I don't react. "It goes in your mouth." I dangle the gag in front of her face, and she snaps her mouth shut. As expected, it doesn't last long. I doubt it ever does.

"What for? What does it do? Why would I want a huge ball in my mouth? How can I tell you to stop if I can't speak?" She gets paler, faster with her words, more frantic with each question, so I withdraw the gag and return it to the shelf.

"Do you want to be released from the restraints?"

She shakes her head.

"Do you want answers to the questions?"

She nods.

"To shut you up."

Her wide eyes narrow, fear and curiosity giving way to the flames of fire I've seen glimpses of since I met her. "I'd shout louder."

I bet she would.

"What happened to you to make you…? Why do you…? I don't."

Watching her brain short circuit might be my favorite part of our interaction so far. Each question causing a flash of something across her face.

"Sometimes nothing happened to make us this way, you know. We're dirty fuckers with no damn good reason." I revel in her flinch like my words smacked her face.

I fucking hate being judged; for my work, for my appearance, for my race, for my sexual deviances. This prissy little snob's preconceptions make me want to get all up in her space and give her a lesson in my proclivities.

Many of us in the kink community are used to judgment, but something about it from this woman in particular irritates me more than usual. She doesn't give off "better than you" vibes, but her words are charged with a deep lack of understanding I'm exhausted by.

People like what they like. We aren't all tall, dark, and handsome billionaires with troubled pasts and unresolved trauma. It gets tiresome having to explain to people who don't get it.

Without another word, I crouch down in front of her, taking my time to open the straps without breaking eye contact. She nibbles on her bottom lip as I unbuckle her first leg. Her chest heaves with heavy breaths as I open the second.

"I didn't mean to imply." Her voice is barely a whisper on the cool air.

Except she did. The tone of her voice, the edge of judgmental hardness in her eyes, the quiver in her words, it all conveyed her thoughts loud and clear.

People fear what they don't know. People are also conditioned to think anything outside of 'normal' is bad, dirty, and something to scorn.

If I had to put money on it, I'd say she's from a religious upbringing. And while I have nothing against religion, I'm tired of all the things it seems to have against me.

The weight of other people's religious expectations on my shoulders is stifling.

As I lean forward to reach the straps around her left arm, her voice skates across my skin. "I'm sorry. I should know better than to judge a book by its cover."

My continued quiet seems to be unsettling her, making her feel guilty, filling her with regret.

When I unbuckle the final restraint, the warmth of her breath grazes across my face. Has she leaned in? Or have I?

We're close. Too close.

The air is thick with tension, charged with an unspoken argument, and my retort dies on the back of my tongue as I inhale. The irony in her smelling like vanilla would make me laugh if I wasn't acutely aware her legs are now free and close enough to swing into my nuts. Bet she would, too.

My urge to kiss this woman seems to grow proportionately with how close I am to her. The need to show her how pleasurable my deviance can be is bubbling in my soul. But I don't owe her anything. If she wants to live in judgment, it's not on me to show her a different way.

Her tongue slipping out to wet her bottom lip is almost my undoing, until a shrill sound echoes around the room. Half-Pint shrieks, jumps up, and cracks my head with hers as she bounds out of the throne.

I'm already tipping back when it hits me, I'm going down. Half-Pint's wide eyes register my fear as I splat hard against the floor of the club with a thud that steals the air from my lungs. I manage not to crack my head, but only just.

When she lands on my chest, I shouldn't be surprised. This chick is as coordinated as a newborn fucking foal. No amount of trying to save her from falling was going to work. I bet she falls over air on the regular. She braces her hands on my chest to push off and stand, which makes her hips rock against my groin.

We both realize at the same time, I have a semi, and her exaggerated movement doesn't help. I swallow a groan. My dick believes it's go-time while this tiny terror is now muttering "Oh no," to herself over and over as she tries to dismount my splayed out body on the floor.

"For fuck's sake." I pluck her off me and plop her on the floor next to me then roll over to stand accidentally kicking her discarded bag over.

A notebook and some loose pages stutter out across the floor as her phone starts ringing again. She launches herself at the bag while I set about collecting the debris. Why the fuck did she leave the damn bag open and on the floor in the first place? There are perfectly good hooks and shelves around the room.

"No!" Her shriek only makes me infinitely more curious about what she doesn't want me to see on the pages, but apparently, the phone seems to be the priority. It's tangled in something in the pocket, so she's now not-swearing under her breath, her irritation building with every utterance.

I've never heard someone use the words "sugar drops" with such vehemence before, but Half-Pint makes it work. I collect the pages, and as I hold the pile out to her, the top sheet catches my attention.

"Talia's Bedroom Bucket List."

CHAPTER 6
Talia

"Hi, Mama." My whole body is on fire from shame and embarrassment. The pitch of my voice is so unusually high if any dogs are passing this building they'd understand what I'm saying. And I can't take my eyes away from the piece of paper held outstretched in Jagger's hand.

"Talia Marie Barclay, what in the good Lord's name do you think you're doing?"

The cringe is so strong, I almost drop the phone. Her voice is so loud, there's no way Jagger can't hear her. Now, he knows my name, too. My full name.

"Mama, I can't talk right now. I'm stranded in Minnesota 'cause of the storm." Apparently my accent goes even more full-blown Kentucky when I'm chatting to my Mama. If such a thing was even possible.

"Sweetheart, if you're stranded, seems all you can do is talk right now. Where else you gotta be?"

She's got a point. But I can't think logically when Jagger, the most beautiful, grumpy, and intriguing man I've ever met, Mr. Dominant himself, stands staring at my meager and embarrassing 'Bucket List' of things I wanted to try with Harry when we tied the knot.

#1 Oral Sex

Turns out, Mr. Harry the Cheater had already tried all-the-s-e-x before I made my list. But I couldn't ever get him to try much of anything. He liked it when I did number one on the list to him, but he never returned the favor. Something always came up; he was tired, someone on his phone needed him, he needed to eat. Looking back, the timing was always suspicious but I never figured it out. I was already the dutiful wife, taking care of my man while unbeknownst to me, he was taking care of someone else.

All the heroines in the books I read love when a guy does it with his tongue. I'd be lying if I said I wasn't curious.

I'm staring at Jagger's mouth. He's probably past reading number one on my list but I wonder if he gives his girlfriends —plural, because there's no way a man like that hasn't had a gazillion lovers, probably even in the last month—oral.

"Talia?"

"I'm here Mama."

Here, but not really paying attention. Jagger's face is impassive. My face is so hot I want to peel the skin off my cheeks and dangle it outside in the snow.

"The Winslow's aren't happy."

Jagger's face twitches. I can't tell if it's because of the name Mama said, or something on the list.

"I don't care, Mama." That's a lie. I do care. I love Harry's mom a lot. His dad has always been a bit aloof and quiet for my liking, but his mom has always made time for me.

"You need to fix this, Talia." There's a sharp edge to her voice, saying if I'd made my flight I might be threatened with a spanking if I didn't do what she said.

"I did fix it. I broke up with the man who cheated on me and broke my heart." My voice wobbles, but I don't crack.

The weight of her sigh can be felt worldwide. "Talia." Another sigh. "So dramatic. So unyielding and unreasonable. What about forgiveness?"

Harry doesn't want my forgiveness, he's never asked for it. Even if he did, though, doesn't mean I'd give it to him, or marry him despite what he's done.

"What about 'Do not commit adultery'?" We aren't married yet, but we've been as good as, since I lost my V-card to him when I was sixteen. My parents made sure of that.

"Talia." There's warning laced in one word. She's got the parental inflection down pat.

"Yes, Mama?" I'm not playing dumb, but I'm also not going to let her manipulate or force me to stay in an unhappy relationship anymore. My parents may be unhappy, Harry and his parents may be unhappy, Pastor Rick may be unhappy, heck, even God himself might be unhappy, but I can't do it anymore.

Jagger seems hugely interested in my list. Is he being polite? Or could he really be *that* interested?

I'm pretty sure he almost tried to kiss me while he unbuckled my ties on the throne.

"I'm not playing. Fix this. Or Harry Winslow is going to find himself a new bride." Part of me wishes Jagger *had* kissed me. Can you imagine what a kiss from the hulking great brute would be like? There's no way he doesn't own anyone he kisses. That passion, burning fire that must scorch when his lips touches someone's. That's the love I want some day.

"I have a gorgeous Vera Wang she could have for her wedding."

"Talia!"

If Jagger didn't hear my name the first time, there's no way he's missed it now with that shriek. Will he call me Talia? Or will he keep calling me Half-Pint?

Either way, he smothers a snort with his hand. Our eyes

meet for a fraction of a second and the gold flecks in his brown eyes sparkle. He nods at me. Is that encouragement? Support? An accidental head movement that means nothing at all, and I'm reading too far into it? I have no idea.

Am I experiencing a somewhat false sense of bravado right now because he's standing watching me? Absolutely. Undeniably. Positively.

But I'd like to think I won't backpedal when I eventually get home to Louisville. I should probably have walked into another room when the call connected, but I didn't want to leave Jagger with my stuff. I didn't want to snatch my pages from him and flee in case Mama heard the commotion and asked about where, and who, I was with. And part of me didn't want to explore any more rooms in this dungeon. I have no idea what I might find, but I know for sure I've had my fill of self-discovery for the day, for the whole gosh dang month, even.

There's a long silence on the line. The air between us is heavy. The way he's looking at me doesn't make me feel like the scolded child the phone call is leaving me feeling.

A thick strand of bright blue hair falls across my face, reminding me of the strength I had to get a chunk of my hair buzzed off with clippers and dyed a bright color. I can't back down. I just can't. It's time for me to learn the word "no," and to say it.

"Mama, I'm sorry you think I should stay in a relationship with a man who doesn't respect me or treat me right. That makes me sad for you. But I know my worth, and Harold Winslow the Third, isn't it."

More silence greets me on the line, and for a moment, I check the call is even connected. It is. That lack of noise tells me Mama is less than happy. She's furious. And since I've combatted her logic with her own life lessons she's bestowed on me through the years, I can only imagine she's madder than a wet hen.

My future marriage with Harry wasn't simply about saving face. I learned a few years after my forced betrothal to him it was also part of some business deal between Dad and Harry's Granddaddy and Dad—the trio of Harry's. I don't know the particulars, didn't need to because I was the cherry on top according to Harry the night we broke up.

I don't want to be anyone's cherry. I don't even like cherries. And I'm really darn peeved I let him pop my cherry.

"Mama?"

"We'll talk about this when you get home, Talia Marie."

"No, Mama. We won't. I've made my decision. If you and Dad can't accept that." A lump grows so big in my throat it makes my eyes water. "Then we don't really have anything else to talk about. And if Mr. Winslow makes life harder for Dad because his son is a no good, cheating piece of dirt, then he's every bit as bad as his son."

It's not untrue, but my whole body aches with the stress of speaking my mind to my mother. It's probably a first. My whole life I've done what my parents said, when they said it. There was no delay, no room for independent thinking, no asserting my opinion.

I learned early in life if I didn't jump to attention and do what they asked, there were stern consequences ranging from being grounded to spanked and everything in between.

So I became the "Yes" girl.

If Dad cuts me off, I have my trust fund to tide me over until I can figure something out. Now that I'm twenty two they don't have control of that either. They have nothing on me.

I follow so many "step into your power" people on social media I could parrot back their teachings if Mama comes at me again. It won't be easy, but I need to hold that boundary. I won't be given away like chattel to a man who doesn't value our relationship enough to stay faithful to the woman he's supposed to spend forever with.

Jagger's still staring, saying nothing. His presence is demanding, consuming, and takes up every inch of space in here. He's truly something to look at. His muscles fill out his clothes, and those tattoos peeking out from underneath the fabric make me want to explore and see what they are and where they go.

Curiosity is my downfall. Despite the fact I'm afraid to go wandering the halls of this sex club, I generally enjoy snooping. And learning.

"We'll talk about it when you get home." Mama's voice is hard, cold, unwavering. I've never heard her so disconnected. I guess not marrying Harry is going to make life complicated for both of them.

Old Talia would have acquiesced.

Old Talia would have said "Yes, Mama. I'll be right there."

But the blue hair dangling in my face reminds me yet again I'm not Old Talia. I'm transforming into New Talia. She's stronger, more self-assured, knows her worth, and even says "no" sometimes.

This is one of those times.

"I'm stranded in a snow storm, I won't be making it back to Kentucky for at least a few days I'd guess." Hopefully more. If the snow doesn't last, I'll find a different reason to keep me here in Minnesota. It's easier not to bend to my parent's wishes from a distance. "But when I do come home, this won't be a topic I'm entertaining discussion on. It's done. I'm not taking Harry back. You and Dad need to accept that."

My voice wavers, but somehow manages to hold out. My insides are like mush. Jagger's appraisal crawls all over my skin as he silently assesses me with his eyes. Mama's judgment beds in a layer deeper, with barbs that sting, seeping into my bloodstream and poisoning my whole body.

I'm exhausted from this one conversation of setting and holding boundaries. How the heck am I supposed to do this more regularly?

I feel like I need a builder to lay concrete in front of me. Surely, that's the only way I'm going to be able to maintain these lines?

"Mama, I've got to go."

More silence. I tug at the neck on my sweater. I can't take the heat engulfing my body. My head's getting light, my skin clammy, and there's a thump-thump brewing behind my eyeballs. Not even the faint smell of pine from Jagger is soothing right now. Though since I met him on the plane there's a part of me that wants to stick my nose in his neck and breathe him in.

But I'd never do that.

Not because of me, I'd totally do that. But because his "stay the heck away" vibes are so strong he'd probably crumple me like a potato chip packet if I tried it. He'd do it one handed, too. And he wouldn't even break a sweat.

Mama hasn't said a word. I've always known my parents could be difficult, but this? Forcing their daughter into a marriage she couldn't possibly be happy in simply to suit themselves?

I'm simultaneously surer than ever they want what's best for me, while also questioning everything I've ever learned. Because Harry certainly isn't what's best.

"I love you."

More silence. It's rare Mama wouldn't say "I love you," back to me when I say it. In fact, this might be a first. Tears fill my eyes. Is she really not saying it back?

Jagger holds his hand out. Does he want my phone?

I take a step back, holding my hand out like a stop sign,

while shaking my head. I mouth "no," giving him the sternest, most crankypants look I can muster.

Jeez. It's exhausting being angry and grumpy.

"Mama?"

Nothing. Another check, the call is connected.

Jagger advances, hand still outstretched. How does he know if he doesn't end the call, I never will?

Closing my eyes releases the brimming sea of tears, and streams course down my cheeks. "Bye, Mama."

I can't even look at him as I hand him the phone. He places something soft in my palm in its place. Without opening my eyes, I know it's another handkerchief. He's giving me space, not hugging me to feel better, or giving me a "there, there," pat like I would if someone was crying in front of me, but he gave me his hanky and that counts for something.

I think.

Maybe I'm just hoping he's not the cold, Grumpypants he was on the plane, and in the car, and the whole time we've been here because I've never felt more alone. And I really could use a friend.

When I dab my eyes and face dry and blink away the blurriness, Jagger has a crown in his hand. It's the prettiest, sparkliest, and most pink rhinestone crown I've ever seen, and he's putting it on my head.

"You can probably mark off number thirteen now, Half-Pint."

CHAPTER 7
Jagger

I LIKE TO THINK I'M A NICE PERSON.

Fine, I'm a grumpy bastard. But I pay my taxes, help old people cross the street, keep myself to myself and don't get in anyone's way. So when my chatterbox, bubbly Half-Pint seatmate from the plane turns out to be my college rival's woman, I can't help but feel like the universe is playing some wild trick on me.

She's in the bathroom, giving me time to figure out what the fuck my next move should be.

Harry Winslow the Third—that piece of shit never let us forget his lineage when we spoke to him—is an asshole scumbag across the board. His name was a bulletproof shield he hid behind to get whatever the fuck he wanted.

The guy was untouchable.

He paid people to write his assignments for him. He used 'roids to get the Quarterback spot. There were at least two rape accusations against him that he made go away. The guy's literally the scum of the earth.

And yet, here's his woman, seemingly in pristine condition, completely untouched with a bucket list that's as laughable as it is despicable. That piece of shit made her wait to have sex while he was boning everything that moved and never even went down on her?

And she fucking took it?

I can't fathom how she thought it was okay for someone to treat her like this. How did she not know what he was like? Or does she? And she's sparing her mom's feelings by protecting her from the truth?

If she knew the depths of his crimes, this blue-haired shortcake in front of me would have spat them out to silence her aggressive mother. She mustn't know.

It's unsurprising the prick hid it from her, maintaining a double life, but did he keep her untouched for a reason? Was he saving her like some a trophy on a shelf?

My blood bubbles under my skin as my heart hardens even more. She's not my problem. But the opportunity to stick it to that fucker Harry wells inside me, making it hard not to rip her clothes off and bury my face in her basically untouched pussy.

I'd be doing her a favor, giving her the time of her life. So what if my motives are impure, right? She's single, fair game. A grown-ass adult who can make her own decisions.

She doesn't need to know her asshole ex cheated his way through college, winning damn near everything I worked my ass off to achieve right out from under me. She doesn't need to know this is personal, just that I'm willing to help her.

Would she tell him, though? If they got back together, would she be open and say "hey there was this guy Jagger who I let do some things to me."? I doubt it. I'll have to convince her to put a picture of the two of us on social media or something. He's my 'friend' on a few platforms, but I doubt he'd pay close enough attention to notice his woman on my page.

If *she* shared it, though, he'd see that for sure.

I fucking hate photos. And I rarely post anything on

socials about my private life. I use them for my auto shop and nothing else. But I could be swayed to make an exception for flipping the bird to Harry fucking Winslow.

It's a win-win, right?

Right.

So why's there a tingle of guilt nagging in my chest?

If she agrees, this pint-sized queen will get the most mind blowing orgasms of her life. And when Harry gets her back—which he will, because he always gets what he wants, and he wouldn't have kept her for this long without actually wanting her—she'll have had most of her firsts with me. I'll have defiled his most prized possession.

It's a perfect plan all-around. But trust won't be enough with this one. People don't generally have to like me for them to sit on my cock. But this girl, she's not "people." And the fact I'm a house dom in an upscale sex club with a reputation to uphold isn't going to cut it.

Upside is she's hot, so I don't even have to fake an attraction to her.

"I don't think number thirteen counts." She's blowing between her hands, rubbing them like she's still cold. "I mean, they are restraints, sure. Technically speaking my list said furry handcuffs. But also, I was fully clothed and it wasn't in bed." Her face is so adorably red, and she's back to flicking her gaze to anything that isn't me.

"If you want to try something," I gesture around the room. "This is the place to do it."

Her brows shoot up. "I'm good." Her voice is squeaky as she shakes her head.

Nodding, I hold up my hands. "We're probably here for the night. It hasn't let up outside, so if you change your mind let me know. I won't instigate anything with you, though."

The way she nibbles on her bottom lip makes me want to release it with my thumb. Knowing she hasn't tried anything on the list sends sparks of excitement through my body. Can you imagine having oral for the first time? By someone who knows what they're doing?

She might not let me make her scream, but damn do I want to.

"Have you really not done anything on your list?"

She huffs, blusters, and covers her face with both hands before shaking her head. "No." The word is half-groan half-wail.

"Your ex is a dick."

When her eyes meet mine they're full of fire. "He cheated."

"That's only part of why he's a dick. These things on your list? They aren't anything to be ashamed of. You should feel like you're allowed to ask for every one of them, even just to try. In any relationship." I don't know why I'm suddenly the chatty Cathy in the room, but I need to somehow make sure she has her eyes fully opened before her parents convince her to go back and marry the asshole who treats her like shit.

"I should?" She's so fucking sweet and innocent it makes my balls hurt.

"Yes, Half-Pint. You should. There's nothing on that list I wouldn't be only too happy to do to a lover." I take a step back from her, not wanting to crowd her. "Hell, as a house dom in this place, that means sometimes I put on demonstrations, or I'm there to step in and help people experience their fantasies."

"People you don't even know?" Her teeth are chattering. I turned the heat on, but it doesn't feel like the building's getting any warmer. If it is, it's marginal, and Shortie over there looks like she might freeze at any moment.

"People I don't even know." I drag my hand over my face. I don't remember the last time I talked this much to a stranger, but she's curious, and I want her more so, so perhaps it's what

I've got to do. "The beauty of a place like this is you can come here and try things, with your partner, with strangers. It's the perfect place to learn, and it has the perfect people to learn with.

"What do you mean?" She looks around the room, probably for a chair, but there's nothing but the throne.

I pick up her bag, jerking my head at the door. "Come on, we'll find somewhere more comfortable to sit."

When I get her settled in the cafe, her lips and fingers are almost translucent, so I go behind the counter and set about making her a hot drink. "Tea, coffee, or hot chocolate?"

Her eyes light up. "Hot chocolate please. A giant one." She pauses. "You got whipped cream and marshmallows back there?"

I arch a brow. "What kind of place do you take this for?"

She shrugs, casting a slow glance around the room. "I'm not sure. Is this where people come after?"

"After they do dirty things?" My lips twitch as her blush darkens. "It is. We have snacks and drinks, couches for people to rest and recoup, chat and do some of their aftercare before heading back into reality."

"Aftercare." Her voice is quiet as she taps her finger on her lips.

I am so glad we all got a lesson in how to use this complicated as fuck drinks machine. Otherwise the chattering Smurf wouldn't last much longer. "That's—"

"I know what that is." Her quick shut down now makes *my* brows shoot up. She shrugs again. "I read."

Now I want a peek in her eReader. What is it, exactly, she's reading?

"I figured I should at least be mentally prepared for some of the things Harry might want to try." She swings her legs. The fact they don't touch the floor on those chairs makes me swallow a laugh. "I didn't want to be blindsided by him, or freak out when he suggested something and ruin, uh, the bedroom experience."

She hasn't done a goddamn thing on the list, and she's already perfectly submissive. What the fuck was Harry thinking to fuck it up so badly with her?

He doesn't deserve her. Not that it makes a difference to him. He thinks he deserves everything he wants.

"You're too kind." My admission makes her head snap up from twiddling her thumbs, or assessing her nails, or looking wherever it was she was looking, and the emotion in her eyes makes me damn near pour hot milk over my hand. "He really is a dick, you know. He doesn't deserve you."

She nods, but she doesn't seem convinced.

"The things on your list, are they things you read about and figured you might like? Or?"

She nods again, more enthusiastically. "The people in the books like it, so I thought it's probably not a bad place to start, right?"

Can't fault her logic.

"There's a reason these things come up time and again in romance novels."

The reminder she reads romance and probably has an unachievable view of what a relationship should be hits me in the face like a smack. A quick reminder I'm not trying to date this woman, just ensure she either never goes back to Harry, or, if she does go back, she's already past where he wants her to be sexually.

There's a reason he sexually controlled her for as long as he did. I don't know what he's been waiting for, but clearly he's had his reasons.

"Romance novels don't always emulate real life experiences you know."

She snorts. "Are you telling me oral isn't good?" When she folds her arms I come close to throwing her over my shoulder and taking her to one of the beds in this place and showing her how good it can be.

"That's not what I'm saying."

She hums, like "I told you so."

"Chocolate sprinkles?" I hold up the tub, and she gives me a thumbs up. This woman.

When I place two of the mugs down in front of her, she grins.

"I didn't have a giant mug, so you got two medium mugs."

"Thank you." She skims her finger across the top of the whipped cream before popping it into her mouth with a small moan that makes my dick twitch, then she takes a long drink.

I put my mug on the table facing her, but she's shivering so hard I need to do something. "I'll be right back."

She bolts to her feet. "Where are you going?" Her voice is tight, brittle, and her face is pale.

I can't help myself when I reach out to brush my fingers across the apple of her cheek. "To find some blankets. You're freezing."

She giggles.

"What?"

"You're this giant, grumpy dude who has handkerchiefs and who makes hot chocolate, and who goes to find blankets for blue haired pixies." She presses my chest with her index finger, and I fight not to suck in a deep breath. I want more contact. Touching her face with my fingers was a mistake. Her touching my chest in return, another mistake.

Something flares in my chest. "I'm not a nice guy, Talia, and this isn't a romance novel. We're two people trapped in weird circumstances by a snow storm. I don't do making love. I don't do soft and gentle. I fuck."

Heat fills her eyes, and warm satisfaction seeps into my skin.

"It's in my nature as a dominant to be caring, but don't

mistake my responsibility as some soft and mushy bullshit. You won't find that here." I'm towering over her. Her head's tipped back, mine's bent forward, and there's a large gap between our faces.

Her chest is rising and falling with heavy breaths that match my own. If she was taller, our chests might even brush against each other. She's not staring at the floor. Her shoulders are squared, her eyes flaring with heat and focused on my lips.

At the same moment she whispers "kiss me," I'm already in motion backing her against the wall. Caging her in, I brace my hands either side of her face.

Her head's craned up to me. "What are you waiting for? Don't you want to kiss me?" Her lip catches between her teeth. "Kind of feels like you might." She rocks against me, drawing a growl from deep within my chest.

I lean down so our noses are almost touching. My breath makes her hair ripple, and I can smell the hot chocolate and sugar on her tongue and lips. "Of course I want to kiss you. You're a beautiful woman, Talia. My problem is I want to do more than kiss you, and once I start, it'll be hard to stop."

Her sharp intake of air would be comical if I couldn't see the flicker of lust that shimmers in her eyes.

"And kissing isn't on your to-do list." I can't help but play with her, just a little.

She smirks, and I'll be fucking damned if it doesn't speak right to my crotch. She might be vanilla, but that spark, that glimmer of fight, that steel backbone she keeps flashing glimpses of, drives me fucking wild.

As I lean down to brush my lips against hers, I'm met with the palm of her hand.

"Wait!"

CHAPTER 8
Talia

My heart thuds against my ribcage as his head pulls away from mine.

"What's wrong?" He backs up away from me without hesitation. Holding his hands up like he doesn't want his actions to be misconstrued. Is this club procedure, or a him thing? Either way, it's cute. And all-the-way reassuring.

"I don't want you to kiss me like I've never been kissed before."

His head cants, and he gestures like I should continue.

"Kiss me like you've kissed me a million times over."

He takes a step toward me, the air around him becoming electric, sizzling with anticipation.

"Kiss me like I'm a seasoned submissive who knows what she's doing."

Another step, and my inclination is to retreat. But there's a solid wall behind me, so all I do is remind myself I'm trapped as this animalistic man prowls toward me.

"Are you sure that's what you want?" His question is almost a snarl, a warning, a threat, all wrapped up with a lust-charged bow. His eyes hold me hostage, I'm defenseless, can't look away.

I might draw blood if I bite down on my lip any harder, but I nod, despite myself. What the heck am I doing? It's one thing to read about these kinds of experiences in a book, it's another to talk about doing them, it's yet another still to actually invite a man into my space to touch my person.

But the way he looks at me, still holding me captive, the untamed glint in his eye, the hunger, the way his lips curl at one side, the way his pants tent from his growing erection... it all leads me to believe he wants me. And that feels nice.

Plus, when in my life will I ever get this opportunity again? The chance for no strings, no judgment learning? I never have to see this man again beyond later tonight, or tomorrow when I leave this place.

What happens at the dark and mysterious s-e-x club, stays at the dark and mysterious s-e-x club, right?

And just because I'm inviting him to kiss me, doesn't mean I'm inviting him to do more than that. What's in a kiss? It's not like he can make me lose all sense of self and convince me to do anything more untoward with a stranger. Right? I know who he is, and where he works, and while it's naive as all get out to trust him... I can't help it.

There's that feral glimmer in his chocolate-brown eyes again. I'm not actually sure anymore. I'm already off-balance.

"What do you do for a living?"

"Other than work here?" He's not looking away, in fact, he's looking at me like he knows I'm stalling for time. But the air thickens. He's so close, his breath's tickling my skin. There's that scent again, too, pine needles and something else.

I nod my head.

"I'm a mechanic."

Ah ha! Motor oil. That's what the undertones in his scent

are. It explains the black streaks across his dark wash jeans, and the dirt under his nails.

"Kiss me like I'm someone you just met here in the club that you want to take to bed."

He doesn't move, only stares. Not looking away from him takes all I have. The way his eyes capture my attention and don't let go makes me feel vulnerable, like he's peering inside my soul to see everything about me.

I lick my lips, his stare flickers for a second, and when his eyes meet mine again they're even more intense, filled with more heat, more lust, more everything.

Our chests rise and fall together, brushing against each other as we breathe in the silence. What's holding him back? Indecision?

My body's being tugged toward him like I'm possessed. Is he going to kiss me?

I don't know. But I want him to. With every cell in my body I want this man to kiss me.

I almost close the distance. But before I can say another word, or think, or even breathe, his hand cups my throat, my back firm against the wall. His thumb glides across my jaw, sending goosebumps spreading all over my body. He frees my lip from between my teeth, staring me down like a hunter pausing before striking.

"Kiss you like I don't know how pure you are, you mean?"

Pure. Chaste. Innocent. Ignorant. Whatever word you choose, I feel all of those things right now. My body's tingling, sensations spreading throughout muscles I've never felt before, even while reading the dirtiest scenes in my spicy books.

There's an ache between my thighs that's driving me closer to doing something stupid with this strange man in a stranger place.

"Yes." My voice is breathy, his scent invading my senses.

"Kiss me like I'm the woman on the throne. Not the chaste girl on a pedestal."

He leans closer to me, his thumb sweeping gently back and forth across my bottom lip. "So soft, Talia."

"Half-Pint." If he doesn't use my name, I can't be reminded of all the things I *should* be and instead can be all the things I *want* to be.

He grinds out a dark chuckle as his gaze flickers to my lips and back to my eyes. He doesn't question why I correct him, he doesn't hesitate, and he's not the least bit gentle as his hand tightens around my throat, and he crashes his lips against mine.

There's nothing soft about this kiss, nothing exploratory or tentative. It's hungry, demanding, possessive. His tongue spears my lips apart, and my mouth falls open on a gasp. If I thought he might slow down, I was wrong.

There's no educating in his kiss, only consuming. In this moment, Jagger owns me. Not just my lips, my tongue, my mouth, but all of me. My whole being is being manipulated into giving him every ounce of myself in one kiss. I'm a puppet, and this stranger, this mechanic from the plane is pulling my strings.

His tongue surges between my teeth, digging into my mouth until he finds my tongue and massages it like he's trying to coax something out of it, a moan, a response, all my lifelong secrets. I have no idea. But he's not letting up. He tilts my head, his thumb still caressing my jaw.

I've never wanted someone's hand around my throat before. Even reading about it in my books, the 'hand necklace' in a lot of stories doesn't make it sound as arousing and thrilling as having Jagger's giant hand curled around my fragile neck.

Part of me knows it's unsafe, and yet, the same part almost feels exhilarated, like I want to push that boundary further, I want his hand to tighten even more. The idea of not being in control of my own breaths is equal parts terrifying and electrifying.

Has he done it before? Choked someone? Controlled the very breath that enters into their lungs? I bet he has.

His teeth clash against mine as his kiss intensifies. Need bubbles under my skin, scorching, pulsing, a hunger so deep I couldn't reach it even if I tried.

Pressing my thighs together isn't helping. The heat, the damp between my legs, this pulsing ache... I might die.

When he releases my mouth, my lips are swollen and puffy, tingling from every lick, suck, and nibble Jagger subjected them to. But he's not finished. He drags his tongue along the length of my jaw before trailing his teeth down the opposite side of my neck to where his hand is.

The scraping of his hard teeth against my soft, sensitive skin makes me shiver. My heavy breaths have turned into moans and whimpers. His dark enticing presence looms over me, caging me against the wall.

I'm a fly in a spider web, stuck, helpless, and staring down my demise with no way of escaping his snare. But I don't care. He can take me, own me, use me, do whatever he wants to me if he can fix this throbbing hunger between my thighs.

"Please." It's a single word, panted out of my exhausted body on a huff of warm air.

"Please, what, Half-Pint?"

"Do something."

CHAPTER 9
Jagger

The only thing I need to do right now is stand the fuck down. My dick has this woman pinned to the wall by her goddamn stomach like a spear. There's no telling it that it's not go time. It's leaking precum into my boxer-briefs. The heavy pulsing and tightness in my balls demands release, and my head is spinning from how delicious this little sprite tastes.

"Jagger." She rolls her hips against me, drawing a slow hiss of breath from between my teeth. "Do. *Something.*"

"What do you want me to do?" Open communication is important to me, especially in a scene or with a lover. I'm not thinking with my brain, all my blood's pooled in my rod-stiff cock. This is what I wanted, her to need me, want me, crave me, beg me to take care of her so I could send her back to Harry de-flowered in as many ways as I can manage.

But this isn't how it's done. We sit, we talk, we make a list of limits, soft and hard, we discuss aftercare, and all manner of things. I don't just grab a woman and pin her to the wall, assaulting her with my tongue.

But she tastes so fucking sweet, I want to do it all over again.

I didn't expect a burning in my chest to want to make her feel good, but I can use it to my advantage.

"Anything. I don't care."

I dot kisses along her neck, across her jaw, over her chin, lips, nose, and forehead as she rolls her hips against me. "You do care. You *should* care." I stop dead, no more kisses. Bracing my hands on either side of her head I lower my face so our noses are almost touching and we're eye to eye. "What. Do. You. *Want.* Half-Pint?"

Her breaths are loud, sharp, heavy, weighed with indecision and shame. I don't care if it takes all night, this woman will ask me for something she needs, or wants, in her own damn words.

Her cheeks are flushed, eyes glassy, hair sticking up in places. We need to reset. Need to breathe, do this properly. Any of the other doms in here approached a situation this way, I'd lay them out.

I'm not this person. I'm grounded, level-set, and practical.

Don't lead with emotion, or my dick. It's one of the reasons I'm so good at what I do. I don't have space in my life to be unbalanced. I face every sexual interaction systematically.

Her breath tickles my skin as she trembles against the wall. Is it fear? Need? Curiosity? What makes every muscle in her body shake like this? And how can I make it happen again?

Taking a step back, she heaves out a slow hiss of breath. Is that relief?

"Are you afraid of me?"

Her tooth is pierced into her bottom lip so deeply it may draw blood. She shakes her head. "I don't think so."

That's not the same as not being afraid, so I take another step back, pulling out a chair for her to sit in before I round the table and take a seat myself.

"Should I be afraid of you?" She's leaning against the wall, her tiny stature quivering.

She probably should be afraid of me, yes. I want to ruin her, not just for Harry the Prick, but for any man ever to come after me. I want to make her scream so loudly, experience every sensation so intensely, make her crave self-exploration and discovery, guide her until she knows herself and every kink and fetish too well to settle, for the rest of her life.

"I won't do anything to you that you don't ask me to do."

"That's not a no." She tips her head. "It's not a yes either." She takes a seat, scraping the chair across the tiles as she drags it closer to the table.

"I can't answer that question for you." It's true, I can't. I don't want her to fear me, but if she's afraid, I'll need to take it slowly. "But we'll need a conversation before I do anything to you, or with you."

Her face falls. "Like, t-t-talk about it? Out loud?" She's fucking adorable, and the way she shifts her weight in the chair suggests she's every bit as wound up as she was against the wall.

"Yes, Talia."

Her eyes flinch wider at my use of her real name.

"Talk. Out loud. About sex." I wasn't sure it was possible for her face to get any redder, but here we are. I lean forward. "We're the only people in the building you know."

She nods.

"There's nothing to be ashamed of, or embarrassed about."

She tips her chin upward, straightening her spine as she does. "I'm not embarrassed. I read... things."

"Tell me."

She clamps her lips shut, shaking her head, making her hair jiggle, sending a waft of her vanilla scent my direction. It's hard to fight the urge to close my eyes and breathe her in.

"You've seen my, my list." She swallows, then takes a drink.

"I have." I anchor my elbows to the table before I steeple my fingers. "But that doesn't tell me a lot."

"It tells you what I'd like to try." It's these flashes of stubborn, silent strength that makes me both curious about this woman and hard in my pants.

"You're right, it does. It tells me you've got little experience. Or you held back on your list." I lean back in my seat. "Do you masturbate, Half-Pint?"

Her jaw drops, mouth hanging open for a long moment before it snaps shut. I could fry a fucking egg on her sizzling cheeks if I was so inclined.

"I used to." She's twisting her hands in her lap so much she might pop off a digit.

Giving her foot a nudge under the table makes her eyes meet mine, but only for a moment. "What do you mean you used to?" How long has it been since this woman had an orgasm?

I'd ask who hurt her, but I already know the answer. Harry takes everything good from people and uses it to make his own life better. He hurt her. He's clearly controlled her sexually, and not in a positive way. And certainly not for her benefit.

She clears her throat, her jaw trembling. Suddenly, my rivalry with her ex feels petty. Who gives a fuck what happened in college? This woman has been broken down, she's a shell. She's insecure and self-conscious and in this moment, the bright and bubbly pixie from the plane is nowhere to be seen. It makes my blood boil and my insides liquefy.

I want to kill him.

"He caught me doing it once." She snorts, a bitter sound juxtaposing the tears trickling down her face. "At least I was alone, unlike when I caught him." She brushes the tears from her jawline with the back of her hand.

"He told me it was dirty, disgusting even, and that I should be ashamed of myself. He made me feel so gross I haven't done it since."

I can't stop the growl rattling at the back of my throat. Her eyes flex wide like she's sitting with a wild animal, and I can hardly blame her. I didn't need a reason to hate her ex more than I already did, but this... this is too much, too far.

Minutes ago I wanted to ruin her for Harry. Now I want to destroy the asshole.

I can't ask her when she last got off. Those expressive eyes, those pouty lips, that trembling chin. I don't stand a chance against her if she asks me again to do something.

She sniffs, drawing my attention to her button nose. My hand moves without instruction to collect the tears dangling from the tip, ready to drop onto her lap. "He doesn't deserve your tears." My voice sounds like it's been dragged over broken glass.

"This isn't like Fifty Shades."

Her declaration takes me aback. Literally. I almost cuff her nose as I retract my hand. "What do you mean?" That movie is generally frowned upon in the kink community. If this is the extent of her kink education, we definitely have our work cut out for us.

"Their negotiation scene was much more fun. She had a contract and everything." She's trying to lighten the mood, but it does little to dull the bitterness pooling at the back of my mouth, or the ice charging through my veins.

"There are basic contracts in the office upstairs if you'd like to look one over. But we aren't at that point yet."

Her shoulders curl, chin dips, eyes fall to the floor like I rejected her and something sharp stabs my chest.

Not sure if it's Harry the asshat or the fact we're sitting in something of an ice box that makes me shiver, but we're approaching seeing-your-breath-on-the-air level of cold inside Club Protocol so we need to find somewhere warm.

"Let's find a room to bunk in for the night, and we can start over in the morning." It's been a day already. And I don't typically like to do things with play partners if they're overly emotional, drained, dehydrated, or not well rested. Those things only contribute to the risk of error.

I can tell from the way she's forcing her face into a smile—or what she thinks is a smile, it's definitely more than a grimace—she's disappointed, which only makes my cock even more intrigued.

We pick up our crap, and I lead her two doors down the hall to another room. It's got two beds in it, but beds made up for playing, and beds made up for warmth are not the same thing. So I raid the aftercare closet, returning to the room with a giant stack of blankets. Hopefully that'll be enough to stop her teeth from chattering and her lips from turning blue.

When I step into the room we're staying in, she's still staring at the bed. "Why are there two in the same room?"

She helps me lay blankets on top of each other over the dark satin sheets.

"Sometimes couples come together, and they like to fuck beside each other." It's the only explanation I have, it might not be the real reason, I have no idea, I'm just guessing. I should probably ask someone.

She glances behind her at the glass. "And other people watch." She hooks a thumb back to the window.

I hitch a shoulder. "Yeah. Though there's a switch on the wall that can make that two way glass opaque for those who want to fuck next to their friends."

The way she flinches every time I drop the F-bomb is so cute. It makes me want to say it in every sentence until she becomes desensitized to it. Wonder if she'd flinch as hard if my mouth was on her when I said it.

No amount of trying to force pure thoughts is making my boner deflate. I'm like a fucking high schooler in gym class.

When we're done layering blankets on her bed, I fold back the sheets for her to climb in. She looks at her bed, then mine. "You didn't put any blankets on your bed."

I'm hoping the cold will make my cock shrivel overnight. "I'll be fine. I run warm." There's a fucking blizzard outside, no one's warm. But this tiny elf woman is so cold she definitely needs them more than I do.

She doesn't look convinced, but she slips off her shoes and climbs into bed fully dressed. She's there half a beat before she bounds back off the mattress. "Where's the bathroom? I need to pee."

After a short trip to the restroom, we both climb into bed. My fingers, toes, and nose are really starting to realize it's fucking cold out. I steady myself for Little Miss Chatty Cathy to start a rapid round of questions now that she's settled for the night, but she stays quiet, which makes me even more uncomfortable than her prying into my fucking life.

A few long, quiet moments pass between us before I hear it. Her fucking teeth are still chattering. Either that or she's crying.

Another moment later, and it sounds like she's running a marathon inside the bed under all those blankets.

"The fuck?"

Something resembling a giggle bursts out of her. "I'm sorry. I'm trying to get warm, I think the cold settled all the way in my bone marrow." Her whiny voice makes me smile in the darkness.

"I could come over there."

Her gasp damn near shreds the air between us. "No, it's fine."

There. I offered. I've done my due diligence. If I wake up six feet from a beautiful corpse in the morning that's on her. Not me. Right?

Fuck sake.

I drag my ass off the bed and cross the space. My weight on the mattress is what alerts her to my presence and even though there are only two of us in the building, even though there's a snow storm outside, and even though she knows who I am, she screams like I'm Jack the fucking Ripper.

I end up closer to her ear than I expected as I shush her. "It's only me, Half-Pint."

"I t-t-told you n-n-no." She did tell me no, and under normal circumstances that would be enough.

"I don't want to answer questions from the police about your cold, dead body in the morning."

She giggles, relaxing her back against my chest. I didn't mean for us to snuggle, just to share the same bed, but she's already invading my space. She wastes no time reaching a hand back to grab my arm and curl it around her waist.

"Relax, Mr. Grumpypants, I'm using you for your body... heat." She giggles again, and I'm loath to admit, the sound that grated on every raw nerve earlier feels nice in the cold, dark room.

She smacks the back of my hand, making my eyes snap open. "Just don't get handsy, you hear?"

CHAPTER 10

Talia

Please get handsy.

Please get handsy.

Please get handsy.

I don't know how long I've been lying with a giant grump man curled around me in this bed, but I'm finally starting to get feeling back in my fingers and feet. For a while, I thought he had his phone in bed with him until I realized that thing digging into me was his peen.

Even though we only had s-e-x one time, I've slept in the same bed as Harry sometimes. He was never hard like this for me. So either it's a general guy thing, and Harry was defective —Please Lord let Harry be defective—or the giant grump man is hard for me.

A rumbling growl alerts me to the fact said giant grump man isn't as asleep as I thought he was. His breath tickles my face as he huffs out warm air. "Are you done wiggling and fidgeting?"

"Sorry." My voice is barely a whisper. The place is otherwise empty, I don't have to be quiet, but something about lying in a kinky s-e-x basement with a stranger makes me keep my voice down.

A hysterical laugh bubbles up inside me. This is how people end up on the news. He joked about my cold, dead body being found tomorrow, but didn't specify whether it was from the cold, or the fact that he's a murderer.

My parents are going to be so distracted by the fact I slept in the same bed as a potential killer they will forget all about the fact I shaved my head, and left their beloved Harry.

Misdirection. It's a solid plan.

"For fuck's sake." Jagger's solid hand grips my hip in a bid to still me but it makes me wriggle more. "Should have let you freeze."

"When will it go down?" I'm glad he can't see the color of my face right now, but the heat radiating from my cheeks could probably heat the room just fine.

"What?" His gruff voice makes me smile. Is he always grumpy like this? Or is it something I have a talent of bringing out in him?

I wiggle my hips again, drawing a low groan from him, the noise lighting up my nerves in the darkness. His breath on my skin, his hand on my hip, his voice in my ear, the smell of the forest tickling my nose. It's like a party for my senses.

"That." I can't say it out loud.

He sighs. "How do you expect to tackle number three on your list if you can't even say cock?"

It's like the last word is a switch, and my body is a dormant Christmas tree. The sensation between my thighs takes my breath away.

#3 Talk dirty between the sheets.

Even the thought of saying that word he just said, out loud, makes my whole body shrivel up. It's crass. Dirty. Offensive. And not something a girl like me should say.

My parent's words assault my mind as Jagger's thumb

glides back and forth on the sliver of skin where my shirt has ridden up.

"Whoever told you whatever it is making you tense up like this over the word 'cock' is wrong. Why give words so much power over you anyway?"

He has a point, but I still can't say it. I'm not sure I ever could.

"Th-this list was born from a voracious appetite for reading."

He snorts, making my hair move. "Classic literature has the word 'cock' in it? Huh. Who knew?"

"I read all sorts." I dig him with my elbow, a warm satisfaction spreading through me at his soft grunt. "Don't shame me for what I enjoy."

"I don't need to shame you for anything. You do it more than enough for both of us."

Oof. My body lurches like he punched me in the stomach. He's not wrong. But I don't want to unpack that right now.

"Well? That's not an answer. When does it... uh... deflate? I thought this only happened in the mornings."

He sighs again. Grabs my hand and puts it square-on his junk. Oh, my. It's... uh... girthy? Is that the right word?

"What are you doing?" I feel like I should jump out of bed, get on my knees, and say a million apology prayers to God for the fact I'm touching this man's penis. But if I get on my knees in front of Jagger, only God knows what he'd do with his penis.

"This isn't morning wood, it's not evening wood, it's pure, unadulterated attraction, Talia. When a beautiful woman pulls me up against her pert little ass it's hard to hide the raging boner I've had in my pants all fucking night."

Oh.

You could hear a pin drop in the heavy silence pressing on both of us. My chest rises and falls in the quiet, and I'm focused on filling my lungs with oxygen because if I stop thinking about air circulating in my chest I might think about what his words mean.

He lets go of me and rolls onto his back. "Ugh. Your self-loathing is so fucking loud." I can't see what he's doing, but the sound of friction suggests he's rubbing his forehead. At least, I sure hope that's what he's rubbing.

"Stop making assumptions about me." I don't mean to snap, but I've had assumptions made about me my whole life. This man doesn't know me, and yet he's guessing what's going through my head.

New Talia made the conscious choice to be curious, and to leave her years of conditioning to be ashamed in the past. It's not always going to work, it's going to poke through here and there, but New Talia is exhausted from a lifetime of shame.

I can't lie still. Between his protruding... extension, and the heat pooling between my legs, my body keeps twitching. My nipples are making a bid for freedom through all the layers of clothing—like the princess and the pea I can feel them poking through my shirt.

I'm not sure if embarrassment or lust is winning, but my whole body prickles with sweat. If I wasn't so cold I'd kick him back to his own bed, or another room, but in truth, I'm kinda freaked out by spending the night in a dungeon and don't really want to be alone.

"Jagger?"

He grunts.

"Can't you make it go away?"

"Not without making a mess."

I can hear the smirk in his voice, it sends a shiver snaking up each bone in my spine making me squirm.

"Like that idea do you, Half-Pint?"

My stupid body's betraying me, even in the darkness.

"We could take care of number nine on your list together."

#9 Mutual masturbation

Blinking, I'm not sure I've heard him right. Did he suggest we both…?

He grunts again, and I squeak, scooting closer to the edge of the bed, the silky soft sheets making it easy to slide. His chuckle is savage, and once again I feel like I'm food for a predator, and he's messing with me before biting my head off.

"We don't even have to turn the light on if you don't want to. But I have to admit, Half-Pint." His breath is on my face again, his voice so close to my ear it's sending waves of goosebumps all over my body. "I'd love to see you finger that tight little cunt of yours."

The moan slips out between my lips before I can cover my mouth with both hands. Am I more embarrassed that he heard it? Or that it happened at all? The way he's speaking shouldn't turn me on, but we now *both* know it is most definitely getting me aroused.

His tongue tickles the shell of my ear. In the darkness, the slight touch is heightened and I feel it everywhere, my nipples, my chest, between my legs, and all the way down to my toes. "Do your steamy books have safewords, Talia?"

I nod.

"Out loud, Half-Pint."

"Y-yes."

"Good. If you decide you want to play with me, we'll need a safeword. You should start thinking about one."

"Unicorn." It's almost inaudible, but the room is so quiet he picks it up.

"Unicorn. I like it."

He said we could do it in the dark, I don't even have to turn the lights on or take my clothes off. And I already know squeezing my legs together isn't doing a darn thing to ease the ache shimmering inside me.

What happens in the weird kinky dungeon, stays in the weird kinky dungeon, right?

The heat under the blankets is unbearable. And also largely imaginary. It's cold. It's freezing outside, and the room is cold, but the heat from my core is warming up the space between us, between the sheets, at an unbelievable pace.

This is new and improved Talia. Blue haired, strong spine, confident Talia. And a beautiful man has told me he's turned on by me. That's a heady, empowering feeling.

My fingers glide across my stomach, hesitating at the waistband of my pants. The battle between pushing my parent's and pastor's words out of my mind and succumbing to the desire building in my core is consuming.

"There's no one here but us."

I know that. Every time he speaks, his warm breath dances across my skin.

"After tomorrow you never have to see me again."

Also true.

The bed shifts like he's inching closer toward me, so I hold my breath.

"I won't judge."

I believe him.

"Just let yourself feel good."

It's harder than he seems to think.

"Would it help or hurt if I touched myself first?" His voice sounds like he's grinding it out between his teeth. Is he that turned on? A seasoned dominant like Jagger, turned on by someone as vanilla as me? How?

The thought of him touching himself in the darkness lying next to me makes my breath catch in my chest.

"Would you rather I left you alone?"

I reach a hand out to grab his arm so he doesn't leave, and I grab, uh, something else. The guttural sound that comes out of him at the contact sounds more animal than human.

"I, oh no, I'm so sorry. I didn't mean to." I snap my hand away, but part of me wants to make him make that noise again.

"It's fine."

It doesn't sound fine. The grump sounds like he's in pain, actual, physical pain.

"What can I do?" My hand jerks out again, but I pull it back before it comes into contact with anything.

"Make yourself come, Half-Pint. For both our sakes." The strain in his voice sends me over the edge.

My fingers are almost at my clit when I stop dead. "I want the light on." I don't know that I do, but new Talia thinks it might be hotter if we can see each other. I want to see the strain in his face, not just hear it in his words. I want to see his body reacting to what I do with mine.

His face lights up when he picks up his phone and hits the screen. A low-level lighting comes on, not the harsh, bright lights we had earlier.

"You can control the lights from your phone?"

He winks at me, his face serious. "You can control a lot of things from your phone. We can talk more about that if we get to do number six. Fingers, pussy, now."

I shimmy my pants down to my knees, but his hand covers mine.

"Repeat your safeword to me."

I frown at him. "I just did."

"Do it again." Something about how his words implore me with a simple inflection.

"Unicorn."

"Good."

Another dart of pleasure shoots up my spine, softening my shoulders.

"You know you can stop at any time, right?"

I sink my teeth into my lip and nod, but his thumb unhooks it. "No nodding, speak up."

"I do."

"Good."

Every kinky book boyfriend I've ever read says "Good girl," and Jagger not giving me the full thing is making me ache in a deep place I didn't even know existed.

What do I have to do to make him tell me I'm a good girl?

CHAPTER 11

Jagger

Is death by balls exploding a thing?

Because if I don't get to take the edge off this soon, I may very well find out.

The lights are on. Despite the cold, the blankets flipped back off her completely, her pants are shucked all the way down to her ankles, and the gorgeous woman lying next to me with flushed cheeks and wide eyes is just... staring.

"Tell me what to do." Her voice is quiet, soft, not pleading, but there's a firmness to it that makes me want to test her.

"Do it how you usually do it."

Her brows flinch like she's processing what I said, before she licks her bottom lip.

I prop myself up on my elbow, hand gripped around my pulsing cock. It's leaking, aching, begging for release, but I don't want to scare the sprite. If she decides she wants to stop, I'll figure myself out in a bathroom, but for now, I'm enjoying watching her face. "Can I look?"

She flickers her gaze to my cock, then back to my face. "I'd like that." Legs spread further apart, she sighs, her eyes drifting closed. Her hand is resting above her pubic bone. Tufts of blonde curly hair lead down to a perfectly glistening pussy I'd love to sink into.

"So beautiful, Talia."

She rolls her lips between her teeth but doesn't argue. She walks her fingers through her hair until she finds her clit. She's slick, slippery, completely soaked and when her fingers move in a circle and makes a noise, she covers her eyes with her free hand.

I pluck her hand off her face and put it on her chest. "There's nothing to be ashamed of."

Her questioning eyes flicker open and find mine.

"There's no sound your body can make that's going to pull a reaction from me that isn't desire." I pause. "Unless you fart. Sometimes farts are funny."

Her lips flicker like she's going to smile. The skin of her neck flickers quickly as her pulse races below the surface.

"And even then, if you fart, you fart. When you sign up to play, you sign up for the fluids, and the sounds, the queefs, the farts, the squelches."

She tries to cover her face again.

"Don't hide, Half-Pint. Sex isn't neat and tidy, it's not pretty, it's not clean. It's messy, and raw, and loud. It's nothing to be ashamed of. It's nothing to hide from or fear. Exploring yourself and your sexuality isn't only normal, but it's completely healthy. Don't let anyone tell you it isn't. Do you want to stop?"

She shakes her head. Then, as though she realizes I'm about to ask for vocal confirmation, she says 'no' out loud.

"Good. Just make yourself feel good. That's all you need to do, right? Don't hold back. Don't let embarrassment, or shame, or self-consciousness stop you from feeling nice, okay?"

She hums, but her fingers are moving fast. They're sliding in jerky up and down movements skimming faster and faster across the top of her clit. Her hips are bucking, her breath is fractured, and while her eyes are closed, she's scowling, so I know she's not getting the desired result from fingering herself.

When I put my huge hand over hers, she stills. "Am I doing it wrong?" Her voice is strained, layered with frustration.

"There's no wrong way to get yourself off. But can I make a suggestion?"

"Please."

That sounds like a plea, and it makes my dick twitch.

"Try a gentler touch, and try circles." I move my hand over hers, guiding her. Her body shakes with a shiver as she begins touching herself again. When she's found a rhythm, I take my hand off hers and plant it firmly on my cock.

I want to touch her. I want to stroke her cheek, push her hair out of her face, and tell her how she looks like a goddess lying next to me as she touches herself. I wish she'd open her eyes, though I understand her reluctance to look at me. This isn't a small deal for her.

Her pace is steady, and as she circles her clit, her free hand makes its way up under her shirt, and I bite my lip to stop any noise coming from my body. I don't want to spook her. I don't want her to stop.

My dick is painfully hard, precum weeping from the tip as my tight hand pumps up and down in time with her circles.

When she moans, her breath catching, it almost sends me over the edge.

"Fuck." My teeth are gritted, my balls so heavy I'm not sure how I haven't blown my load yet, and my dick is throbbing, so hard and ready for release.

Her hips are rolling, slowly lifting off the mattress with every swirl of her hand on her pussy. Her face is pinker, her fingers slicker, her breathing coming faster and faster as she charges toward her orgasm.

I'm barely touching myself, and I'm close. It's brewing all the way to the base of my spine, release so sweet I can almost taste it.

Something's holding her back from letting go. It's like she needs more, or she's starting to get in her head. Her fingers splutter, stop-starting, her eyes flutter open, and she holds my stare.

"That's it, pretty girl. You're doing so well."

Her eyes search my face. I don't know what she's looking for, or if I can give it to her, but when my fingers skim her soft, smooth cheekbone I want her to come.

Shit, I need her to come.

"Come for me, beautiful. Just let it go."

"So close." Her words hiss out on a whoosh of air through clenched teeth. Her body is rigid, muscles tense and poised for ecstasy. "C-can't."

"Do you need me to step out?" I'm not sure I can walk in my current state, but I need to offer. Whatever she needs to make it happen.

"N-n-no. S-s-stay. Please?"

I sweep her hair off her forehead, gliding my lips across her temple in the gentlest of kisses. "Okay. I'll stay. But I need you to be a good girl for me, and let it all go. Just com—"

An ear piercing scream rips through the quiet air as her body bucks off the bed. Her shrill cry of release is unfettered, her eyes roll back in her head, mouth drops open, and I'll be damned if my little Half-Pint doesn't squirt over the bed.

She's still coming when I curl my fist around my cock and pump myself over and over.

"You have no idea how gorgeous you are when you come, Talia. So fucking beautiful." It doesn't take long before I'm spraying jets of thick, warm cum all over my stomach on a grunt. Relief weaves through all my muscles, relaxing them through my orgasm.

The urge to cover her in it was strong, but we didn't discuss it beforehand so I made a mess of myself.

Her body trembles, every muscle quivering. She hasn't stopped, her fingers circling her soaking wet clit. Her hips buck again, legs jerking, sliding on the silky sheets. "I-i-aaaaaaaaahhhhhhhh." Another wave crashes into her, and it's fucking glorious. Her head tips back, hair fans across the pillow case.

Her body goes limp as she sighs, collapsing onto the mattress.

When her legs hit the mattress, she whimpers. Cold satin sheets against skin isn't nice. I didn't plan for this, clean up supplies are out of arm's reach, and I didn't grab a towel. I'm normally better prepared than this.

Leaning over her, I brush another soft kiss against her temple. "I'll be right back. Don't move, okay?"

She yawns. "But I need to clean up. I'm all sticky. I made a mess." Her voice is thick and heavy, slow and adorably mumbly.

"Just stay where you are. I've got you." I tuck my cock away, climb off the bed, and walk over to the clean-up station where I pick up two towels. In the bathroom, I grab some warm water and head back to the bed.

She's almost asleep, but when I touch her calf, she gasps, then crosses her legs. "You can't clean me up."

"Shhhhh. I can, and I will." I dip the towel into the water and squeeze most of it out before I dab the inside of her thighs, cleaning up. "Sleep, Talia. It's okay. I'm here, and I've got you."

She hums contentedly. "Mmmk."

After I've cleaned her, I move her and the pile of blankets to the dry bed, and climb in beside her. When I've curled myself around her, she takes my hand. "You don't need to do this."

"After care is important to me, Half-Pint. You don't get to steal my fun."

She smiles. "You're too grumpy to have fun."

She's not wrong. I don't do fun. Tomorrow's probably going to bring regret and shame from her, but for right now, the sprite is quiet, warm, and if I don't cuddle her I could end up losing body parts to the weather.

But I'll face tomorrow, tomorrow.

CHAPTER 12
Talia

I'M SO COLD MY NOSE MIGHT FALL OFF.

When we woke up this morning, the heat hadn't magically kicked on overnight in the club. And despite the giant's warmth, and the mountain of blankets, we were both still cold. Turns out, Mr. Grumpypants is also Mr. Protectivepants, and despite the fact there was a fresh helping of snow overnight, and another one on the way, he's determined we should at least move to the hotel half a mile down the road.

It's half a mile, he said. We'd be fine, he said.

The snow plows haven't been able to keep up with the inclement weather. It's coming down faster than they're clearing it. And as scary as it was to ride in the car with him through the ice, snow, and wind, the prospect of staying another night in that ice box wasn't an enticing one.

Okay, fine. Maybe it was a little enticing.

Did I want to be forced to stay snowed in at a sex club with a gorgeous man who watched me make myself come last night?

Yes. Yes, I did. And both old Talia and new Talia feel very strongly about it. It was the best orgasm I've ever had.

Orgasms.

Plural.

And when he came, the look of pure relief, of sheer bliss that crossed his face as he coated his stomach in his cum was everything I've ever dreamed of when it came to finding a lover.

He was invested in my pleasure. An almost complete stranger who barely laid a hand on me wanted me to come first. And when I did, he let go, and my pleasure fed into his own.

That's what I always thought was supposed to happen. It's what always happens in the books I read.

"You going to stay out here to freeze?" The man in question holds the car door open. He had contemplated taking his car, because he clearly abhors my poor dear Bessie, but his car isn't designed for the snow. And after a lengthy discussion about not being a stubborn idiot, he agreed that Bessie was the better choice for the weather.

Did she fishtail on the road a few times on our short journey? Absolutely. But she also got us where we needed to be without incident. So I'm more than a little smug right now.

"No! I'm coming." I dart out of the car, albeit too fast, and my feet slide across the sheet of ice underfoot. "Whooop" My wobble and imminent collision with the frosty ground is blocked, yet again, by Jagger. He grabs me just in time.

The last thing I need right now is a wet and bruised booty from falling.

"You know how to walk, right?" His gruffness almost sounds amused. Almost. His brow is furrowed and his lips are downturned, though, so it's probably wishful thinking on my part.

"Only since I was a year old." I snatch my arm from him, instantly regretting that life choice as I wobble again. I refuse to fall. So I scoot forward on the ice like I meant to do that the whole time.

A couple minutes later, he's handing over his credit card to Melanie, the very friendly lady at the check in counter. They only have one room left, but contrary to all the books I read, it has two beds. No snuggling for me tonight. Not unless we end up freezing like we did last night.

The disappointment that makes my stomach drop is too obvious to avoid, but I try to push it aside. Melanie is smiling widely at Jagger as she programs our key cards. I don't blame her, he's a stunning human being. But there's a slight twinge of something inside me. I want to learn more from him, do more with him.

To say I have a crush on the man who saved me from freezing to death would be an understatement. But I'm not that naive. Guys like Mr. Grumpypants don't pick girls like me.

Even if after last night, I kind of want him to.

While I follow him into the elevator and stare at the back of his feet as we make our way up to our room, I try to convince myself his bad boy persona is attractive to me right now. My plans for the future turned on their head, everything I thought I knew and wanted exploded, and I lost the man I thought I'd spend forever with.

Jagger is the antithesis of Harry. It stands to reason I'd love to rebound into a man who's everything Harry isn't. But there's no way Jagger wants anything more than a little fun with me.

Could I be okay with that? No strings attached?

As someone who, until very recently, was essentially keeping herself for marriage, I'm not sure I can go all the way with someone I have no plans to marry. But that leaves a heck of a lot of stuff I could try.

My bucket list is pretty long, and only some of them involve full pene—

"You coming?" Jagger's holding the elevator open, staring at me with impatience in his eyes, his lips in a flat line.

I bet he's regretting bringing me along on his adventure into the warmth. Following him into the room, I shrug off the dirty thoughts of my roommate for the rest of the day and all night. He probably thought we weren't going to survive the night so needed one last orgasm before his peen froze.

Nothing else is going to happen between us.

The room is small, cozy, and while the woman at the desk told us there were two beds, she was overshooting. The second bed is a pull-out couch. And twenty minutes of trying to figure the dang thing out doesn't help. I'm pretty sure it's broken.

"I'll take the couch." Jagger's voice is hard.

"No! I couldn't let you do that."

He didn't let me pay for the room. I spied an ATM in the lobby though, so I'll withdraw cash and pay him for my half before we leave. But I draw the line at him taking the world's smallest couch that doesn't even pull out into a bed like we were promised when we got here.

"It wasn't a question." He grunts, drops his bag, and settles on the couch like the decision has been made. Without discussion.

The audacity.

"What if I want the couch?" I pop my knee, planting my hands on my hips like I mean business. Which I do. But staring down the man who barely fits on the couch, even I have to admit it's laughable.

Just a little though. I've got a pretty good mean mug.

He doesn't even dignify me with an answer. In fact, he glares right through me. If I wasn't so mad at him not even letting me make my own decision, I'd put up more of a fight.

But if the big, cranky oaf wants to make his creaky, broken, couch-bed, then he can lie in it.

"Fine. Be a stubborn mule. I'm taking a shower." I gesture at my clothes. "I wonder if they have a laundry service. I'm running out of clean clothes."

My carryon bag didn't have a lot in it since I was going to my parent's house and I have clothes there. But I have the clothes from the plane, today's clothes, and a pair of pjs I didn't wear last night because it was so cold.

He doesn't answer, he's too busy digging in his bag for something, so I leave him to it. While I'm in the shower, I try to remind myself he's always been grumpy, from the minute he sat down next to me on the plane.

Our little, uh, session last night didn't make him less grumpy. Did I expect it to soften him some? I don't know. But I'm hugely self-conscious for some reason. And I'm definitely feeling... things, things I don't quite understand.

Tears stream down my face under the jets of steaming hot water. The warmth wraps around me, but doesn't reach all the way into my bones. I don't know how long has passed, but when there's a soft knock on the door, the bathroom's full of thick steam.

"Yeah?" I sniff, hoping it's not too obvious I'm crying.

"Are you okay?" His voice is as gruff as always, but there's an element of concern that warms my insides. "Do you need help?"

It's hard not to snort. "Help? Showering? I think I'm good."

Something tells me he's still lingering at the door.

"What is it?"

"Do you need me to wash your hair?"

What the heck is this guy's deal?

"No, thanks, it's already done. I'll be out in a sec."

When I emerge from the bathroom, a towel wrapped

around my body and another curled around my head, he's sitting on the edge of the bed like he's been waiting for me.

"Do you need a hug?" His voice is soft, sincere.

"Why?"

"Aftercare." It's one word, and it seems to blanket-cover a variety of things. I might need him to explain it to me more.

"And the hair washing?"

He nods. "Aftercare."

"And the bed?"

He nods again but this time doesn't speak.

"Aftercare." It's not a question, but a statement. I say the word slowly like I'm testing it out in my mouth.

I've read a lot of books. Some have aftercare, some don't. But I've never given much thought to what I might need for my own aftercare. "I don't know what I need." Voicing my thoughts out loud makes me feel incredibly vulnerable. I try to wrap my arms around myself, but I'm standing in a towel, which makes everything worse.

"That's okay. Even if you had a whole list of things written, sometimes after a scene you still don't know what you need. It's okay to not know. Sometimes drops can last weeks, or even take a while to hit after a scene. But if you're with the right kind of partner they'll be happy to help you through whatever comes after playing." He points a finger at me. "That's how you can tell if you're with someone you should be with or not. If the person you're with hauls ass after a scene, or doesn't give a fuck, or dismisses your aftercare—those aren't your people."

I nod, trying to absorb the information.

"You hear me? That's non-negotiable, Half-Pint."

I'm still nodding. "Okay." I hug the towel tighter to me. "So you don't mind if I need a hug once I get dressed?"

He flinches like I slapped him. "Of course not."

I really need to dive more into this aftercare thing. He

clearly takes it very seriously. Does he need aftercare? If so, does he want me to give it to him? I'm not sure I want to open that door to conversation, but he's so adamant about helping me with my aftercare, it only feels right I should ask him.

Thankfully, I have travel toiletries too, so my teeth are clean, and I don't stink. It's warmer here, so I pull out my pjs and point to the bathroom. "Be right back."

It's a quick dry, change, and towel dry of my hair before I'm back in the bedroom. My pjs aren't anything sexy or revealing. In fact, they're pretty frumpy. But I'm not trying to make him fall for me. I need him to squeeze me for bit, and I'll be fine.

"You sure you're down for cuddles?"

He doesn't dignify that with an answer either, he plucks me up off the floor and drops me into his lap on the bed before curling his arms around me. Okay, fine. This is nice. It's more than nice.

The tightness of his arms banded around me, the warmth of his breath tickling my neck as he breathes, the way my muscles melt. Tipping my head back so it hits his shoulder, I feel like a doll sitting on him.

"You okay?" He's gruff, but the concern etched into those two words has me welling up.

I nod, afraid if I open my mouth to answer, a sob will come out. I don't even know what's wrong with me.

"You know, it's really easy to hit drop sometimes. Those hormones that hit during a scene drop and leave you feeling inexplicably sad and emotional. It's totally okay. Last night was a lot. And it's not something you've experienced before. Just let yourself feel." He's stroking my forearm with his thumb, and his voice is so soothing, so calming, it's almost hard to believe he's so grumpy.

I yawn, closing my eyes and settling in. Taking a quick nap won't do any harm, right?

"That's it. Just relax."

"You're really nice for a grumpy guy." I'm mumbling, but he must make out what I say because his chest rumbles against my back as he chuckles.

"I'm a responsible dominant. I wouldn't have encouraged you last night if I wasn't prepared for the potential fall out today."

"Aftercare." My voice is thick with sleep.

"That's right, Half-Pint. Aftercare."

I don't know how long he lets me nap for, or what wakes me up, but one of his thumbs is stroking the side of my face, while he's typing on his phone with the other when I wake up.

He hums, like he knows I'm awake. "You can sleep more if you need it."

I didn't think a mutual masturbation session was all that big of a deal, but it clearly took its toll on me. Even thinking about it is making my body react, and I can't afford that when I'm curled into him like this. What if he notices?

"Easy." His thumb skims my face. "Just breathe and relax. You're safe."

My phone rings across the room, and when I jump out of my skin, my head catches his chin.

"Fuck." He cups his face, muttering cuss words as I scramble to find and answer my phone.

"Shhhh" I'm flapping a hand at him to simmer down. Mama's name is on the screen, and if she hears a gruff man in the background cussing, she's going to have questions. "Mama?"

"Did you book a new flight? Harry is here, and he wants to talk to you."

Turning my back to Jagger doesn't dull the blazing scorch of his stare on my body.

"No, mama. I'm still snowed in. And I have no intention

of talking to Harry. I told you already. Mama. I need you to hear me when I tell you I'm done with him."

She snorts, like it's the most absurd thing she's ever heard. "You're never done with him, Tali. He's your one, forever. So stop being childish and talk to the boy. The sooner you figure this out the sooner we can plan your wedding and get to the fun things."

She's not listening. Pinching the bridge of my nose isn't doing much to help the fact my temples are now pounding. I felt great after the nap. Like, "I could take on the world" great. And now, now I feel like a scolded seven-year-old for taking grammy's snickerdoodles off the cooling rack.

I heave out a huge sigh. It's not only that she's not listening, she doesn't *want* to hear. There's nothing I can say to her that will make her hear my words, or my meaning. It's going to take actions. Which means not going back to see my parents. If I go back, they'll assume I consent to being shoved back into a relationship with a man I don't love, a man who doesn't respect me, and a man who can't keep it in his pants.

That's not happening.

I open my mouth to say something else. I'm not even sure what, but before I can get a word out, Jagger clears his throat.

"Who's that?" Mama has had bat-like hearing since I was born.

My breath stops in my chest, my brain short circuits, and my heart thump-thumps so loud against my ribs, Mama can probably hear it.

"Hey, Talia. Are you ready for lunch?" His silky smooth voice carries across the small hotel room. My stomach turns to lead, my muscles tense, and before Mama can grill me about the man's voice in the background, I panic and hang up the phone.

In fact, I go one step further and turn it all-the-way off. I can tell her my battery died. Considering I'm stranded in a public place, it's not out of the realm of possibility.

When I turn to face Jagger, he's got a casual smirk smeared across his smugly beautiful face. If I was a violent woman, I'd smack him. This isn't funny. It's not even smirk-y funny. This is a disaster. My Mama is going to think I'm a floozy. Even from being in the company of another man when she's so desperate for me to fix things with Harry.

She's going to assume I don't want to get back together with Harry because I'm with some mysterious man. She's going to think I'm not on a plane right now because of him, not because of the weather. She's going to—

Warm hands cup my face and redirect my spiraling attention. "Breathe."

He's not the boss of me. And anyway, I can't breathe. It's not that easy. You'd think considering it's something I've done for over twenty years on this earth it would be something that comes easily. In this moment, however, my chest is so tight I'm afraid my head might pop off my body.

"Breathe, Half-Pint. With me." He sucks in a breath, holds it, and releases it.

It takes, actually I have no idea how long it takes, but after some time I become aware we're breathing together.

"You don't understand my parents. Y-you shouldn't have done that." Even as I say it I don't fully believe it. Part of me is glad he did it, but another is really, really mad.

"Is she why masturbation is okay, but sex isn't?"

Wow. Talk about not pulling any punches. "Strict religious upbringing. My parents drilled it into me from a young age that sex isn't something you do before you get married." I shrug. That's really all there is to it. When you peel back the layers, I don't have sex because my parents told me not to. But those voices are really freakin' loud. I've never felt empowered like the heroines in my books either.

To his credit, he doesn't snicker, or mock my upbringing, or my parents. He simply boops my nose. "Your accent is stronger when you talk to your mama." He mimics my Kentucky. It's exaggerated, and sounds more like he's from Georgia than Kentucky but he tried his best.

Bless his heart.

Clearing my throat, I pop my knee again, planting my hands on my hips. This is becoming a habit with this guy. "You ain't seen nuthin' yet, big boy."

His nostrils flicker. It's the closest I'm getting to him laughing, that is until he chuckles. "Wow. That's so... southern." He bops my jaw. "Keep breathing. New Talia, remember? We aren't entertaining assholes."

I have a tendency to babble out loud, I must have said something about being New Talia that he could hear because I certainly never said anything to him directly. Wait.

He called my mama an A-hole. And from the defiant look in his eye, and the firm set of his jaw, he doesn't care.

"You're either real brave, or real stupid to insult a southern woman's mama, Jagger." I poke his giant chest. Oh. Oh my. He's got muscles under that shirt.

"I'm real hungry, ma'am. That's what I am." His accent is terrible, but I can't help giggling at him. "You comin' to eat?"

I shove his arm but he barely moves. "I don't talk like that. Let me get out of my pjs and we'll go eat."

It's somewhere between lunch and dinner. Too late for lunch, too early for dinner. But when we hit the restaurant, there are a few tables of people dotted around. There's a young couple with two kids in the corner closest to the door. The mom's arguing with a little boy with unruly red hair about a screen, while the dad guides food toward a baby in a high chair while making airplane noises.

It must be awful to be trapped in a hotel with kids. Not having their toys, or clothes, or space to roam freely. Hopefully the hotel has diapers and things in case the mom runs out. If this was a flood, I'd contemplate trying to hit up a pharmacy, but there's no way I'm braving Bessie on the roads. Not even for an adorable baby whose mouth, hair, and entire body is covered in tomato sauce. She's still super cute, though.

Two old men play backgammon on one table, another two are playing Battleship, it seems when one lands a hit they make exploding noises. I'm here for it.

At another table, a group of half a dozen old ladies sit with pots of tea and fancy china cups on the table. They've got the remnants of afternoon tea scattered around, half eaten sandwiches and decadent pastries, while they sit and knit or crochet.

Grammy used to love her weekly stitch 'n bitch group. Something tweaks inside my chest. What if Grammy follows my parents with her opinion on Harry? Will she disown me if I don't do as they say?

A warm hand meets my lower back and guides me forward. The hostess is gesturing to a table for two in the far corner, away from the bustle of the main restaurant. It's definitely not my vibes that's causing her to isolate us from the rest of the group.

Jagger radiates 'leave me alone' waves into the air around him. It's his natural vibration frequency.

"One of the servers will be over to take your drinks order in a moment." The hostess's smile lights up the room as she hands Jagger both our menus.

"Thank you." I match her smile with a smile of my own.

As with most chairs, my feet don't quite touch the ground when I sit all the way back. So I scoot forward. "What looks good?"

He doesn't even glance at the menu. "Pancake stack, with a triple side of bacon."

Wow. This man doesn't play around when it comes to

food. Granted, we haven't eaten anything but a granola bar for breakfast since our drive through last night.

"Sounds good." I skim the menu, keeping one eye on my dinner buddy over the edge of the large card. He doesn't make conversation, he doesn't scroll on his phone, he doesn't read, doesn't ask what I'm having to eat, or, I dunno, anything. He just sits.

What's going on inside his beautiful brain?

Placing the menu on the table, I clasp my hands together on top of it, leaning toward him. "Would you rather be forced to sing along, or dance to every single song you hear?"

He looks at me like I've grown three heads, my skin has changed to blue, and I've sprouted scales all over my body. "Neither."

"Are y'all ready to order?" Our server is tall, has athletic shoulders like she might be a swimmer, and looks like someone Jagger would be better suited to be having dinner with.

Something stirs in my stomach. This man isn't mine, I have no claim to him. All we've done is kiss, and get off side-by-side in bed last night, but that seedling of a crush I had on him seems to be sprouting teeny tiny roots in my chest, and I don't like it.

We order our meal, and the server leaves with one parting, toothpaste ad smile.

I level him with an eye roll. "You can't pick neither, that's not how the game works."

"I don't play games."

Another eye roll. "Look, we're stuck here together. How else do you suggest we pass the time if not getting to know each other?"

There's that bemused look in his eye again. "Would you rather questions isn't exactly getting to know each other, Half-Pint."

I mean, he has a point. But what does knowing his favorite color, or food tell me about him?

"Indulge me?"

He sighs with a shake of his head. The Battleship's table erupts into a chorus of explosion noises as one old guy leaps to his feet, arms raised above his head in triumph. His wiry glasses slide off his nose and onto the table with a plop. Part of me wants to go high five him for his success.

"Singing. I can do it quietly and not draw attention to myself."

That tracks. This hulking great guy wants nothing more than to blend into the background and go unnoticed.

He doesn't ask my answer, or rush to give me more information, so I throw another one at him. "Would you rather be in Disney Land for five years, or be in a coma for a decade?"

He arches a brow, accentuating those golden flecks in his brown eyes.

Holding up a hand, I shake my head. "I know, I know. Silly question. You'd pick the coma, right? No one can bug you when you're asleep."

He grunts. Seems that's the only answer I'm going to get, and I can't help but giggle. I'm going to have to get creative to tease some conversation out of this man. Out of everyone on the planet, my chatty self gets landed with the world's most stoic, quiet and sensible man alive.

It's just my luck.

Thankfully, he's pretty to look at.

"Would you rather uhhh swim in a pool full of Nutella or a pool of maple syrup?"

That makes the corner of his lip twitch. "Maple syrup. Nutella would be too hard to swim through."

I indulge his silence for a long moment. When his phone rings, I find myself paying attention to his long, thick dark lashes, his flawless brown skin, and the size of his hands as he takes a call on his phone.

If this was a date, I'd scold him for being rude. But since all this amounts to is a situationally convenient meal between almost strangers, I bite my tongue.

"Yeah. I'm fine. You?" His conversation skills are even limited on the phone. Or perhaps it's because he's in front of me that he doesn't want to demonstrate he's actually great with the chit chat.

He falls silent for a beat. "Cool. I spent last night at the club." Another beat. "Heat is broken. All the blankets I used are in the laundry baskets."

Am I mildly disgruntled he didn't mention I was with him when he almost froze to death? I am. But I'm also aware it's irrational.

He's not my captor, but perhaps this is early onset Stockholm syndrome or something. It's coming up to the holidays, that weird space of time between Thanksgiving and Christmas, there's a thick blanket of snow pouring down onto the city, and I'm stuck in a hotel with the most beautiful man I've ever met.

That's it, right? It's got to be the only reason a billion bumble bees start humming in my stomach every time he looks in my direction. It is.

That and my cheating, scumbag ex-fiancé.

He snickers. "Yes, sir. I'm sure I know how to work it. I reset the whole system. Still nothing."

The guy on the other end of the phone cusses so loudly even I can hear him. I wince, drawing attention to myself. Jagger stares at me with his piercing dark eyes.

"I moved to the hotel half a mile away."

"Pancake stack for the gentleman." The server appears with our food, placing the tower of bacon in front of Jagger.

"And a club sandwich with fries for the lady." She flashes

me the dazzling smile, and the idea I could switch my sexual preferences for this woman flickers through my mind. I've never questioned my sexuality before, but this woman is so blindingly stunning, I'd consider it. Maybe.

"Thank you." I keep my voice low because I don't want to interrupt his call.

She asks if we need anything else, then leaves. As she retreats, Jagger's lips fall into a flat line, a muscle feathering in his cheek as his eyes hold mine. "No one."

Oof. The wind deflates from my lungs.

He's right. In the grand scheme of things, I am no one to him. But until those words left his lips, I thought, I dunno, maybe I thought I could maybe be someone.

CHAPTER 13

Jagger

HALF-PINT'S BODY COLLAPSES LIKE AN ACCORDION right in front of my eyes. Her chest caves, her shoulders sag, her head droops. I'm not sure she realizes she's doing it, but she's literally crumpling into herself.

My boss, and probably the closest thing I have to a friend, Slade, asked who I was eating with, and I said no one. Realistically, she isn't anyone. I've known her for less than forty eight hours, I've had meals last longer than my interaction with this woman. Why's she so crushed?

Is she so starved for attention she fixates on anyone who shows it to her? She can't be attracted to my winning personality. What the hell is this woman's damage? What did he do to her?

The more I pay attention to her, her gaze falling to the floor, her quivering chin, her trembling fingers as she picks up her food, the more I realize she's probably been hurt before. She's clearly upset. And I don't like that maybe I had something to do with that. It *was* kind of a jerkish thing to call her no one. But that slight rejection from a damn near stranger derailed her.

That fucker. Flexing my fingers under the table, I want to destroy him. The rage surging through my veins like a live wire makes my knee jump. I want to pound on his face with my fist until he's unrecognizable.

He's not a murderer, at least not that I know of, but he's such a scumbag it wouldn't surprise me if he was. He'd deserve whatever punishment I could bestow on him. I know that for damn sure.

Talia seems to be pure hearted, and kind; sure, she talks too much and she is irritatingly upbeat and positive, but she's a good person. And watching her wilt in front of me revives my determination to destroy her ex.

I make light work of ending the call with Slade before trying to come up with something to draw her back into my space. "Would you rather have skin that changes color based on your emotions, or tattoos that appear all over your body depicting what you did yesterday?"

Her head snaps up. "Excuse me?"

"I said, would you rather have skin that changes color based on your emotions, or tattoos that appear all over your body depicting what you did yesterday?"

She tilts her head. "You don't have to do that."

The sigh that comes out of my body is so heavy it makes the table cloth and napkin flutter. "I don't have to, I want to. Yes, you heard me tell my boss you're no one. After knowing people for a day, that's a pretty normal reaction."

She flinches.

"That's not to say you're a bad person. Or I don't like you. I don't know you." I shrug, hoping to convey my nonchalance. It's not personal, it's no big deal, it's just I don't know her from Adam.

She holds my stare for a long moment, and I'll be damned if I don't want to kiss her. She licks her lower lip like she's thinking the same thing. "Color changing skin. I've never been allowed to get tattoos, my parents always forbade them so I made do with glittery temporary tattoos where they wouldn't see. I don't think I'd want my whole body covered in tattoos of what I did yesterday. That would be terribly boring."

Her eyes flit to my arms where she's seen pieces of my ink before. "Would you choose tattoos?" Her tongue curls her bottom lip back. It's like she's deliberately drawing my attention to her mouth.

"Nah. You're right. Too boring. I'd go with the color changing skin but since I don't have many emotions, that would be boring, too."

She shakes her head before taking a giant bite of her sandwich. She may be small, but she sure can fit a lot in that mouth.

Oh, fuck.

I swallow a groan with a mouthful of bacon.

We eat in silence. I pretend to ignore when she squirts ketchup all over her sweatshirt, even if she looks like she might cry. "I'm definitely going to need to do laundry." She balls up the shirt like it did her dirty.

"I've got an extra." It takes a beat before it hits me. "Okay, so it'll probably come down to your knees, but I've got a hoodie upstairs you can borrow."

That settles her back into silence. When a notification disrupts the quiet, I pull out my phone and start tracking orders for work. There's a shipping update for parts that have been delayed. The snowstorm is going to put me behind schedule, even with my scheduled trip out of town. Weather reports say it's due to start clearing tomorrow at the earliest. I'll tack on another day to be sure and hope the car parts start to arrive at the shop by then.

When we finish up, Talia opts to stick around for a while reading her book and drinking the world's biggest hot cocoa

I've ever seen. I don't want to disturb her by making calls, so I step into the lobby.

Chasing down car parts and rescheduling customers isn't my job, but my front of house person is out on her honeymoon, so I've got to run the gauntlet of talking to people. It's an exhausting twenty minutes. My clients are all very nice people, but talking to this many of them is a lot for one day.

Hell, talking to even a single one of them is a lot for one day.

I'm going to head upstairs to shower. I need to wash off all the 'being social' from my skin. I should tell Half-Pint where I'm going so she doesn't believe I braved the elements to get away from her. Going by what little I know of her, she would probably think just that.

She's not at the table where we were. A quick scan of the room leaves me unsurprised to find her at the table of old ladies who are all knitting or crocheting shit.

She's not sitting down, at least not yet. She's helping the server clear the table of all the afternoon tea remnants. She's chattering away to the server, who seems only too happy to have an extra set of hands. I bet the weather has left them somewhat shorthanded here.

It's sweet of Talia to be so considerate. Midwesterners are nice, but there's certainly something to be said for Southern hospitality. Has she done this before? She's carrying so many plates, and other than her face being screwed up in intense concentration, she looks wholly at ease.

When she emerges from the door to the kitchen, one of the old ladies, with hair as blue as Talia's, beckons her to sit with them. She hesitates for a moment before smoothing down the front of her shirt and taking a seat.

Where has her sweatshirt gone? She's probably made fast friends with the staff, and they took her ketchup-stained shirt to get cleaned. Wouldn't be surprised.

Either way, she sits, cradling her mug of hot chocolate under her chin and inhaling what must be delicious chocolatey goodness. Her eyes flicker closed to a stretched out moment, before she giggles at something someone said.

"Look Betty, young love."

"I remember when my Alfred used to look at me like that."

Two of the old women are shuffling toward where I'm standing in the doorway to the restaurant giving me serious side-eye.

The urge to tell them I'm not with Talia tickles the tip of my tongue, but I stay quiet. I've learned it's best to let people do their thing and not give them the satisfaction of engaging.

"Ladies." I tip my head.

"Don't remember the last time anyone called me a lady, do you, Philomena?"

"Alfred called me an old battle-axe yesterday. They'll never find his body." The old woman gives me a wink of her twinkling eye as they pass me. I believe her. What did she do to Alfred to make him disappear? Bet she dismembered the poor fucker.

"Talia's quite a catch, Jagger." Philomena's voice is light and airy.

"Just don't hurt her like that bastard Harry did."

"That's right." Philomena waves a finger over her head as she walks away. "Or they won't find your body either."

I chuckle despite myself. Of course Talia has already told the table of old ladies our entire story. I bet she's gone all the way back to elementary school in her life story. Dunno how she does it. I'd be happy to live in a cabin in the middle of nowhere if I could. But Talia comes alive as she chats with the strangers around the table. Her eyes dance as her mouth moves at the speed of light. I'm half concerned she's going to slap one of the women with her hands, they're moving so fast, I can't imagine her accident prone self being able to keep up.

She's animated, smile wide, and sitting on the edge of her seat. The women are all engaged, knitting away, but wrapped up in Hurricane Talia's orbit. I've never seen anything like it. She doesn't look exhausted from the interaction, hell, if anything she looks energized and deliriously happy.

What a weirdo.

With a scratch of the back of my neck, I leave her to it. She's going to be there a while. I could take an hour long shower and circle back, she'd probably still be sitting here talking to this group of women. Bet they'd all have knitted double blankets by the time I got back, too.

A few short minutes later, I'm stripped off and standing under jets of steaming hot water. The contrast of the cold, winter wonderland out the window and water so hot it's almost painful is one of my absolute favorite parts of winter.

I'm on the second chorus of Raspberry Beret by Prince, working up a good lather—or rather, attempting to—what is it about hotel toiletries that don't lather right?

There's a dull thud in the distance. Sounds like the room next door. Hopefully it's not housekeeping here in our room, or they're about to get the shock of their lives.

I let myself enjoy another few minutes of the hot water before stepping out into the steam. Hotel towels are another thing I take issue with. Why are they always like postage stamps? If I'm gonna pay you a couple hundred bucks a night, least you can do is give me a towel big enough to cover my fucking junk.

I'm drying my face and head as I step through the bathroom door toward the bedroom and straight into something. The something shrieks, then falls on her ass.

Half-Pint's eyes are wide, her mouth open, then both snap shut. As I drape the towel around the back of my neck, a smile making the edges of my lips twitch, and she reaches out to grab my leg, pulling herself onto her knees.

I'm not sure she quite knows what she's doing. My body's slippery, so her hands slide down my thighs, which of course wakes up my cock. But it's when she tries again I can't fight the chuckle brewing inside me. She looks so perfect on her knees, her skin so flawlessly creamy and pale, pure, pouty lips that would look sinful wrapped around my dick.

She grumbles, heaving out a sigh, then peeks out from one eye slit. Her gasp is comical. "Oh. My. Goodness." She flaps her hands. "It's hard."

"Of course it's hard, you keep trying to touch it."

"I'm doing no such thing! I'm *trying* to get up off the floor."

I've never met someone so accident prone before. This woman has probably spent more time *almost* on her ass than she has on her feet since I met her.

She hasn't broken eye contact with my cock. I dunno if she's intrigued by it, or intimidated by it.

"If you'd come back a few minutes earlier, we'd have been able to check number four off your bucket list."

It takes a minute for her to register that number four is having sex in the shower. She gasps again. Does this woman do anything other than trip over herself and gasp?

"Does it hurt?" She stretches a finger toward one of the piercings in my cock. The urge to yell "boo" at her is so strong, I flex my fists at my sides. Her curiosity strokes something in my chest as she tips her head, looking up to me for permission.

How can I say no to her? She's beautiful, inquisitive, and as soon as I nod my head, her fingers touch the first of my piercings.

It takes a second before it hits me that the slow hiss of breath is coming from my body as she rolls her thumb over the metal beads and bars. It's like slow torture.

"What do they feel like?"

My fingers burn with an ache to slide into her hair, to caress her porcelain skin, and to hold her head while she takes my cock down her throat.

"You tell me. You've got your fingers on them."

She licks her lips, and without saying another word she sticks her tongue out and laps at my magic cross. It's not what I expected, but I can't say the warmth of her mouth as she closes it around the head of my dick isn't welcome.

It's too fast, though, and my dominant brain kicks into high gear as I struggle to gather up the words I need before things go too far.

"I need for you to say out loud that this is what you want, Half-Pint. I don't want you swept along with something you don't want to participate in. My dick's right there, in your pretty little mouth. I'm naked, but that doesn't mean you have to touch me, or do anything with me you don't want to do. I need for you to consent, but only if this is what you want."

She hums, rolling the metal of my frenum piercing around on her tongue. Her tongue is every bit as curious as her mind. It explores every inch of my hardware until my balls ache with a familiar heaviness.

She pulls back, taking her mouth off my cock, and if it could speak it would be yelling at me right now. She grins up at me. "Of course I want to do it, I did it, didn't I?"

She did. But it's not the same as giving straight up consent. Being swept up in the moment is one thing, but I don't want her to regret this in fifteen minutes. I guess she sees something on my face, because she rocks back on her heels. "I'm curious, and..." She casts her eyes at the floor. "Excited. I'd like to keep going if that's okay?"

Running my fingers through her hair is quickly becoming second nature, and I tip her head back so she meets my gaze again. "I want it. I need us *both* to be sure that you do."

Nodding, she licks her lips. "I do. I'm making a choice, not being swept in a current."

That's all I need to hear, so I nod at her, and before I can blink, her lips are wrapped around my cock once again. When she curls her hand around my shaft and pumps it to meet her bobbing head, I almost lose my mind. She adds her other hand, even with both her hands and her mouth, there's part of me uncovered. Could she fit more of me in her mouth? Would she take instruction well or would she bite my balls off?

Guess there's only one way to find out.

Brushing her hair back from her face, my eyes roll back as she hollows out her cheeks around my dick.

"Relax your jaw, Half-Pint."

She looks up at me, those big, innocent eyes piercing through all my defenses, and she does exactly what I ask her to. Her jaw slackens, and as though she's figured out my ask, she guides my cock a little further into her throat.

"That's it. Perfect. So sweet, aren't you, pretty girl?"

Her eyes water then tears stream down her face as she gags against my hardness. I expect her to stop, and for me to need an emergency trip to the bathroom to finish what she's started. But she doesn't stop, doesn't even slow. She takes more of me into her mouth. There's nowhere for the pool of spit to go except down. Strings of drool hang from her chin as she gags and pushes me deeper.

"You look so goddamn beautiful with my cock in your mouth." I can't take my eyes off how blissed out she looks on her knees with those perfectly pouting lips spread wide to accommodate me.

Her throat is tight, hot, and the eagerness in her eyes as she stares up at me makes me want to reward her all night long. I don't know what she sees on my face. Is my self-control showing? It's taking all I have not to grip her by her head and buck my hips until I shoot cum down her throat.

But this is on her terms. I'm a toy to her right now, a real-life prop helping satisfy what is very clearly a deep curiosity.

"Such a good girl." I stroke her face, my hips jerking more and more as she drives me closer to the edge.

She somehow manages to make a noise that isn't gagging, a low rumble that makes my cock vibrate in her mouth.

Pretty little Half-Pint has about three seconds before I'm gonna shoot my load.

CHAPTER 14
Talia

Everything hurts, and I'm dying.

My knees ache from where they're pressed into the cheap, scratchy hotel carpet.

My back hurts from arching myself into Jagger.

My throat hurts from his giant penis being wedged up in there.

My jaw throbs from holding it open for so long.

My eyes burn from the constant refilling of tears before they spill down my face.

But, I think he's close. He's struggling to keep his eyes open, the muscles in his thighs as I wrap my hands around them to pull him even deeper down my throat are tight and poised for release.

I have no idea what I'm doing. But I must be doing something right because his hips keep bucking and jerking, his breath is quickening, and instead of stroking my hair, his fingers have wrapped strands around them, and he's holding on for dear life.

Despite the pain radiating through me, there's a deep sense of satisfaction. What started as a seedling of curiosity is now straight up raw determination. I need this man to finish. I need the validation someone as inexperienced as I am can make a guy like this, someone as breath-taking and practiced as Jagger, climax.

He hums again. Even if I heard that sound every day for the rest of my life I wouldn't tire of it. There's something about the frequency of the sound that nestles deep in my bones. His contentment, his approval is warm, welcoming, and steadfast. The way he strokes my face and hair, the way he enunciates his praise even through his grunts and moans, the way he stares down at me like I hung the freakin' moon.

This is what I need. I need to find someone like Jagger. Someone who looks at me and talks to me the way this man does. I've known him a couple days and already he's made me feel like a queen. Already he's made me realize how taken for granted I've been for the entirety of my relationship with Harry.

"Half-Pint." His breath hisses out on a slow release. "Close."

The fact Mr. Grumpasaurus can't form coherent sentences fills my every cell with glee. So I suck harder, push deeper. There's probably a pool of drool on the floor under me but in this moment I don't care about the mess, just about making this man come undone in my mouth.

"Feels so good." His voice is raw, gravelly, strained.

I don't give him the chance to say another word, I'm making him cross the finish line whether he's ready or not.

"Fuuuuuuuuuuuuuuuck." It's a low moan, a grunt as he cups my head, spraying cum on my tongue.

I should have thought this through better. I don't like to swallow. But what if that makes him angry?

It takes him what feels like ten minutes to recover enough to catch his breath. He drops onto his knees in front of me. "That was amazing, Half-Pint. Such a good fucking girl for me, aren't you?" The warmth of his palm as he cradles my face makes my eyes close.

He plants a firm kiss on my forehead before he rocks back enough to take me in. "You haven't swallowed?"

I shake my head, my eyes dropping to his chest. Maybe if I pretend to be staring at all his intricate tattoos I won't see the disappointment stirring in his eyes.

He hooks a knuckle under my chin, tipping my head so I have no choice but to face him square in the eye.

"Don't like to swallow?"

Another head shake.

The disappointment I've prepared myself to see on his face, doesn't come. Instead, he flips himself onto his back, somehow avoiding the wet patch on the ground, and opens his mouth. "Give it to me."

Wh-what? He can't possibly be serious, can he?

"Give it to me, Half-Pint. I'll get rid of it for you." His face softens. "I'll never make you do anything you're not comfortable doing. Give. It. To. Me."

Leaning over, I drop the mouthful of cum into his open mouth. After licking my lips, I whisper "thank you," but he's already on his feet and heading into the bathroom. I'm frozen in place. Did he really take his cum out of my mouth?

When I look up again, he's leaning on the doorframe on his forearm with a lazy smirk on his face. "Guess you had your first snowball."

I don't know what that means, but I nod anyway.

"When your partner comes in your mouth, and you spit it back into their mouth."

Oh! I definitely did that.

"And my first piercing." I gesture at his dangling peen. Harry's wasn't pierced. I like the sparkling piercings, there's something pretty about them, and they're smoother, more flexible than I expected them to be.

My voice sounds weird, croaky, and my throat burns with every word.

"Neither of those were on your to-do list." The corners of his mouth quirk.

"True." I need to get up, but I can't move. It's as though my knees have welded to the floor, and I can't feel anything below my waist.

"Let me help you." He darts toward me from the door, arms outstretched and picks me up, placing me on the bed with such care I'd cry if I wasn't drained of all my tears from sucking him off.

He turns to the counter, grabs a water, and cracks it open. "Drink."

I look at the water, back at his face which wrinkles as he scrunches it up.

"I said drink, Talia." His stern voice makes me want to tell him to stick his bottle of water where the sun don't shine. But the scratching at the back of my throat tells me to drink the dang water.

So I do.

"Good." He caresses my face.

I'd be lying if I said even the room temperature water didn't feel good against my raw throat. I clear my throat a few times, but it feels like it's not helping.

He strokes my face again. "It'll get easier the more you do it."

I arch a brow.

"I mean, you know, with other people." Mr. Grumpy may be blushing, but it's probably my oxygen deprived brain seeing things that aren't there.

I sip at the water until my tummy sloshes. He takes what's left of it and sets it aside.

My phone rings, breaking me out of my fierce eye-to-eye contact with the butt-nekkid man I gave a blow job to in a hotel room.

Shaking off the stupor, I dig out my phone. Harry's name appears on the screen, and my stomach drops. I expect shame, guilt, regret, but all I feel are prickles of annoyance he's interrupting this time with Jagger.

What does that mean?

Jagger's staring at me expectantly. There's something in his eyes, something dark, challenging. I'm pretty sure it's murder, there's murder in Jagger's eyes. Is he challenging me not to answer? Or does he want to murder Harry?

One of those things I might be on board with.

Okay, fine. I don't want Harry to die. But if he got some kind of sexually transmitted infection, or someone stole all his pantry goods labels, I wouldn't be mad about it.

The call drops off, Jagger's shoulders relax enough to be noticeable. And when it starts to ring again, there's a muscle twitching in his face like he's clenching his teeth. What could he possibly have against Harry?

"Hey, Harry."

"Why didn't you pick up?"

Ugh. Has he always been so self-important?

Jagger steps back. I assumed to go get dressed, except he's opening my pants. The swift jerk of them as he pulls them down throws me backward onto the bed with a whoop.

"What's wrong?" Harry doesn't sound concerned, just mildly inconvenienced.

"Nothing, I tripped over something." Considering my accident prone nature, it's not out of the realm of possibility.

I've officially tuned out of what Harry is saying because Jagger's stroking the outside of my thighs. His giant hands gliding across my skin send sheets of goose bumps all over my body. When he presses my knees apart, I lean up on my elbow to be met by a devilish grin from the man between my thighs.

He wouldn't, would he?

When he dots a soft kiss on the inside of my knee, he follows it up with a nip of his teeth that makes me yelp.

"What on earth are you doing, Talia?" Harry's impatience is growing. If I'm lucky, it'll grow quicker, and he'll leave me the heck alone to enjoy whatever it is Jagger's about to do to me.

"Nothing."

He goes back to talking. Jagger grins and my insides almost explode from the sheer beauty of the man. He kisses again, a little higher, and again, higher still. If he keeps this up he's going to—a gasp escapes me. Oh, no, no, no. He can't put his tongue there when I'm on a call with Harry. He can't. Can he?

"I know, right? Can you believe they won't let me buy a new car?" Harry's prattling on in my ear, but my focus is on the fact Jagger is staring at my crotch like he's about to eat the best dessert in town.

"What's your safeword, Half-Pint?" It's a husky whisper. Harry's talking so loud there's no way he heard it.

"Unicorn." I mouth back at him.

He scowls, his gorgeous face contorting. I can't help giggling.

"It's not funny, Talia." Harry scolds me. Not having the faintest idea what I'm truly laughing at. But if he thinks I'm laughing at him throwing a tantrum because he's not allowed to buy another new car, what do I care?

I mute the call. "Unicorn."

"Good girl." The satisfaction smooths out the wrinkled crankiness on Jagger's face. "Are you okay for me to continue?"

There's a piece of me wanting to say no. It's small. And for all the wrong reasons. I'm on the phone with Harry. It's rude. But the allure of having Jagger be sexual with me while I'm on the phone to another person, especially Harry, is strong. So I nod.

"Use your words, Talia." The sternness in his voice would make me wet if I wasn't already soaking.

"Yes, *sir.*" It's what all the girls in the books say, so why shouldn't I try it?

I unmute Captain Chats-too-much—which is ironic coming from me—and when Jagger grips my knees and jerks me across the bed toward his face, I immediately regret that decision.

"Talia? Talia? What the hell's going on over there? It's like you're not even paying attention to me."

"Harry, now isn't a good time."

Jagger dips a finger between my lips. He's probably seeing if I'm wet, though how he couldn't see that by looking at it is anyone's guess. The squelchy noise I make down there makes me groan. My face is hot, I cover my eyes with my forearm.

"But I need to talk to you."

When Jagger's finger skims across my clit, I have to bite my bottom lip to keep from letting the noises out that are building inside me.

"I have nothing to say to you, Harry."

Jagger hums, curling his arms around my thighs like he's settling in for the entire night and buries his face between my legs. Oh. My. Goodness. From the second his tongue connects with my sensitive skin, my body tingles all over.

"Well I have things to say to you, Talia. We need to fix this. To sort things out between us, for both our family's sakes."

I can't help the urge to hold Jagger's head right where it is, and there's a tickle of surprise when he lets me. He doesn't have hair for me to hold onto, it's buzzed short against his head, but I press him against me all the same.

"Talia? Talia? Are you listening to me?"

It's as though Harry's moved further away, like, down a corridor or something. He's growing more distant.

In this moment, Jagger owns me. With each sweep of his

tongue against my clit he's not even driving me closer to release, he's commanding it. This man knows what he's doing. His licks are firm, paced, rhythmic, and my body shivers and jerks in response.

I'm going to draw blood if I bite my lip much longer.

"Talia? Are you...? Talia? What the fuck are you doing?" Harry's almost shouting through the phone.

"Harry, I told you it's not a good time." Not for Harry at least.

"But we need to fix this."

"No, Harry. We're done. Finished. I never want to see you again. I told you that before. And I'd really rather you didn't call again."

He snickers. "Be reasonable, Tali."

Jagger flattens his tongue, long sweeping motions against my clit have beads of sweat creeping across my forehead. I want to let go. I want to toss my head back, open my mouth, and scream through my orgasm on this talented man's face.

"Talia...? Are you...? Masturbating?" Harry's suddenly curious, but I'm past the point of caring about Harry. All there is, is my impending orgasm.

I hang up the phone, silence it, and drop it off the edge of the bed.

"It's about fucking time." At least that's what it sounds like Jagger's mumbling against my girl parts.

It's as though he's been holding back, waiting to have my full attention before he delivers his full and ferocious onslaught on my body. He picks up the pace, one, two, three swipes of his tongue and my whole body shudders. Sweat trickles down my face as Jagger's demands get more and more... intense.

I thought I was prepared for the orgasm he was sending me toward but when it crashes into me, my whole body levitates, and I hear colors. My already raw throat burns with the scream he rips from me with his mouth.

The more I scream, the more he continues his attack on my clit with his tongue.

There's a heavy smell of sweat in the now warm air around us. My body is damp, the bed probably soaked.

Twitching muscles, racing heart, heavy limbs, my body sags into the mattress as the shockwaves slow. But Jagger doesn't seem like he's stopping anytime soon.

He's still down there, still fluttering at my clit with his tongue, still licking and sucking and biting all those sensitive nerve endings. He's pushing me, exploring me, devouring me. With every second he's down there it's like he's drawing a map of... me. It doesn't take long before I'm fisting the fabric on either side of my waist, my feet scramble on the sheets, desperate for traction as my hips buck against his face.

I can't come again. I can't. My body doesn't have the strength left to do *that* all over again.

Jagger is ravaging me, consuming me, possessing me. And all I can do is lie here and let him.

Another scream when I bend in half, my back bolting up off the bed as my muscles react without instruction. I don't control my body anymore, my reactions, my movements, that's all him. Jagger and his skilled and smooth tongue.

When I scream his name, he doubles down, his tongue flickering against me harder, faster, like he knows exactly what's building inside my core. Is this what it's like to be a volcano? Molten hot lava brewing inside my entire body until he lets me release it?

Without moving his mouth, he somehow manages to speak. "Again." He demands.

"I c-c-can't." I can't come again. Maybe his magic tongue won't work on me like it does all his other conquests.

I expect him to stop, to pull back, to give up, but he

doesn't. Like the words I just said to him never left my mouth, he resets, throws my legs over his shoulders and goes back to eating me like I'm a lifetime supply of his favorite flavor of ice cream.

"Jag-ger-it's-okay." All my words run together. "Y-y-you d-don't have to k-keep—"

He stops dead, his head bobbing up from between my legs. If his expression wasn't so stern, I'd laugh.

"Talia?"

My stomach tightens. I prefer when he calls me Half-Pint, and he knows it.

"Yes?" My voice is a whisper.

"Are you asking me to stop? Are you using your safeword?"

"Wh-what? N-no." I'm trembling all over, my muscles are having uncontrollable spasms making me jerk and twitch. I'm still not recovered from the first one.

"Then lie back and let me enjoy myself. Okay?"

"Yes, *sir*."

He growls at that, replacing his head between my legs and sucking at my sensitive clit. I've never had anyone down there with their tongue. What does it taste like? It can't be too bad if he's still down there, right?

A groan. "Talia?"

"Yeah?"

"Get the fuck out of your head."

"Yes, *sir*." I keep waiting for him to tell me to stop that, but he hasn't. I need to be careful not to get too attached to it.

Dropping my head back onto the bed, I clear my mind, focusing only on Jagger's fluttering licks against my clit. A shiver skates up my spine, and something deep inside me starts to grow.

When he hums his approval against me, I know he knows I'm close. My hips buck, knuckles whiten from gripping the bed on either side of me as he drives me relentlessly closer and closer to my second orgasm.

Like the first, it hits out of nowhere. A wild, fractured shriek breaks from me as liquid pours from my body. Another hum of approval, but I have no time to enjoy it because he's already slipping his fingers inside me.

When he presses what I think is my G-spot, it's game over. I come again, harder, deeper, wailing and mumbling, shaking, trembling, sweat coating my entire body, my hair stuck to my face, my legs locked so tightly around his head I'm not sure how he's still breathing.

I can't go on, but I don't want to stop. I've never had three in a row before. Shouldn't that be enough? Isn't more than one greedy? If Jagger thought I was being greedy wouldn't he have stopped by now? Does he expect me to give him more blow jobs to make up the balance?

He growls, a visceral, feral, noise as he thrusts his hand in and out against my G-spot making me whimper. I'm a passenger. My body won't quit until he does. And I have no idea how much staying power he's got, but considering I'm on three, I'd say a lot.

He's not letting up, his fingers and tongue move together in a blissful harmony that resonates at my body's favorite frequency. I'm close again, I don't know how. I've never come so many times in such a short space of time, but I'm not going to ask how he does it.

My toes lock up, my calves tighten, my legs lock around his head as my body starts bouncing off the mattress. I don't have energy for screaming, but my mouth opens in a silent wail as he thrusts me over the edge of ecstasy once again.

I must fall asleep. All I get are flashes of warmth between my legs as something brushes against my skin, sweet, soft kisses across my forehead, warmth of praise being whispered while Jagger takes care of me.

At some point I'm in his arms. I don't think I have legs anymore.

"Aftercare?"

He shushes me, tightening his arms around my body, curling himself around me.

"The bed's wet. I ruined the bed."

"Shhhhh. Come on, pretty girl. Slow your mind. I've taken care of everything. It's okay."

"But—"

He sighs. Putting something to my mouth and encouraging me to drink. After a few gulps of water, he resettles me in his arms. "I put my towel under you while you were talking to Harry. I've cleaned you up, put your pants back on, and I'd really like for you to take a nap for me. Please? That was a lot."

"Mmmkay." I melt into his hold.

"That's a good girl. Just sleep." He strokes my face with his thumb. "I've got you."

CHAPTER 15
Jagger

Fucking fuck fuck fuckity fucking mother fucking fuck.

I'm in trouble.

I probably should have stopped at making her come once. But I guess her relentless curiosity rubbed off on me in such close quarters because I couldn't help but wonder how she'd react to multiples. And once I got a taste of her... It was out of my control. I was a man possessed.

She was amazing. From the salty-sweet musk of her sopping wet pussy, to her communication, her noises, her reactions, her relenting, giving in to my demands and letting me lead. Everything, from start to finish she was perfect.

And let's not even talk about how eager she was to suck me dry.

A growl rolls through my chest as I flush and wash my hands. She can't be perfect. She's vanilla, Harry's ex, Miss. Prim-and-proper and everything handed to her on a silver platter.

I know Harry's type. I bet she graduated with something fru-fru from college just to say she has a degree and is taking time out to find herself, to Eat, Pray, Love herself all on Dad's dime.

Girls like her don't get together with guys like me.

And even if they did, I don't do vanilla.

Except... Maybe I had forgotten what really good vanilla tastes like. The pure stuff, the quality stuff, made from the most exceptional vanilla beans planet earth has to offer. And now, fuck. Vanilla might be my favorite flavor of them all.

We're both quiet during dinner. It's not abnormal for me, but the fact Ms. Chatterbox is quiet concerns me. Is she having regrets? Is she dropping? Is there a tug of shame in her veins for having done something "dirty"?

As we head back up to the bedroom in the elevator, the air is thick with tension and unspoken words. My gut tells me she wants space, but it's contradicting everything in my body to pick her up and hold her until whatever's going through her mind slows down and fucks all-the-way off.

It feels like longer than a day since we met on the plane, it feels like weeks. I'm not used to someone being in my space like this, or feelings escaping from the box of the great beyond I've kept well-guarded in my chest. And for good reason. Having feelings is dangerous, and as much as I don't mind being grumpy and mysterious, I don't tend to take unnecessary risks.

Talia is an unnecessary risk. And while she's currently full of that liberated feeling of fierce independence, Harry always gets what he wants. And from the sounds of that phone call, he wants her. He won't let up until he gets her.

Clearing my throat seems to startle her from her thoughts. She jumps as she turns to me.

"You need anything?"

She shakes her head, curling her arms across her body. "I'm good. Thanks."

It doesn't feel good, but if she says she's good, I need to be able to trust her. Communication is key in kink, and if she says she's fine, I need to believe it.

"I'm going to do some reading then turn in for the night." I gesture at the sofa which is probably half my size. It's comical, but after our scene earlier, she needs her rest and she won't get that tossing and turning on a beat up old sofa-bed.

I open my backpack, but my book isn't there. It's not in the living space, or next to the bed, it's not next to the now empty bottles of water. Where the fuck is it?

It appears in my periphery, attached to the daintiest little hand compared to my enormous ones. "You left it in the bathroom." She says this like she's been picking up after me for years, there's a weary sarcasm leveling her tone that almost makes me smile. Almost.

She changes into her grandpa pjs and climbs into bed leaving the lamp on. She rolls on her side to face the wall. There's plenty of space in the bed, and I can almost hear her teeth chattering from across the wall, but I'm not violating her airspace without permission. No matter how badly I want to.

I don't know how long I'm lost in my book, but a slap on the bedspread draws my attention back to the bed.

"Oh!" Her indignation seems to deflate like the puffy blanket she pummeled. "You wear glasses?"

That much is clear by the fact they're sitting on my face.

"Of course you do, that's why you're wearing them."

I arch an eyebrow. If I wasn't needed for this conversation she could have left me to my book.

"The couch is creaky. You're making so much noise I can't sleep."

To be honest, I'd tuned it out when I got sucked into this police procedural. But I guess now that she's mentioned it, even when I breathe the damn thing makes a squeak under my ass.

I slide off the edge onto the floor. It'll probably be more comfortable down here anyway.

"What do you think you're doing?"

"Not making noise?"

She huffs out an audible breath, throwing back the covers. "That's not what I meant." She shuffles around the bed to me and thrusts her hand out.

I look at her hand, then at her adorable scowly face. She won't be able to pull me up from down here. I'm twice her size. But she's being sweet so I let her try.

"What did you mean?"

She sweeps her hand at the bed. "There's a whole half a bed over here." She's right, there is. But I don't want her to feel uncomfortable.

"Are you sure? I can build a comfortable enough space on the floor if you'd rather."

She rolls her eyes. "Just get in the bed, Grumpasaurus." She leaps back into her side of the bed and waits for me to climb in and turn on my lamp before she turns off hers.

I've only been reading for fifteen minutes, but she's moved herself right to the edge of the bed and is clinging on for dear life. If she moves, sneezes, or even coughs, she's gonna eat dirt.

"Half-Pint?"

"Mmm?"

"Get your ass over here."

"Aftercare?"

"Aftercare."

She backs herself up toward me, but doesn't turn over. I put my book down, pick her up and turn her so her head is resting on my chest.

"So bossy." She's giggling.

"You're cold. And you're gonna fall on your face if you stay all the way over there."

"And I give good cuddles." She tilts her head so she's looking up at me.

"You do give good cuddles."

She nods like she's won something, places her hand on my chest and strokes gentle circles on my skin. "I know. I wasn't expecting you to admit it."

"I have no problem admitting when I like something. Or need something. You need to learn to use your voice, Half-Pint. I can't read your mind. You've been quiet all afternoon. Do you regret what we did earlier?"

She jumps, but I've learned to move my head so she doesn't crack my skull. "No. Of course not."

The knot I didn't know was sitting in my chest loosens. "You sure?"

She nods. I shiver when something cool hits my chest. It turns out to be a ring on her finger. "What's this?"

She pulls her hand back before I can see what it is. "It's nothing."

I sigh. Again. This woman is going to be the death of me. "Half-Pint. You don't have to hide anything from me. You have nothing to be embarrassed about. If you don't feel like sharing, that's fine. But if you're holding back for some other reason, I'm going to call bullshit."

It's her turn to sigh. She buries her head in my chest before she mumbles against my skin. "It's the promise ring Harry gave me right before we, uh, I lost my virginity to him."

This woman has dirty talk on her to do list, but she can barely grind out the word virginity. I have my work cut out for me with this one.

"And you're embarrassed that you're still wearing it?"

She nods, her hair tickling my nose.

"Half-Pint, you don't need to be embarrassed for having feelings. Those are well out of our control. If you want to wear the ring, wear the ring. If you want to take it off, take it off.

You're your own person, and you can make your own decisions and choices."

The way her brows shoot up her forehead suggest she's never been told that before in all her life, which makes my stomach sink.

"What are you reading?" She's clearly trying to re-direct her discomfort, so I'm going to let her. At least this time.

"The latest Erica Swift novel by M K Farrar."

"Mmm." She hums like she knows who Erika Swift is.

"Would you like me to read it to you?"

She nods.

"Even though you'll be lost and have no idea what's going on?"

She nods again, pressing her fist over her mouth as she yawns.

"Okay, but it's going to make you want to go back and read the whole series."

"I've never heard of M K Farrar."

"She's a British indie author. I like supporting the little guys."

She smiles, and settles her head right over my heart like she wants to hear the thump-thump in my chest. "Your glasses suit you, you know. You should wear them more often."

Holding the book open with one hand, I take the opportunity to stroke the fabric of her pjs with my free hand. "My eyes were scratchy. I guess I left my other contacts at home on the bathroom counter."

"What were you going to Chicago for?"

"I was going for a kink event."

Her muscles noticeably tense up. "Like a group type thing?"

"We have events all the time, Half-Pint, all over the country. Sometimes even in the club where you stayed last night. It's really not as seedy and dirty as people think. My favorite is

RopeCraft, it's in Chicago in May. I find that to be the best dominant I can be, I need to educate myself and regularly work on honing my skills."

She settles again. "Sounds so intimidatin'." Her Southern accent gets thicker as she gets more tired. She falls quiet, so I read to her. It's not long before she speaks again, so I put the damn book on the bedside table. There's no use burning energy to hold the thing if she's not going to shut up enough to let me read it.

"Jagger?" She's mumbling, so she's almost asleep.

I don't answer, but she doesn't need me to. Girl's a verbal steam train. Even when she's sleepy. "Why are you single?"

My muscles start to clench despite my breathing not changing. She's breathing evenly in seconds. Her heavy, measured breaths suggesting she's fallen asleep but that doesn't stop my thoughts from churning.

Unfortunately, it's a question I get asked a lot. I don't like to talk about why I choose to stay single, why I choose to keep the commitment piece of myself locked away. Not even my colleagues at Protocol or at the auto shop know I'm a widower.

Stroking Half-Pint's face, I pick up the book. Her contented sigh warms my insides. Turns out, this woman hasn't waited for an invitation into my space. She's ninja-kicked the door down and made herself at home. Problem is, I'm not sure I'm even mad about it.

"Because there's a piece of me that will always love my wife." My voice is quiet, but saying the words out loud in the presence of another human being feels freeing somehow.

I'd love to say my wife would be pissed, but Caitlin would absolutely want me to be happy. She said as much leading up to her death. And worse than that, she and this force of nature curled in the crook of my arm would get along like a house on fire. They'd get up to all kinds of trouble.

Which means she's all kinds of trouble.

For both our sakes, I should let her go. Except she's tugging on pieces of me which have been dormant for so long, I forgot they existed.

And it feels kind of nice.

CHAPTER 16

Talia

When I wake up, the bed next to me is cold. Bolting out of bed doesn't help. Jagger's not in the bathroom, on the couch, and I don't have his cell phone to check if he's even still in the hotel.

Yanking back the curtains makes my stomach hurt. The roads seem much clearer today, clear enough we could go our separate ways and never speak to each other again.

That makes my stomach hurt even more.

I didn't realize it as it was happening, but I've grown attached to the giant Grumpasaurus from the plane. Which was helped along last night by his heart shredding confession he has a wife. From the sorrow in his voice it sounded like she's an ex, but his voice was so heavy, his body so tense, all I wanted to do was take away his pain and make him feel better.

I put on my freshly laundered yoga pants and brush my teeth. There's not much of anything that can be done for my unruly hair, but it still makes me smile when I catch a glimpse of myself in a reflective surface. So it was definitely the right thing to do.

When I get downstairs, my feet stutter to a stop as I enter

the restaurant where breakfast is being served. My old lady friends from yesterday are all standing around the same table they sat at for most of the day. Jagger holds out a chair for one of them to sit down. As she sits, he pushes the chair in, and when she's seated, he drapes her napkin over her lap.

He does this for all the ladies at the table. Before he turns to leave, one of the ladies grabs his forearm. From the firm-set of his jaw, he's not thrilled with the contact, but he can hardly deck an old woman, so he pauses patiently as she asks him something.

He nods, blesses himself, and as his mouth moves in what seems to be a prayer, all the women around the table bow their head.

Then he goes back to the same table we were at and picks up the menu.

Huh. This man is an enigma. I guess it says more about me than him I assumed he wasn't a religious man because he was, well, a dirty one, but he at least knows enough to say a prayer before eating.

There's so much about him I don't know, so much I want to know. The thaw outside has been less impressive than how Jagger has melted my preconceived notions about a guy like him, a guy with oily jeans, tattoos, and who lives the kink life.

I like him.

Okay, I more than like him. There's this expanding crush blooming in my chest that's potentially problematic. But we aren't gonna think about that.

We're not going to think about how Jagger's expansive chest stretches that black shirt nicely, or how his biceps fill out the armholes. We're certainly not going to think about how cute his butt looks in those jeans. Or the fact I had his manhood in my mouth yesterday.

Nope.

Definitely not going to think about that.

"Ma'am? Are you okay, ma'am?"

A new server approaches, suggesting the roads have cleared enough for the staff to change over, and my guy clenches a lil bit more.

"What? Yes, I'm fine thank you. I was looking for my friend."

"Are you sure? You look flushed."

So much for not thinking about Jagger choking me with his enormous eggplant yesterday.

"Yes. I'm sure. Thank you, though." Before I head over to where Jagger's sitting, I venture toward the table of women who are already pouring coffee and sipping on OJ. They've made themselves right at home.

"Good morning, Talia!" Julia waves at me.

"Good morning, ladies. Don't mind me. I'm over here pickin' up after that forgetful man over there." I grab his novel from the table top, tucking it under my arm.

"He's quite a man, isn't he though?" Alma winks at me.

My face is on fire. There's no hiding it. "Yes, ma'am. He is."

"Fixin' to leave today?" Gertie asked the question, but the whole table is waiting for my answer.

"Think so. Yes, Ms. Gertie."

Someone nudges my behind. "Go get him, girl. Don't let that catch leave."

The eyes of the whole table are on my back as I make my way across the dining room.

"Morning." I sit, sad he didn't push my chair in for me like he did for the nosy old ladies who are all watching me intently from across the room.

"Good morning."

I hand him his book. "You left this over with the ladies." I pause. "Thought you might have been gone, gone." The way I'm nibbling on my lip is pathetic. But I want him to acknowledge that he feels for me. Something, anything. Even a flutter. I can work with a flutter.

His brow creases as he frowns. “Definitely not.”

“Aftercare.”

“Well, that, and you know, it’s rude.”

Rude. Okay. It’s not the proclamation of undying love I was going for. It’s not even a flutter. It’s hey, I’d do the same for any of those women sitting across the room. The pulse ringing in my ears gets louder and louder as the server takes my order and brings me a drink.

I need to deflect. To move the awkwardness from the fact I want him to like me to something else. “So, uh. You go to church?”

Wow. If I thought things couldn’t get more uncomfortable at our table, that definitely did it. Probably doesn’t help that he’s trying to read.

“I do.”

“Cool. Uh. Me too.”

“I figured.”

He figured. Cool. Great. Wonderful.

I turn my attention out the window. There’s a truck plowing snow out of the way on the main road, and spraying salt from the back.

“Is there anything else on your list you’d like to do before we part ways?” He doesn’t lift his line of sight from the page he’s reading, but his glasses shift on his nose. I definitely like when he’s all bookwormy and studious with those specs.

Part of me wants to say no. Again. I mean, he’s licked me, I’ve licked him, and we both orgasmed. What else is there to do other than The Deed?—which I’m absolutely not doing with a man who’s about to walk out of this hotel without a second thought about me for the rest of his days.

But I’m curious. If I say no all-the-way, what’s he going to suggest.

"If I said yes, what would you suggest?"

He drags his tongue over his bottom lip sending a shiver up my spine and a bolt of lust straight to my core. I can't help squeezing my thighs together in case my coochie sends out some kind of signal to him to tell him I'm thinking about having his tongue between my legs.

"I don't think you could handle what I'd do to you, Half-Pint." That wolfish grin is back on his face like he's playing with his prey, but the Southern Woman rises up inside me, my toes curling with the indignation of the challenge that he believes I can't do something.

"Prove it. I can take anything you throw at me." Regret curdles the coffee in my stomach as soon as the words are out. And the glint in his eye tells me he already expected me to rise to his bait.

He jerks his chin at my plate. "Finish up, and I will."

My whole body shakes with nervous energy and anticipation as we head up to our room in the elevator. We're surrounded by people, but that doesn't stop him from running his fingers across my lower back, inching higher and higher up the curve of my spine.

When he gets to my bra strap, I'm not sure what I'm expecting, but when he essentially clicks his fingers and the dang thing bursts open in the back, I can't help but gasp.

When three people turn to look at me, I duck my head.

When his hand skates down my back, dipping into the waistband of my pants, I grit my teeth.

Maybe he's gonna feel up my butt cheeks or something? Maybe he's, oh. Oh. My. Goodness. His hand's sliding between my cheeks.

He wouldn't.

He can't.

He's not going to attempt number twelve on my bucket list right here in the elevator. Is he?

When his finger touches my butt hole, I tense up. His quiet murmurs in my ear tickle my skin, I can't fight my eyes as they roll back and drift closed. "Come on, Half-Pint. Show me how you can take anything I throw at you."

The elevator wall is cold as I reach a hand out to stabilize myself. My legs are trembling, my arms aren't much more secure. And all he's done is put his finger there. Is he going to, like, go inside?

I clench my butt, and he chuckles. The low rumble sending sparks straight to all my girl bits. It's like he picked up the erotic phone tree, dialed 1-800-nips, and my nipples only too eagerly answered the call. They're picking up whatever this guy is putting down. Even though we're surrounded by people.

All he does is run his finger around my booty hole. He doesn't penetrate, doesn't put all that much pressure on me, but I can already tell I'm getting wet. And I hate myself for it. But I can't let it go.

When I bend myself back, trying to press against his finger for more pressure, there's a contented hum rolling around his chest that warms me all over.

"Such an eager little thing, aren't you, Half-Pint?" His whisper next to my ear makes every hair on my body stand upright.

I can't answer him. If I open my mouth, I'm not sure what unladylike thing will come spraying out. So I sink my teeth into my lower lip, nod, and try to push the thoughts right out of my brain that I'm doing the devil's bidding by letting a gorgeous man finger my behind in an elevator full of people.

Because it feels so dang good.

By the time the last people step off the elevator, a bead of sweat is making its way down my neck. My body sags.

His tongue picks up the bead of sweat, and he sweeps it

along the column of my neck. I should be grossed out. But I'm only growing more and more needy.

I grab his shirt, fisting it in my balled up hand, stretching that pristine black tee covering all his beautiful ink. "Jagger."

The pressure on my hole builds a little, enough to make me whimper.

"You like that, don't you baby girl?"

Oh, Lord.

Is it possible to climax from a simple pet name? It's right at the back of my throat to answer "Yes, Daddy." But I force myself to swallow it down. I've seen it in books. I've seen the groups where women says it gives them the ick, but I'm curious about it. So curious, in fact, that's why it made it onto the list.

I've never actually wanted to say it out loud to someone before, until now.

What is this man doing to me?

By the time the elevator door opens, my knees are shaking so hard I'm not sure I can walk to our room. I don't need to, however. Jagger takes his hand out of my pants, wipes it on something in his pocket—likely another handkerchief—then swoops under me to pull me up into his arms.

It takes me a fragment of a second to curl into his chest. My head fits right into the front of his shoulder, like a jigsaw puzzle clicking into place.

In our room, he plops me down next to the bed. "Get naked."

He steps back. I don't need to look at him to know he's watching my every move, every reaction, every breath.

I step out of my clothes and kick them a few feet away with a sweep of my foot.

"Kneel."

I obey. And the sound that rattles in the back of his throat makes me want to grind on the floor to finish what he started in the elevator.

He opens his luggage. "What's your safeword, Talia?"

When he's all business, he uses my real name. It's like he's checking to make sure I'm paying attention. I guess he hasn't figured out there hasn't been a time when he's spoken, that I haven't paid attention. It's something people assume about chatty folk, that because we talk a lot, we never listen.

"Unicorn." I speak loudly and clearly so he can hear that even though my voice is wavering, I'm not afraid. Even though I'm most definitely afraid.

"Good girl."

Do those shivers ever end? Those words of pleasure dancing all over your skin like someone turned on fairy lights? I can't imagine hearing him say those words and them not having this impact to my body. Even my nipples are tingling.

Something clicks, twice, but I resist the urge to look over at what he's doing.

When he stands behind me, my insides burn. It's like something triggered a chain reaction inside my body, and he's the only one who can stop it, or fix it, or make it better, or worse? I don't know.

But I know he's the only one that can do *something*.

Smooth, cool, fabric covers my eyes.

#2 Blindfolds

Something soft and furry touches my wrists as he clicks cold, hard handcuffs around them behind my back.

#13 Restraints

There's a moment of silence, shuffling, and then a click. "Yes, hi. Could you send me up some strawberries and whipped cream, please?"

#5 Playing with food

If my body wasn't awake before, it is now. It's like having my sight removed has dialed up the simmering energy buzzing across the surface of my skin. I don't hear him walk back toward me, so when something grazes my nipple, I squeak, then moan.

The urgency with which I need this man to touch me should be shameful. But the burning ache between my thighs makes me not care. I don't. I just need him. There's probably a swimming pool on the carpet between my thighs.

He kneels beside me, keeping one hand on my shoulder, stroking back and forth. "I'm right here, Half-Pint, okay? If you get anxious or scared, or you feel weirded out by the silence and lack of sight, drop your safeword, and I'll make it better. How are you doing? Are you okay?"

"Yes... sir." I drop my voice. "Is that okay? Can I call you sir?"

He sweeps his lips across my forehead, making me lean into his kiss. "Yeah, baby girl. It's fine."

I don't want to call him sir. There's a Talia inside a cage in my chest screaming something else, but I ignore her. I need to focus on proving Jagger wrong. I can totally take this. In fact, the anticipation feels like the moment right before you step out onto a stage in a room full of people. My stomach is flapping, my breath rapid, and my skin shimmering like he's running textured fabric over it.

"Easy. Slow that breathing down, please."

As I comply, there's a knock at the door.

"I'll be right back. I swear I'm not going to show anyone any piece of your naked body, okay?"

For some reason, I trust him. "Yes, sir."

The exchange at the door takes only seconds before it clicks shut, and he slides the extra bar over to lock it with a soft thud.

He's back by my side in seconds, his fingertips on my skin, a silent reassurance I'm not alone, he's not leaving me, and that I'm safe.

"Can you stand up?"

It takes a little work, but I keep my balance and stand.

"Good. Lean forward onto the bed." His hand splays on my stomach and spine like he's guiding me face down onto the bed. "Bring your knees up so that pretty ass is in the air. Good. So responsive."

When my ass is in the air, he clicks something around my ankles. Handcuffs I'd guess? Then my feet shoot away from each other on a gasp.

"Is that the bar thingie from Fifty Shades?"

He snorts. "A spreader bar. It is. What else have you learned from those smutty books of yours, Half-Pint?"

"And you just so happened to have that in your bag?"

A deep chuckle makes my body tingle. "I just so happened to have this in my bag."

My mind goes blank. The only thought consuming my mind is how on display I am, how vulnerable, exposed, fragile. And I can almost hear the smile on his face as he assesses me.

His hand cups my butt cheek, the squeeze is firm, but not painful. I never expected to be the needy woman who ached for someone to touch her butt, but after the elevator, I want his finger back. What would it feel like for him to slide in, just a little bit?

Oh, boy. Is that whining coming from me?

"All in good time, baby girl. Patience. All those noises are making me want to give you everything all at once. We both need patience."

Before I can answer or even take a breath, I'm flat on my back on the bed. He flipped me like a buttermilk pancake. There's no way the neighbors didn't hear my squeal.

"I wish you could see yourself, Talia. Bound, sightless, naked and so very, very beautiful."

I can't squeeze my thighs together, but his words suck the oxygen from my lungs, leaving my chest to heave under the strain of trying to breathe. His voice is almost serene, like he's praying, worshiping.

"Are you wet for me?"

"Yes, s-s-sir." Without question. I'm soaked.

"I'm going to put cream on your body now, okay?" Then a bag shakes, plastic crinkles and something hard rattles inside. "Then I'm going to eat these M&M's off your body before I make you scream my name so fucking loudly everyone's going to know I'm making you come for me in this room. Are we clear?"

"Yes, sir." Wow. It's not quite ticking off *Dirty talk*, but it's on its way. How can he sound so encouraging, so soft and warm, and also so dirty? It does things to my body I shouldn't be proud of.

"I have a packet of Pop Rocks we can try if you like the cream and M&Ms."

I don't have time to ponder how Pop Rocks might feel against my skin before something cold lands on my nipples, and I wiggle.

He drops a kiss on my lips. "Stay still, please, Half-Pint. My appetite is voracious. Can I touch that soaking wet pussy of yours?"

When I nod but don't answer, his fingers barely skim my pubic hair. "Out loud, Talia."

"Yes, sir. Please. Please touch me."

There's no warm up, no soft touch, he rams a couple fingers inside me and curls them so they press hard against my G-spot, knocking my breath away yet again. The urge to rock my hips is overwhelming, but he asked me not to move.

Muscles straining with the need to press ahead and charge toward the climax, I try to focus on the sensations he's making me feel other than a bone-deep frustration and longing.

Another dollop of cold cream lands under my belly button toward my pelvic bone as he withdraws his hand. The clink of M&Ms echoes in the quiet before the sound of fabric hitting the floor meets my ears. Hopefully he's getting naked. I've decided I need him to be naked too.

When he moves over the top of me, caging me but not smooshing the cream, something inside me eases. He strokes my face, my upper arm, my forearm, brushes his thumb over my lips.

I've read about this one. I let my mouth fall open, and his thumb finds its way inside. He waits, thumb resting on my tongue, and I don't move, I don't make a sound, all I do is breathe.

It's an age before he moves again, and he moves his thumb to the back of my tongue so I can't swallow, but not far enough that I gag. Before long, saliva pools in my mouth and trickles down my cheeks.

He licks it off me. "Such a good fucking girl, Talia. You're such a good fucking girl."

The warmth between my legs blooms so much I can't breathe. When he shifts down my body, hope shoots up to an eleven on a scale of one to ten. When his tongue meets the cream on my nipple, a soft moan escapes me. The cream is cool, his tongue is warm, and the way he caresses the sensitive tip of my breast with his tongue makes me even wetter.

He repeats the process for the other side, then moves down toward my belly button, and by the time he's licked the line of dessert off my pubic bone, my body's trembling with the need to wiggle, writhe, move so he goes where I need him to go.

Blood's simmering, my crotch is so warm he could probably melt those M&Ms easily, crispy shell and all.

He rocks back on his heels, goes quiet for a moment before smacking his lips. When he leans back over my body, he places a strawberry in my mouth. I love strawberries. But I've never paid attention to how sweet, how juicy, how decadent they can be. When I'm done chewing and swallow, he kisses me so deeply my toes tingle.

It's controlling, consuming, and full of emotion. He can deny it if he wants but he's enticed by me. And that growing hardness pressing against my body tells me he wants me every bit as badly as I want him.

"Such an amazing mouth and all tied up. The temptation to stick my cock in there and make you suck me until I cover your tits in my cum is overwhelming."

Nothing about that sentence doesn't sound hot to me. So I drop my mouth open.

"Fuck. Such a fucking eager submissive, aren't you, baby girl?"

The more he calls me baby girl, the more I want to answer with Daddy. The more he says it, the warmer and more right it feels in every part of my body. But I don't want to say it. I don't want to offend him, or upset him, or make him angry.

When his thighs clamp against my arms, and his peen lands on my lower lip, the urge to touch myself burns my skin. He doesn't let me suck him for long, enough to take the edge off, at least for me.

"Nope." He withdraws, and my mouth pops. "This isn't about me. Though my balls are ready to shoot their load all over that cunt of yours, Half-Pint."

I always thought the C-word would be too far for me. Even in the books I read, it makes me cringe. But there's nothing that could come out of Jagger's mouth I wouldn't love to hear, that wouldn't make me wet, and an aching ball of need.

"Pop Rocks?"

"Please. I'm curious."

"Always so curious." He says it like he's in awe, not like it's a judgment. And when the popping candy lands on my breasts, I give in and arch my back. I need his mouth back on me.

"Please, Jagger." I'm panting.

When his tongue sandwiches the candy between his mouth, and my skin, I can't help the noises that burst out of me. Something about the fizzing, the popping, the way he works his tongue has me on the edge.

"She likes it." Sounds like he's saying it more to himself than to me. "We'll have to do that again sometime, Half-Pint. But as much as I want to tease you with popping candy all day, I have other plans in mind for you."

CHAPTER 17
Jagger

I WANT TO DO EVERYTHING TO THIS WOMAN.

Every damn fucking thing.

Her responses, her curiosity, her eagerness to please, to explore, it's intoxicating, and I want it all.

"You doing okay, Half-Pint?"

She nods. She's not quite hog-tied, but blindfolded, hands cuffed in the small of her back, and legs held wide open by a spreader bar, and she looks like a fucking queen.

"I didn't hear that."

"Yes, sir." The words fall from her lips on a blissed-out sigh. She's so comfortable it warms the brick in my chest. The trust she's placed in me, without question, makes me glad she met me and not some wannabe dominant who would hurt her.

When she calls me sir, it makes my balls throb. When I play with people at the club they call me sir all the time. But not like this, not the way Talia does. Something about how the words fall from her mouth makes my chest expand.

"What do you have planned for me, Jagger?"

Even the way she says my name makes me feel things. It

means "one who cuts," and considering I have a growing curiosity for pretty knives, it seems to fit.

"Do you want me to talk dirty to you, baby girl?" No matter how many times I tell myself to stop calling her that, to stop strengthening whatever that connection is that's sparked between us, it's getting harder to ignore. She's so tiny, so fragile, so innocent I want to protect her at all times when I'm this close to her.

Yet when she's not tripping over her own feet, when she's not making herself small, she has a spine of steel, a sassy mouth, and there's a flicker of strength in her I'd love to see her let fly.

"I like it."

Dragging a finger through her soaking wet pussy tells me as much. "I can tell."

She wiggles her hips. I'd love to fuck her. Even fingering her G-spot gave me a quick taste of what she'd feel like from the inside. Smooth, warm, her muscles so tight and strong. Fuck. My cock is so hard it's weeping.

She's so responsive it's hard not to fuck her senseless until she doesn't remember her own name.

"Brace yourself, Half-Pint. I'm flipping you over." When I grab the bar, I grin. Flipping her onto her face takes less than a second, but she's already scrambling to push herself up onto her knees. Presenting that curious little ass to me.

"What's the matter, baby girl? Your ass feeling empty?"

Her whole body inflates and deflates with her rapid-fire breathing. "Please, I'm so curious. Please, sir. Let me see what it feels like. Please?"

This fucking woman. I can't say no. Not when she pleads so prettily. I have a travel-sized lube in my luggage. I don't warn her I'm squirting it between her cheeks, because her shocked gasps send shivers of pleasure through my body.

I used my pinky in the elevator, but I rub my thumb over

her tight hole, working the lube in as I massage. She's dripping, her pussy glistening like she's been coming for me for hours.

She's fucking perfect.

I've gone from wanting to destroy her for Harry, to needing to make her mine so she can't remember why she ever wanted to be with him.

I want this woman. I want to own her every breath, explore every inch of her body, everything she likes and doesn't.

That fucking ring catches the light, reminding me she's not mine, and the tightness returns to my chest.

Irrational anger wells up in my body. That's fucking it. Caging her in with my body, I dot kisses down her spine, slowly dragging my tongue between each vertebrae. When I get to her hands, I kiss every finger. When I get to her promise ring finger, I take the whole thing in my mouth.

She moans. I flick my tongue around the metal band, wiggling it off her finger slowly. When it's loose, I grip it with my teeth and pull it off completely.

When it's in my hand, her body softens like tension has left her body. Or maybe I want to see that. Perhaps I want her to feel better now that it's off.

I don't ask her how she feels. I simply add it to the chain around my neck, and get back to making my girl writhe on the bed.

The more I rub around her tight hole, the more she's pleading. Her back arches as much as she can with her hands tied behind it. She's not holding back, she's not embarrassed, and she's not in her head—at least not anywhere near as obviously as she was in the club.

It's like she's given herself over to the process. And it makes me oddly proud of her to not only have such an open mind about it all, but also that level of trust in someone when she's just had her heart broken.

Her pureness, her naivety, her goodness all shine through. And the more of it I see, the more I want to protect it.

And kill her fucking ex.

"Please, Jagger. More. Please?"

Pressing the tip of my index finger against her clenched ass makes her whimper, by the time I'm a knuckle deep, her begging's more urgent, more demanding.

"Can you take another finger, baby girl?"

"Yes. Please, yes."

Fuck. I've found that more often than not, women who want to try ass play don't tend to stick with it. They've heard about it, or read about it, and once they try it they figure out it's not their jam. Which is fine. Different strokes for different folks and all that jazz.

I did not expect Talia to enjoy having her ass fingered. Especially since she's so tiny, and my hands are so big.

Another healthy squirt of lubricant makes her shiver. "I like the cold."

I stroke her ass cheek, kneading it in my palm. "Such a good girl for telling me what you like."

Not sure if she knows, but she purrs sometimes when I say things to her. It's the most beautiful soothing sound I've ever heard during a scene. And makes me want to draw that sound out of her every second of every day.

"Second finger. You ready?"

"Yes, sir." Her enthusiasm makes it so easy to be patient and take my time. The slower we go, the easier it'll be to watch her every move, every reaction, to see precisely what she likes and doesn't, and log all her feedback.

When the tip of my middle finger joins my first, she tenses, I move so I'm kneeling perpendicular to her body and can stroke her hair. Leaning down so my lips are almost touching her ears, I reassure her. "You okay, baby girl? You can safeword at any time you know."

"I know. I'm okay. Just scared it's going to hurt."

"That's reasonable, and expected. You haven't had anything back here before, right?"

She nods.

"Lots of lube, super slow, and if it hurts or gets uncomfortable I need you to tell me, okay? We'll take it slow."

"I trust you." The firmness in her voice is like an arrow straight to my heart. She has zero reason to trust me. We barely know each other, and she's giving it to me freely. I refuse to give her reason to take it away.

"And I'm going to take care of you." I can't help stroking her hair, her skin, the urge to take care of her, nurture her, consuming my every breath. "You know that, right?"

She nods. "Yes, Daddy."

I don't want to disrupt the scene, but that hits me like a kick to the solar plexus. It's something I don't want to dig into, not now, maybe never.

I've been called Daddy twice in a scene in my entire life, both by strangers at the club, and both were quickly corrected.

I don't have a Daddy kink. I've never had a Daddy kink. I will never have a Daddy kink.... except...

"Just relax, baby girl. I've got you."

Her muscles unstiffen as I work my middle finger into her ass to join my index finger. It's a slow process, checking in with her each time my finger moves, and her ass stretches to accommodate me. While she adjusts, I use my free hand to circle her clit, trying to help her relax into the experience.

"Still doing okay?"

"Yes, Daddy." Her voice is dreamier, softer, and if I were to put money on it, I'd say this scene is putting my girl into subspace.

Despite the aching in my cock, the pulsing in my balls, I

need to be responsible here. It's her first time. I can't imagine Harry ever even got her to come, let alone pushed her into subspace, and I want to make sure the whole experience is good for her. Even if it means I end up with blue balls.

"You okay to take a little more, baby girl?"

"Mmmhmm."

"Good girl." I stroke her hair. "Show me how good you can be for Daddy, okay?"

The moan those words draw from her has me pumping my cock with my free hand. She's squirting onto the already wet bed.

Then the giggles start.

"You still with me, baby girl?"

She nods.

"I'm going to need you to use your words, Talia."

Using her name seems to break through the haze. "I'm okay. It feels good."

"Such a good girl. You're doing so well. I'm so fucking proud of you."

She hums. Then giggles some more.

"More?"

"Please."

It takes a little time and patience, and a lot more lube, but we work in the second finger.

"More, please." Her politeness, even in her demands, is the most adorable thing. I've always valued good manners, and the fact I don't need to remind her of them is another check in the column that makes me want to explore this woman's every kink.

Instead of adding a third finger, I add even more lube and start finger-fucking her ass. Gently, slowly, but still rhythmically. Her humming, her contented sighs, and her giggles spur me on more and more until she's a soaking wet mess, and her muscles are twitching around my fingers.

"Close, baby girl?"

She's mumbling, seems more to herself than to me. But from the flickers and clenching, the tensing around my fingers, she's not far away.

Watching her like this is the most beautiful thing. The privilege of experiencing someone in their most base level, in their most intimate space, is one of the things I treasure most about being a dominant.

Stripping back the day-to-day life, coaxing someone to shut off their critical inner monologue, and giving themselves over to the process, to the whim of another person.

To truly disengage the way Half-Pint is right now, usually takes longer than this, but it's glorious to witness.

It can be difficult to make someone come anally, and I really want to make her fall apart into a soaking wet puddle on the bed. I move so I can slide my other hand into her slick folds and swirl my fingers around her clit too.

"You're so beautiful, all tied up and blindfolded for me, baby girl. You know that, right?"

She hums.

"And your ass takes my fingers so well. Such a good fucking girl." My fingers work faster, circling her clit and spearing her ass in sync.

Her muttering and mumbling is interspersed with blurts of giggles that make my chest expand with warmth.

It's the scream I've been waiting for. A feral, raw, free wail that bursts from her body, sending her back into the perfect arch as all her muscles spasm through an orgasm that threatens to rip her soul from her body.

"Good girl, Half-Pint. Don't stop. Keep coming for Daddy, okay? Daddy needs all your cum."

She seems to enjoy when I refer to myself as Daddy, and the more I play with the word in my mouth, the deeper into this scene I get with this woman, the more natural it feels. I should have predicted she'd identify as a Little, but I never in my life imagined I'd be considering letting someone call me Daddy beyond the first time.

Her legs tremble, her body quakes, and another wave of pleasure rolls through her body. Everything tenses, her muscles gripping my fingers in a vise making it damn near impossible to fuck her with my fingers. When the second orgasm hits, she's silent, head flung back in ecstasy as cum trickles from her sopping wet and slick pussy for me.

There's nothing about this moment I'd change, even if I was with the most experienced submissive, there's literally nothing that could make this scene any better.

Talia's body sags into the bed, but with the restraints, she can't relax. Pressing my hand between her shoulder blades, I try to re-center myself. I shouldn't get caught up in this woman, but it's too late. I'm feeling feelings, I want to take care of her, and I want to see her again beyond this forced situation due to the weather.

I want to explore this new dynamic to see if once the snow thaws, it'll be as potent, as consuming as it is right now.

"Easy, baby girl. I'll get you out of those cuffs, okay?"

"Yes, Daddy." It's mumbled through a yawn. My girl is understandably exhausted.

I release her arms and legs, throwing the apparatuses across the room onto my bag instead of taking time to put them away, they can wait. She barely moves when I take the blindfold off, or when I go into the bathroom to run a washcloth under warm water to clean her up.

It's only a few minutes, but when I'm done, I work her into one of my t-shirts that falls down below her knees and scoop her into my arms.

The damp patch hasn't made it through the bedspread, so I settle in under the blanket, curling myself around her and talking to her even though she's pretty out of it.

"You did so well, baby girl." I dot kisses on her forehead, stroking the cool, soft skin on her thighs. "Take a nap, okay? We'll get you in the bath in a while when you wake up."

She reaches up like she's trying to grab onto my shirt, but I'm not wearing one. Everything about her draws something strange and new from inside me. I've never been a nurturer, I've never sought out the company of someone else. I've never wanted to be anything than by myself.

Caitlin was like me, it's why we worked so well together. We enjoyed each other's company when it suited us both, but for the most part, we simply existed in the same space. It brought a deep contentment to our short-lived marriage. Finding someone who didn't want inane prattle, or to talk about stupid shit.

This isn't that. This is different. Talia and I are not only from two different worlds, but we're complete opposites of each other. Would that even work in a relationship?

I guess the only thing to do... is to find out.

CHAPTER 18
Talia

When I wake up, it feels like I've slept for a month.

"Shhhh. Easy, baby girl." Jagger's hand holds me tight against him, stroking the skin on my arm as he holds his book in the other hand, off to the side of the bed. I have no idea how he's turning the pages, or how he even reached his glasses and book if I've been on top of him this whole time, but I'm too sleepy to ask.

"You doing okay?"

I nod, nestling my head back into the crook between his head and shoulder. "Mmmhmm."

"Good. You did so well for me, Half-Pint. I'm so proud of you."

It's hard to describe the way his praise lands when he says it. I've never had someone's words seep into my skin and bed so deeply inside my whole being. It's a similar feeling to stepping into a warm home after being out in the snow, and basking in the glow of the heat.

My mouth is dry, throat raw, and I need a shower.

"If you keep wriggling like that, you're going to end up uncomfortable."

The growing hardness under my behind confirms what he's saying.

"Are you sore? Is that why you're fidgeting?"

I clench my butt cheeks. I wasn't sure I was going to enjoy butt-stuff, but I'd be only too happy to explore a bit more in the future.

"Not sore, but there's a definite 'something's been in here' signal. A little discomfort, nothing major."

He hums, and it vibrates against my back. "You want a bath?"

I'd love one. But I'm not sure I'm ready to be alone yet.

He buries his face in my neck, kissing me. "I'll come with you if you want some company."

"Aftercare?" I turn my chin so it's in line with my shoulder.

His shaking head makes my hair move. "Because I want to."

I try not to react, but there's something about the fact he wants to spend time with me rather than it being straight up aftercare he would give to just anyone else that makes me smile. "I'd like that."

"Me too." He kisses my cheek, and it hits me we haven't done a lot of kissing, actual kissing on the mouth. I reach a hand up to caress his jaw, tilt my head back, holding my breath in case he rejects me. The gentleness with which his lips meet mine makes me tremble. He turns me so he can deepen the kiss, our tongues tangled in a slow and lazy dance of emotion.

It's powerful, moving, and so tender I almost need to double check it's really him. Except this is him. Our session earlier showed me the real Jagger, the man inside the grump's body. The sweet, tender, nurturing and caring man who wants to take care of me.

He's like an armadillo. Crunchy and hostile looking on the outside, but once you get to his innards, he's a big soppy ball of goo. Though I'd obviously never tell him that.

When his hand cups my jaw, I melt into him.

Time stops. There's no him and me, just us. His kiss is soft, the bristles of his stubble graze against my skin, his breath tickles my face, and despite the intensity of our kiss, he doesn't rush, or push, or get demanding with his mouth. It's easy, lazy, comfortable, and gives me goosebumps, making my toes curl.

Something in this moment blossoms between us. It's like a seed was planted on the plane, and now that he's stopped fighting it, it's growing in the sunlight. There's a nagging at the back of my mind about his wife, is she ex? Am I helping a man commit adultery? Guilt clutches at my chest, tightening around my body.

Is it awful of me that right now, I don't want to care? But I can't help it. "Are you married?" My voice is a whisper, but from the way his body tenses, there's no doubt in my mind that he heard.

"No." He doesn't offer any further explanation, nor does his body relax, and his answer has only left me with even more questions. Is he divorced? Or just separated?

He kisses me again, probably to stop me from prying further. It's the best kiss of my life. Harry never kissed me like this, and when it finally slows to a stop, I'm more breathless from that kiss than I was from all our sexual activity earlier.

He presses a soft kiss to the tip of my cold nose. "I'll go get the bath started."

I check out his naked booty as he walks away from me. It's like he knows, because he stops for a moment. When he steps out of the room, I hug my knees inside his shirt. It smells of him, and eau de Jagger might be my new favorite scent.

The bath is full and bubbly when Jagger calls me into the bathroom. His hands skim my hips under his shirt as he helps me get naked, and as soon as the shirt is off, his lips and hands are all over my body. Quick, delicate kisses make me shiver as he moves from one shoulder, across the base of my neck to the other.

He steps into the tub before picking me up and settling into the hot water with my back against his chest.

A yawn strangles the words brewing at the back of my throat. I don't want to break this spell or ruin the moment by saying something stupid. I can't remember a time when I felt more comfortable, safe, protected than I do in this moment.

He uses a washcloth to make warm water cascade over my chest while continuously dotting kisses on my cheek and temple.

"I could nap again." It's true, there's a heaviness in my limbs that hasn't gone away with my nap.

"I've got you." His voice is so sure, so confident, I can't help but believe him.

He brushes my arms with the cloth. "Do you want me to wash your hair?"

I've read about this in books, too. I always thought in books it's fine, but in real life I'd never let a guy try to wash my hair. But I'm curious. What's the big deal about it that makes so many smut authors put it in their books?

I'm already sold on the joint bathing. Maybe I should give him a chance to wash my hair, too.

"You might get covered in blue dye."

"I had my fingers in your ass, Half-Pint. I can handle some hair dye." His voice is low and next to my ear.

My body temp shoots up to thermonuclear levels, and my chest gets red. There was no criticism in his voice, no judgment or accusation.

"We both know I like it messy."

The shiver that snakes up my back takes me by surprise.

"And you got so beautifully messy for me, baby girl." I can

feel his smile against my skin. "I love when you make that noise, that purr of contentment. It's my favorite sound."

The risk of popping our bubble of bliss is high, but I can't choke back the questions any longer. "I heard you say about your wife last night."

He stiffens ever so slightly, but he doesn't stop caressing me, and washing me with the cloth. "She passed away from cervical cancer a few years ago. Only six months after we got married."

Oh. A sliver of my heart breaks off for the man of steel who puts a rough facade on for the world.

"I'm so sorry." My chin's trembling, tears already streaming down my cheeks and off my chin into the bathwater. "That's awful."

He nods, his chin scratching against my shoulder blade. "She had no symptoms, right up until the time it was too late to do anything about it."

The fractures in my chest grow with everything he says. "Jagger..." I don't know what to say. There are no words, no comfort I can provide him.

"It's okay. I can't say it gets easier, but it's definitely hard to let people into a more long-term relationship space. It was hard watching her fade away in front of me." His voice is small, fragile, like if I poked him he might fall apart. The strong, confrontational, dominant man I've known for the past couple of days, the man who's held me together, now clings to me for comfort.

I'm afraid to breathe in case he realizes he's vulnerable. But yet I don't want him to think I don't care, or I don't appreciate what he's sharing with me. Because I do, on both counts. It's tragic. No one should ever have to go through something like this, never mind someone so young.

I can't stand my back being to him anymore. I need to look him in the eye, I need him to see that even if I'm quiet,

I'm not awkward or ignoring this conversation. I'm not hiding.

I spin to face him, the water sloshing over the side of the tub as I maneuver around his giant limbs. We sit staring at each other for a long moment. He tenderly sweeps bubbles from my shoulder, and suddenly it's him who can't meet my stare. His eyes flicker to the water.

"I don't know how this is going to go, Half-Pint. I'm not good at more than one-and-done."

I'm still not letting myself breathe. It's like I'm intruding on a private moment right now, and I don't know how to navigate it. His gruffness seems easier to handle than this emotion. For both of us.

"I'd like to pursue something between us. But I need to come clean. I know your ex. Harry is my college rival. He picked on my friends and I, cheated and swindled his way through college and took everything I ever wanted right from within my grasp."

The tears are flowing faster, as my chest heaves with tiny hiccupping sobs. We must have gone to the same school, and I was just younger than they were. But I don't remember Jagger at all.

"When I realized who you were, I wanted to get my revenge on him. I wanted to punish him for everything he put my friends and I through." He sweeps kisses across my wet shoulder. "But when we started playing, started checking things off that bucket list of yours, I realized it wasn't about ruining *you* for *him*, but ruining *him* for *you*. You're too good for him, Talia. You're too good for both of us." His voice hardens.

"You shouldn't be with either of us. But I wanted to expand your world enough for you to not be able to go back and settle with him."

His raw honesty curls itself around my chest, tightening

against my ribs and forcing me to breathe. I should be angry at him, I should be mad he wanted to use me as an implement of vengeance, but the tone of his voice, the way his words are laden with apology and regret soothes over the wound.

"I want you to be my girl, Half-Pint. I know it's been a couple days, I know it's fast, and it's certainly not something I've ever done before, but there's something here. And I hope you feel it too."

The confession makes him quiet for a long moment. "Now would be a good time for your chatterbox to kick in. The universe is off balance with me being the talkative one for a change."

I giggle through my tears. "That's more than you've said to me since we met."

He grunts like he's reached his quota of words.

He washes my hair in silence, rinsing it off after a deep and long head massage that sends me to a space somewhere between sleep and climax. It's a place that's floaty, like I'm levitating outside my body, it's warm and comfortable and safe. It's somewhere I want to visit more often, but I'm not sure how I even got here.

"Are you back in space, baby girl?"

"Space?"

"Little space. Or subspace, but I'm pretty sure you're a little."

I can't figure out how to get my tongue to form questions, so I stay silent.

"A little is a submissive that is more of a child-at-heart submissive. One who leans into their child-like nature."

That definitely sounds like me.

"Do you remember calling me Daddy last night, baby girl?" His voice is soft, like he's talking to an actual child. "You've nothing to be embarrassed about, and I'm not mad, so keep breathing for me, okay?"

"Okay."

"Do you remember?"

I nod, and before I can stop myself words trickle out of my mouth. "I've wanted to say it almost every time."

He nods. "I saw it on your list, but I wasn't sure if you understood the context, or if it was just 'cause you saw it in a book."

"Definitely the latter. I fought it. But earlier, I couldn't fight anything. Not words, not orgasms, not my deep-seated upbringing. It just came out. I'm sorry." My voice sounds distant, lazy and slow almost like I'm drunk.

"Shhhhh." He nuzzles into my wet hair. "That's not why I brought it up." He squeezes his arms around me, making the water slosh against the sides. "I wasn't really kinky with my wife. We dabbled, but I only discovered the lifestyle after she passed. One reason I fell in love with the kink community was because everyone was so accepting. I didn't have to downplay the color of my skin or the way I grew up around them. People took the time to get to know me, not just what I could do for them or give them. The kink community wanted me not just to feel powerful, but to be powerful. No one ever wanted to diminish me. And I never want to diminish you."

He takes a huge breath, like saying all that was physically exhausting. "I can't imagine Caitlin identifying as a little, nor have I ever sought littles out to play with. You're different."

I've always been different. I ready myself for the barb, the backhanded compliment, the 'but' I'm sure is coming.

"Turns out I liked when you called me that earlier. It felt like something clicked into place inside my body. And if you're open to it, I'd like to explore that with you."

His words are warmer on my skin than the pool of water we're lying in.

"Exclusive?"

His chuckle makes my body shudder in the water. "Yes,

baby girl. Exclusive. Just us. And whatever's left on your dirty bucket list and beyond."

I like that idea.

He clears his throat, and I tense. "What is it?"

"I don't want to give up my role as a dominant in Protocol. So if being exclusive with you means I have to give that up, I don't think I can."

I love his honesty. I also hadn't considered that. "I don't want you to give up something you love, just to be with me. But can we set some boundaries?"

"Of course." He sighs as though he's relieved. "We don't have to talk about them right now, but I'd suggest at least no fucking other women and no tongue kissing."

I like that idea, too.

I must fall asleep again. When I come to, the water around me is much cooler than it was when I dozed off. Jagger seems to have been content enough to stay in the tub and sit watching over me while I napped.

We get out, he dries me off, helps me get changed and settles me on the couch with water and the remote before he starts to towel himself off.

A sharp knock sounds at the door, followed by an aggressive tap, tap, tap stream of additional and wholly unnecessary thwaps.

Jagger wraps a towel around his waist as a familiar voice sounds through the room. "Talia? Are you in there?"

Jagger looks at me as the blood drains from my body. Harry is outside the door, and if Jagger doesn't open it soon, my ex-fiancé sounds like he's going to break the dang thing down.

CHAPTER 19

Jagger

I'd know that pretentious prick's voice anywhere. It haunted me for four years of college and beyond.

I probably shouldn't swing the door open, standing balls out, wrapped in a towel with his former fiancée's promise ring dangling from a chain on my chest, but I can't fucking help myself. The urge to stick it to him, and the opportunity, are too good to pass up.

When I swing the door wide, it slams on the wall, bouncing off and making the picture frames shake. "What the fuck do you want?"

Harry, the cowardly fuck, recoils, takes a full step back, and the color drains from his face like he's seen a ghost.

But he's not alone. There's a woman who looks like an older version of Talia, except her hair is long, blonde and wavy, and her clothes scream money.

Talia's parents. Wonderful. This was not on my fucking bingo card for today.

"Is Talia in there?" Harry curls his lip.

The urge to pick him up by his throat and beat him into next week is strong. But these people will press charges and make sure I go away forever. They'd throw the book at me. So I swallow down the burning bile on the back of my tongue, dig deep, and try to find some element of civility in my body.

This isn't for me to drop her in trouble with her family, so I turn to her to see what she wants me to say. She's barefoot, wet hair soaking the shoulders of her t-shirt. Her fresh-face looks pale, and she's balling the front of her t-shirt, shrinking back inside herself right in front of my eyes.

"I'm here." Her voice is small as she steps forward, joining me in the doorway.

The look on Harry's face is comical. His jaw drops, snaps shut, drops, snaps shut, and the more he stares between Talia and I, the more his fists flex at his side.

I'm silently daring the dumb fuck to take a swing. He'd be in a body bag before he lands a single hit.

Talia's dad hasn't taken his eyes off Talia, while her mom's gaze is fixed firmly on my chest. Whether it's the tattoos, the nakedness, or the fact her daughter's promise ring is hanging around my neck, I don't know. But there's a silent staring stand-off, and no one's daring to so much as breathe.

After a long, quiet moment, it's no surprise Harry breaks the silence. Prick never did know when to keep his goddamn mouth shut. "Tali, what the fuck did you do to your hair?"

She visibly bristles. It's not the same shiver she gets when I call her pet names or say dirty things about her pretty pussy in her ear. It looks painful. Her face falls, and her shoulders curl forward.

"Get your things, Talia. We're leaving." From the stern look on her face, Talia's mom seems pretty determined.

Half-Pint's head snaps up, eyes wide for a fleeting beat before she clenches her teeth. "I'm not going anywhere but back to my house, Mama."

"We need to talk, sweetheart." Her dad seems to be good cop.

"I can talk here." Talia folds her arms across her body like she's protecting herself. It takes all the strength in my body not to step in front of her to protect her.

Honestly, I'm not sure whether she needs it or not. And I don't want to piss her off more, or worse, hurt her if she thinks I'm not in her corner, or believe she can't fight her own battles.

She stares at her parents for a long, drawn-out moment. "We can talk downstairs. But I'm not leaving the building with you."

The fire blazing through my veins is out of control. I'm proud of my girl for standing her ground. I'm proud of her for telling them she wasn't leaving with them because they said so, but I can feel from the way she's holding herself that she's going to crack.

"Half-Pint?"

Her watery eyes meet mine.

"You don't have to do anything you don't want to."

Harry huffs out a breath that makes me flex my fingers into a ball at my side. In my periphery, he takes a step back. Good. He should be scared. He might be a controlling prick who has Talia under his thumb, but he doesn't control me.

It's shitty of me, but I take a step toward her, sweeping her hair behind her ear. "You want me to come with you?"

As she's nibbling on her lip, her head tries to turn toward the people at the door, but I hold her chin firm so they can't influence her decision.

"Is this why you refuse to marry Harry? Because you're shacked up with this... man?" Distain drips from her mother's words, making my skin prickle with irritation.

Judging people is human nature. But standing here in nothing but a fucking towel I'm honestly not sure if this woman's issue is that I'm half naked, I have tattoos, or maybe even that I'm black. Either way, fuck her and her judgment.

Talia opens her mouth to answer, but I can't help myself. Stepping in front of her, I shield her from their vitriol.

"Not that she owes you an explanation, since she's a grown-ass woman and all."

Her mom twitches at the word ass. Just wait till I get to the F-bombs.

"But our plane got grounded, and we got snowed in together. There was one room left, so we shared." I gesture at the pile of blankets on the couch, half-dangling onto the floor. "I've been sleeping on the couch. I'm half naked because Talia was napping after her shower, and I was drying myself off when you tried to beat the door down."

My words are pointed, clipped, and the last part is directed to Harry. I point my finger at him. "Watch yourself, asshole. We aren't in college anymore, and I don't care what the fuck connections you have, if you so much as make a single tear trickle down her face, I will end you."

I'm not sure at what point my finger rammed itself into his chest, nor when I stepped forward to tower over him, but my chest is rising and falling with heavy breaths.

"You're letting this lout speak on your behalf now, Talia?" Fuck. Her mother is a piece of work. Daddy dearest stays suspiciously quiet, but the way he's eye-balling me doesn't suggest he shares his wife's opinion, he's more curious than hostile.

"She can speak for herself. I'm simply saying I won't stand for her being treated like shit. So if that's your intention the three of you can fuck off all the way back to Kentucky."

She cringes at that one. Good. It's petty as fuck but I want her to know her hoity-toity bullshit won't fly with me.

Talia's hand touches the small of my back. "Jagger, I'll be okay."

I want her to encourage me. I want her to stand up for herself, to advocate, to use her voice. I need her to communicate with her parents the way she did for me a few short hours ago when my fingers were in her ass.

The mother's face slowly spreads into a slow smirk that drips with victory, and Harry flips me off before reaching a hand out to Talia.

Thankfully, she doesn't take it. If she did I might break the door off its hinges. I try to plead with her silently with my eyes. I try to convince her not to go, to draw the boundary. I mean, what kind of crazy fucker brings his almost-in-laws through a blizzard to scold their grown-ass daughter?

"Wait." I hold my hand out to stop her from going with them. "How did you know where she was?"

Harry avoids my eyes. "Find my phone."

Of course he did.

"Then I had a local P.D friend do a drive by to see if her car was in the parking lot."

The fucking audacity of this guy. I want to snap his neck like a fucking twig.

"Riiiiight. That's red flag as fuck. And it tracks that you want your daughter to marry a sociopath." Stopping the words spitting from my mouth is impossible, and Talia recoils at the insult to her parents like I slapped her across the face. She steps toward her parents, and with one last mournful glance back at me over her shoulder, she goes with them.

Fuck this shit.

CHAPTER 20
Talia

"Did you screw him?" Harry's accusations start before we've even taken our seat in the restaurant. I wanted to stay vaguely public in case things got, well, yelly.

"Everything okay here, Talia?" Maeve, one of the ladies from the knitting group, pats my shoulder.

I force my face into a smile. "Yes, thank you, Maeve."

Her side-eye game as she mean-mugs my parents and Harry is impressive as all get out. She leans toward me. "Where's Jagger?"

My body heats, more from the weight of my parent's stares than from Maeve's cheeky question. "He's upstairs."

"He asked you out on a date yet?" Man, this woman does not let up.

One of the other ladies saves me from having to answer by grabbing Maeve's arm. "Leave the girl alone, clearly she's got things to do."

Maeve tosses me a wink before she lets her friend lead her away from our table.

"Talia, what can I get you?" Steph, the server, is all smiles as she approaches. "Cappuccino?"

"Thanks, Steph, that would be great."

"And what can I get the rest of you?"

"Just a pot of coffee with three mugs please, Steph. And if you have any pastries back there, we'll take a mixed selection."

"Sure thing, sugar." Steph pauses for a moment before leaving. It's like all my new friends are trying to save me from my parents and ex. It's cute, heart-warming, but unnecessary.

I don't need saving.

"Well? Did you?"

I swivel in my seat so I can face Harry square-on. "I don't owe you an answer to that, Harry. Our relationship is over. But no, I haven't had sex with Jagger. I met him a couple days ago. I leave that level of casual frivolity to you."

I don't like sounding like I'm shaming him, but I want him to feel shame. I don't care where he dips his quill, but he dipped in someone else's inkwell while he was with me. *That*, I care about. And he *should* be ashamed of that.

"Talia." Mama's voice holds caution, but she should be on my side, not his.

If she's not, then screw her, too.

"No, Mama."

She balks.

"I am not happy with Harry. I don't love him, I don't want to be with him, and you should certainly not want me to be with someone who cheats on me and disrespects me like that." I turn to Daddy. "I know there's business tied up in this Daddy, but honestly, I've done a lot of thinking, and I'm sorry, but I don't care. That's your problem, not mine. I'm not signing myself away to a cheating scumbag in the name of your business. And while I'm at it, it's despicable that you'd ask me to."

My parents have the decency to at least blush.

"And you." I turn my attention back to Harry-the-butt. "I don't belong to you. I never did."

He counters. "You wore my promise ring, which I so happened to notice hanging around your new fling's neck."

"I didn't need it anymore, Harry. I kept up my side of the promise. I wasn't the one who broke it. You did. That's on you, not me. If you want the ring back..." I shrug, a smile tickling the corners of my mouth. "You'll have to take it up with Jagger."

Harry's mouth drops open. "You get a haircut and whore yourself at the first asshole you meet, and suddenly you're a mouthy slut."

A number of things happen at the same time. Dad jumps to his feet muttering protests and knocking over a glass full of water, Mama gasps, fanning herself with her hand like the S-word has made her so uncomfortable she feels queasy, and Jagger appears beside me and grabs Harry by the throat, picking him up out of his seat like he weighs nothing.

I don't know whether to laugh or cry as I bolt out of my chair. "Jagger." If I'm not mistaken, one of the old ladies across the room whoops. But that might be the buzzing in my ears making me hear things.

He growls. "I warned you, you piece of shit."

Harry's face is already turning red. Jagger isn't playing.

"Jagger, please." I touch his arm, and his eyes swing to mine, they're swimming with an unhinged anger, which if I'm honest, is pretty hot. What the heck is wrong with me? Those dirty books have clearly shifted my moral compass, and I'm not sure how I feel about that.

Harry kicks out a leg, which makes Jagger put him down on the ground, but he keeps hold of his Ralph Lauren sweater like he's afraid Harry might flee.

I don't blame him, Jagger is a scary beast right now. I wouldn't want to cross him. But I'm not afraid of him. I guess it's because there's a voice inside me yelling he's doing this for me. Harry disrespected me, insulted me, and instead of making me marry him, like my parents are trying to do, he's protecting me, avenging me.

Jagger's whole body is vibrating, he's snarling at Harry. "That was your freebie. If I ever hear you speak to her like that again, your life is over. Are we clear?" He snorts. "If it was up to me, you'd be done already."

He slams Harry down onto the chair. "Say whatever the fuck you need to and then leave. I don't care that your parents work together, I don't care that you might see each other at holiday parties or wherever the hell you might cross paths. From now on, her name stays out of your mouth, you hear me? Period. You don't talk about her, to her, or come within fifteen feet of her."

Harry, still shaking and tugging at the collar of his shirt, guffaws out a laugh. "And how are you going to enforce that?" He jerks a thumb at Jagger, looking to my parents for back up. "This prick's a psychopath."

Mama won't look at him, but Daddy's face is so red, and he's scowling so hard I can almost see new frown-lines appearing on his forehead.

Jagger plants a hand on the table in front of Harry and leans over him. The eyes of everyone in this restaurant are on us, the guests, the staff... everyone.

Jagger uses his other hand to dust off Harry's shoulder with a grin that sends chills through my body. "I dare you to test me, Harry. I fucking dare you."

"I want my promise ring back." Harry's voice is small.

"Tough shit. It belongs to me. You want it, come and take it."

The challenge hangs heavy in the air.

"Just as I thought, chicken shit." Jagger snorts again, toying with Harry. There's a dangerous edge to his voice. As much as this feels a gross over reaction to what transpired between Harry and me, I also know this resentment between them has been brewing for years. Jagger needs to get this off his chest and clear the air.

"You never talk to her again, you hear me? Delete her number, delete that Find My Friend shit, and stay the fuck away from her. Even if I never see her again, you're done with her."

I could have set the boundary, but it would have exhausted and wrecked me. I feel like I need to confirm what he says is what I truly want, that he's not speaking for me.

"He's right, Harry. We're done. Move on." I turn to Daddy. "I won't marry him."

"I'm sorry I ever asked you to." Daddy's shaking his head as Mama's head snaps up and spins to face him. "I'm so sorry, sweetheart. I should never have locked you into a relationship with this piece of crap."

A smile pulls on the corner of my lips.

"You should leave." Mama turns to Harry. "Talia's made herself crystal clear. She's done with you, Harry." She holds her hand out.

Harry hands over a little red, velvet box. It's grandma's engagement ring. I guess he thought giving me a family heirloom would make me forget the fact he slipped his eggplant into another woman's vegetable patch.

Jerk.

I'd forgotten he left the ring in to get resized and some of the prongs around the stones reinforced, they were starting to get weak from being so old and well-worn.

Harry gets up and leaves, which makes the table of knitters incredibly happy. I know this because they whoop and cheer, applauding. One of them shouts "good riddance," while another asks Jagger to marry her.

He gives a tight-lipped smile to my parents, sweeps his fingertips over my face, and makes his way over to the knitters. I can't stop myself from following him with my gaze.

"You at least like him." Mama's words are accusatory, with a sharp edge.

"I do, Mama. And if that's a problem for you, then it's precisely that. Your problem."

Her eyes flex wide. None of us are really sure where this backbone has come from, but I'm afraid it's going to run away and leave me if I don't quit while I'm ahead.

After a couple of minutes over at the knitting table, they all get up and give him hugs one at a time. He then comes back over to me, scratches the back of his neck with his palm before tucking his hand into the back pocket of his jeans.

"He *is* a problem." Her voice is hard. And I'm not going to press her to explain what she means, because if she opens her mouth and my racist grandfather comes out, there's going to be bigger problems than Jagger assaulting Harry. I'll throw something at my mother. The disgust in her tone could be for any number of reasons, I wouldn't put it past her to be this unhappy simply because Jagger has a penis.

"I've gotta get going." Speaking of Jagger, he's staring at my mother with a hardness in his eyes.

My stomach sinks. But, what? Aren't we going to figure things out between us? "But..."

"Let him leave, Talia. The man says he needs to go." Mama won't let it drop.

His eyes barely come up off the floor, and all the fight I had in me moments ago evaporates on an exhale. "Okay. Do you need a ride?"

He shakes his head. "It's all good. Slade's outside waiting for me. Thanks though."

I stand up, instantly regretting my action because my legs are shaking. "Jagger."

Another headshake. "I'm sorry Half-Pint."

Tears well in my eyes as a lump swells in my throat.

"Girls like you don't date guys like me." He glances at my

parents a few feet away. "You're too good for both of us, like I said." He doesn't wait for an answer, he plants a chaste kiss on my temple. "Take care of yourself, okay?" His voice cracks, but he's not backing down. I don't know whether to scream or cry right now.

Where is this coming from? My head is spinning.

He's running scared. He's spent two days helping me overcome so many of my fears and now he's listening to his and fleeing because things got tough? The. Audacity.

But did they get tough? He chased off Harry, my parents have at least kind of accepted I doesn't want to marry him. What have I missed? I don't understand.

By the time I find my voice, he's already gone, and tears are trickling down my face.

Mama comes to comfort me, like she finally gets it. "There, there, darling. It's for the best. He's right, you know."

I shrug her off, level her with my best disgusted stare and head back up to my room where I collapse onto the hotel bed, take a deep inhale of Jagger's scent, and burst into waves of tears.

CHAPTER 21
Jagger

"HAS HE STILL NOT SAID ANYTHING?"

"No."

"Has he left the club?"

"No."

"Still hasn't showered yet, either. Pretty sure that funk in the air is him."

If my friends think their voices are in any way quiet, they're sorely mistaken.

It's been two days since I walked out of the hotel, leaving a crushed Talia and her judgmental parents sitting at the table in the dining room. I came straight here to the club, and it's where I've stayed.

Slade is in Iowa checking up on construction of the new club. I need him to get his ass back here so he can tell me what the fuck to do to fix this ache in my chest.

"Does anyone know what happened to him? Is he okay?"

A low rumbling growl brews behind my ribs, making my whole body shake.

"Easy, tiger. We just care about you." Kenzie's hand hits

my back. "You stink, you haven't slept, no one's seen you eat, and you've been here for four days straight."

Four? My head snaps up to meet Kenzie's sympathetic eyes.

Paige and Addison hover behind her, giving me similar looks.

"Wanna talk about it?"

I shake my head. I don't even know what there is to talk about. I had to walk away. I did. If her parents didn't make her leave to be with someone better than me, I'd have lost her some other way.

Deep down, I know it's bullshit. I feel like a prick for leaving her there, but the longer I stayed in the hotel, the more the soles of my feet burned. I needed to get out.

If it's been four days that means Slade should be back soon. If he's not back already.

"The fuck is that smell?"

Three sets of index fingers point my direction.

"Jagger, are you okay?" Austin's voice is loud enough for half the club to hear him, but thankfully, it's just myself and my friends, at least for the moment.

Kenzie smacks his arm. "Of course he's not okay, mon guerrier. You have eyes in your head, right? He's been like this for days."

Slade steps in front of me, and the women all step back. "The fuck happened to you?"

My whole body hardens, and I guess I growl again because he takes a half step back. "Okay. Up. Now." He squares up to me, Austin's behind me, Thor's probably behind the bar getting ready for opening in a few hours. Between the three of them, they could totally take me.

"Downstairs, shower, now." He's barking at me like I'm one of his play things. If I was in any way bi or gay, it would probably be hot.

It's not worth the effort to object, so I haul my ass up off the stool I've been stinking up—apparently for four days—and follow Slade down into the dungeons.

The hot, steaming stream of the shower doesn't help me, either. While I know in my soul I'm no good for that girl, there's something deep inside my chest that's mocking me, making me feel like a goddamn idiot for walking away.

"Is it a woman?"

"Fuck!" I damn near jump out of my skin at Slade's voice. The showers aren't communal, I'm in the staff-only bathroom, and there are three shower stalls next to each other with frosted glass doors.

"So you can still speak. Good. Start talking." His voice is hard, words clipped, tone demanding.

"Fuck off."

"Can't do that, bud. Can't help you if I fuck off."

I grunt. I'd say I don't need help but the pain in my ribs is tangible, and if he doesn't tell me how to get rid of it, it might linger there next to the pain of losing my wife.

"It's a woman." The words are quiet, barely audible over the water streaming down my back.

"What did you do?"

"What makes you think it was me?" As soon as the question leaves my mouth, Slade's laughing.

"My dude, it's seeping from your pores."

"Did something stupid with a woman and now need to figure out how to erase it." Lathering up the body wash on my chest takes a mammoth effort.

He laughs again, and I want to punch him in his smug face. "We both know you can't erase anything. What did you do?"

"Fell for her."

"Sounds pretty good to me so far. What else?"

"Left her." I shut off the water and shake my head.

When I step out of the cubicle, Slade throws a towel at me. "Just like that? You just, up and left?"

I nod, drying my head, neck and shoulders before wrapping the towel around my waist.

"Okay, dumbass, why would you do that?" The more he looks at me, the more uncomfortable I get until I can no longer hold his stern gaze. "I get it. You got scared, you freaked out, and you left. Tale as old as fucking time."

He drops onto a bench next to the lockers before patting the wood next to him. "Sit."

"I'm fine standing."

"Cool, but could you cover your junk a bit better? It's staring at me. It's always hard falling when you've gotten so good at keeping people at arm's length." He crosses his legs. "You let someone get behind the castle walls, you bolted, messed it up, and now you're hurting. Do you feel bad? Do you want her back?"

I grunt again.

He holds up his hands, palms facing me. "Not asking if you don't want to share. You're a private guy and that's okay. But you gotta dig deep, Jagger, figure out what the hell has you so scared, what the root cause is, or you'll just end up in this situation the next time it happens. Stupidity is doing the same things over and expecting different results."

Is he just reciting fortune cookie wisdom at me right now?

"Growth is painful, my friend." He stands up and pats my chest. "But if we aren't growing, then what's the fucking point?" With that, he pats me again. "Let me know if you need or want to talk. I'm always here. But I think you probably know what you need to do, you just don't like your choices."

Fucker isn't wrong. I have no way to contact her, though, and I'm not Harry fucking Winslow. I'm not stalking her.

Best thing I can do for both of us, is put her out of my

mind, let the whole thing blow over, and never make the mistake of letting someone in. Again.

CHAPTER 22
Talia

It's been a week.

Instead of going back to Kentucky with my parents, I chose to extend the lease on my apartment by another year. Thankfully, no one had picked it up.

I have a business degree I have no intention of using, and no idea where I'm destined to head in life. I don't even have the first clue. But I've lost two hundred pounds of dead weight, Harry hasn't so much as texted me since Jagger threatened to kill him dead in front of a room full of people.

I've cried more tears than I care to admit. Not for Harry, but for Jagger. His sweater doesn't smell like him anymore, and something about my whirlwind romance with him last week has left me in a tailspin.

This is what heartbreak is *supposed* to feel like. It's also how I know Harry isn't for me. When I broke up with him, I felt relief, not like every breath entering my body was getting caught on all the broken fragments of my heart.

Has Jagger thought about me? He has no way to find me. Did he pay attention when Mama full-named me in the hotel? How would he find me even if he did? Other than the fact I'm from Kentucky, he doesn't know much else about my life here in Minnesota. Even if he wanted to find me, I'm not sure how he could.

Does he want to find me?

The idea he might sends frissons into my fingertips.

I know how to find him. I just haven't done it.

Yet.

I need to return his sweatshirt. I mean, it's clearly a very important piece of his life he simply can't live without.

Do I also want to tear his head off for being a lily-livered coward? Maybe. My tears have given way to a righteous anger that I need to get out. It's also possible I need to get this sweatshirt out of my house. Doing that might take all these thoughts and feelings toward the man right along with it.

A girl can hope.

Today's the day. I've washed the sweater and placed it in an inoffensive grocery store bag. I'm wearing my sexiest jeans, warm boots because not even Jagger, Mr. Grumpasaurus with the cute butt is worth getting frostbite for, and my nicest sweater. I've picked out my favorite pom beanie, a giant coat because I'm always cold, and as soon as I grab my keys I can head over to the club.

The roads are clearer now that the storm has passed. I mean, it's winter in Minnesota but it's not "get snowed in somewhere with a stranger" level of inclement. Have I checked the traffic cams thirty five times just to make sure? Absolutely I have.

Dad threw a bag of sand and a bag of salt in the trunk before he left, just in case I need traction, or to melt a giant snow man I guess. Mama dragged me out to buy an electric blanket for the car and made me put together a snack bag because she said the winter emergency kit in my car was lacking.

They weren't wrong, but now poor Bessie groans when we turn corners because she's so heavy.

Club Protocol looks different from the outside when there isn't a million feet high pile of snow covering everything.

Okay. Okay, fine. Yes. Slight exaggeration. But my point stands. Things look different when you're not stuck in a Hallmark movie winter wonderland.

Huh. Maybe Jagger will look different, too.

Perhaps he won't be the tall, dark, and handsome giant I remember from last week. Rubbing my clammy palms on the thighs of my jeans doesn't help the sweating.

It's early evening, some cars are in the parking lot, but I don't remember what Jagger drives. I didn't ask him if he was here every night, which probably would have been a good plan. But I didn't have that level of foresight.

I didn't want to come later. I'm not sure I'm willing to witness the level of... sexy things that happen behind this door every evening.

On my way in, I'm directed to a locker and asked to place at least my phone in there. When I take my coat off, the hostess looks me up and down and shakes her head. "I'm sorry, but we have a dress code."

My jaw drops. I'm in a sex club where most people will end up naked anyway so what the heck does it matter what I'm wearing on my body? Biting back the judgy quip at the back of my tongue, I shake my head back at her. "I'm not staying. I just need to see Jagger, uh," Shoot. I don't remember man's last name. But there can't be more than one Jagger working here, right? That would be a weird coincidence. Matt, or Brad, maybe. But surely not Jagger?

"You're here to see Jagger?" A gorgeous blonde steps into view, from her accent, she's a southern girl like me, and when she smiles, I want to be her friend.

"Yeah, I have something of his to return."

"He's not here. I'm not sure if he'll be in tonight or not."

My heart sinks a little. It's probably for the best, even if it doesn't feel like it. I should leave the sweatshirt with this woman and leave.

"If you want, you can sit with my friends and I for bit in case he comes in."

I shouldn't.

A quick scan of the place tells me this is not my kind of space. The few people who are here are wearing things I wouldn't know where to shop for, or how to put on. But this woman is so warm and friendly, and yes there's an element of desperation to see the man who broke my heart after only two days, so why the heck not?

"Okay."

She guides me over to the bar where two women are standing talking to the bartender. "I'm Mackenzie. Most people call me Kenzie. And these are my besties Paige and Addison. We're all she/her." She gestures to the bartender. "This is Nyx."

Nyx reaches a hand across the bar. "They-them. Nice to meet you."

We all exchange handshakes. "I'm Talia." I self-consciously touch my chest. "I stopped by to drop something off. I won't be staying long."

Nyx shrugs her shoulder like it's no big deal. Shoot. Their shoulder. I don't know any non-binary people, and I'm suddenly afraid to open my mouth in case I offend her. Them. Double shoot.

It's not hard, Talia. Figure it out.

"Can I get you something to drink?"

"I'm driving, so I shouldn't. Thanks, though."

They smile at me. "It's a non-alcoholic bar. We don't serve alcohol before play, it messes with consent. But we have a non-alcoholic range of drinks, beer, wine..."

That's a pretty darn good point. Alcohol and sex could get incredibly messy. I like the responsible nature of not letting people dull their inhibitions with substances before going down into the dungeon.

"Oh. In that case, I'll take a glass of white wine please."

Nyx nods and walks away from us, slinging a towel over their shoulder.

"Talia's here to see Jagger."

Three sets of eyes burn the side of my face with their curiosity before I even turn to face them.

"Is that so?" The redhead—Addison, I think Kenzie said her name was—leans toward me.

The other lady shakes her head. "In the few years I've known Jagger, I've never known a girl to come looking for him." Her voice is so coated in wonder it makes me giggle.

"I'm returning something of his back."

They all exchange looks that tell me they know that's not the only reason I'm here.

"Let's move over there." Kenzie gestures to a table a few feet away that doesn't require a ladder for me to get onto the chairs like the bar stools would have done.

Nyx hands me my wine and turns their attention to the next customer.

It takes twenty minutes after we settle at our new table, and a second round of non-alcoholic drinks before these three women know everything about me. They know the entire story of Jagger and I, well, aside from the dirty pieces. They know the Harry Chronicles, and Kenzie in particular seems sympathetic to my parental issues.

She's patting my forearm as I tell them my woes.

I end on a giant sigh. "So I'm pathetically here to give him back his shirt, and a piece of my mind." I shrug. "Or I was. Now, I'm going to have to leave it with y'all to give back to him."

Kenzie shakes her head. "You're more than welcome to stay here. Even if you're not appropriately dressed. I mean, if you want to go down into The Dungeon, you'll have to find something to change into, but up here you're okay. Right?" She turns to the girls who nod.

"Absolutely." Paige circles the rim of her glass with her finger. "And if you ever want to explore your kinks." She pauses to wink at me. "Archer is a relatively new dominant who's finding his feet around here. If you want a safe place to play, we can hook you up."

My face is on fire. I might have mentioned the kinky bucket list while I was ranting about how at one time, I'd have done anything for Harry. The offer is tempting, but this is Jagger's space, and I can't muscle my way into it.

I'm also not sure I could play with someone else while Jagger stands and watches. That would be... weird? Even if he doesn't feel anything for me, even if he doesn't care, I care.

"What are you doing here?"

My back is to the door, but that grumbly, low voice is easily identifiable and speaks straight to my core sending waves of shivers all over my body.

"I brought back your sweatshirt." I have no idea how my voice doesn't crack, waver, or shake, but I'm super proud of myself as I pick the bag up from my feet and hold it out to the side. I can't turn to face him, not yet.

Addison raises a questioning eyebrow. "You're returning his shirt, but you didn't do the deed?"

I shrug. "I got ketchup on my shirt."

She sits back, love hearts dancing around her head. "Awwwww. That's sweet."

"And so unlike Jagger." Paige turns her attention to the man in question, who unsurprisingly grunts.

"Right, you've returned it. You can leave now."

Kenzie gasps, Paige looks like she might rip his throat out.

Is this guy for real? He doesn't get to just... dismiss me because he's done with me. My face burns with embarrassment in front of these glorious, strong women I just met, and all that righteous indignation and anger bubbles over inside me.

I squeak my chair back on the tiles, brace my hands on the table, and push to stand before rounding on him. "Listen here, you hulking great brute. You don't own the universe. I came here to return something to you out of the goodness of my heart. And now, I'm half inclined to keep it because you're being rude. And I don't like rude." I cross my arms. Maybe that'll keep the pain from sinking into my chest.

"I realize I'm blindsiding you at your place of work but it's the only place I knew where to come to return it to you. And these lovely ladies invited me to join them for a drink. I'm not here to stalk you, nor was I waiting for you. I was happy to drop the bag here and leave but they convinced me to stay, and I was more than enjoying chatting with them."

I take a step toward him, pointer finger outstretched. "You don't deserve me returning your shirt, Grumpasaurus Rex. Maybe I should hold onto it until your attitude changes."

A man to his left snorts. "You'll be waiting a long time for that to happen." When he realizes I heard him and turned my attention to him, he steps toward me, hand outstretched. "Slade. Protocol is my establishment. It's a pleasure."

"Oh. Well, apologies for my outburst, Mr. Slade. I'll be done and out of your hair in a minute."

He waves me off before taking a seat at the next table, kicking his feet onto it and crossing his ankles. "Don't let me stop you. This is the most fun I've had in a while. Please, continue."

Paige rolls her eyes, but the other two women giggle. Jagger's scowly scowl gets even scowlier.

"You should leave." His jaw is tense, his words clipped, and a muscle is feathering in his cheek.

"Is that so?" Hands planted firmly on my hips, I square my shoulders.

He nods.

"Bless your heart."

"Uh oh. He's activated the southern woman." Kenzie's whisper isn't as quiet as she might have thought.

Rolling my lips so I don't end up in jail for tearing this beautiful man's beautiful head off his shoulders, I instead pick my purse up off the floor. Digging around in my purse, I realize everyone around me is silent, waiting for what's going to happen. It's too late now, I'm committed and can't back down. If I do, then another butt-face-boy is walking over me, and I've had quite enough of that this year already.

In fact, didn't Mr. Grumpasaurus help me find myself juuuust a bit during our time together? Darn tootin' he did. So this is pretty much his own fault.

I walk over to Mr. Slade and present him with my credit card. "I'd like to join your club please, Mr. Slade."

"We don't have memberships here, Half-Pint. It's not that kind of club." His voice has that edge to it, you know the tone that says you're about to get an ass-whoopin?

Mr. Slade nods. "He's right. There's a cover fee for the dungeon. But we're an inclusive club. I don't like exclusionary membership policies." he whispers. "And it's just Slade. First name, not last." He's not condescending, but there's mischief written all over his face. His eyes twinkle. "I mean, I'm tempted to start memberships right here, right now. You're a very convincing woman, Talia, was it?"

I nod, mute, my mouth dry, brain scrambling for what the heck to do now. My neck is on fire, I'm pretty sure tendrils of steam are coming out of the back of my shirt from the embarrassment cooking me alive from the inside out.

"Don't even think about it, Half-Pint."

The way he uses that term of endearment tugs on my insides. Hasn't he lost the right to be familiar with me when he walked away last week?

I don't even know what he's talking about. Think about what? I'm not thinking about anything except perhaps kneeing him in the nuts.

Then it hits me like cold water to the face, and I spin to the table of women watching the exchange with amusement. "Did you say your friend Archer was here tonight?"

Jagger grunts behind me.

Slade erupts into a deep chuckle. "I like this one."

"He is." Mackenzie's nod is solemn, like she knows exactly what I'm doing, and she's playing along.

"Could you introduce me?" I can't stop my fingers playing with the bottom of my shirt.

Slade slaps his thigh, doubling over as he's laughing.

"Talia." It's a growled word, almost under his breath, but it sends a cascade of goosebumps all over me.

"Yes, Jagger?" I keep my voice level and sweet and don't turn to look at him. If those brown eyes were to stare me down, I'd lose my nerve. And right now, I'm on my last nerve. I need it.

"Why do you need to talk to Archer?"

I shrug, nonchalant, my eyes locked in a "do not laugh, do not laugh" grip-stare with Mackenzie.

"What's it to you anyway?" Paige kicks her foot up onto the table, revealing the tallest heels I've ever seen. Those should be classified as a weapon.

"Stay out of it, Paige."

That doesn't make her back down. In fact, I'm pretty sure he waved a red rag to a bull. She bounds out of her chair, pulling out her cell phone from her cleavage. She presses something, puts the phone to her ear. "Hey, can you come out to the bar please?"

I can't see Jagger, but I can feel his frustration bubbling like someone shook up a pop bottle. "Why do you need to talk to Archer, Talia?"

Clearing my throat takes an age. "The girls tell me he's a relatively new dominant."

"This is true." Slade points at me, then ushers me to continue.

I spin to face Jagger, my chest is getting hammered by the erratic thump of my heart, my ears are ringing, my lungs tight, and all I want to do is kiss him.

Dang it. Why do I still want to kiss him? I cross my arms. Maybe whatever juju he's working on me won't be able to penetrate my forearms over my chest.

"So, I was thinking, maybe he could help me with completing my bucket list."

His frown gets frownier, and that super sexy glower gets almost a dangerous edge to it. In the moment, everyone else disappears, the bar, the ambient noise, everything. It's just him and me, staring each other down in a long, drawn-out moment of chicken.

"Like hell he will."

"Just because you don't want me, doesn't mean no one else will, Jagger." As soon as the words slip out from between my lips I want to cram them back inside. Someone gasps, pretty sure it's Mackenzie because she seems such an emotional sweetheart that my words probably smacked her pretty good.

Jagger's face twitches, and his foot moves toward me like he's contemplating closing this distance. "You're not playing with Archer, Half-Pint." His voice softens when he uses the nickname, but it only makes me madder.

"And why the hell not?" My trembling hands are on my hips. I've never been one to air my dirty laundry, it's not the southern girl way. Mama would spank my butt if she were here, not least of all because I said hell, out loud, but it actually felt pretty good, and if I'm honest with myself, the situation calls for much worse.

"Because you're mine." He punctuates each word, like he's struggling to keep his composure. Good. He should be mad. I'm mad too.

"Ha." It's out of my open mouth before I can engage my filter. "I've seen how you treat your toys, Jagger. And your toy box isn't where I want to be." I kinda went too far with the toy thing, but I ran out of steam halfway through the sentence and didn't know where to go with it.

I've barely rotated my body, the intention was logged in my brain but my feet hadn't yet made the movement, when Jagger lurches forward, scoops me up, and throws me over his shoulder.

"Put me down you Neanderthal!"

"That's not your safeword." He pops me on the butt with an open palm, and I'll be damned if I didn't like it. "Simmer down." He says it as though he knows it's like pouring gasoline on an open flame and doesn't care.

I wiggle harder—but not too hard—if I actually break free of the angry man's grasp my face is going to hit the floor first. Arching my back helps me get a view of the rest of the group. They're watching, but no one's moving. I have no clue where Jagger's taking me until we go behind the bar. He kick-slams the door of a room behind him, and plops me onto my feet.

"You can't keep me forever, it's kidnapping. And all those people out there witnessed my abduction. And I'm sure those women like me better than they like you, so they'll totally tell the police you have me when they come looking. And they will come looking you know." If I don't stop talking, he can't tell me he doesn't want me. At least that's what my brain keeps repeating to me as each sentence tumbles out of my mouth. When I come to a grinding halt, the air hangs heavy between us. After a long beat, he purses his lips.

"You are not playing with Archer." He's pointing at me.

"You're not the boss of me, Jagger." I point right back. "You gave up the right to decide who touches me when you ran away scared last week and left me at the hotel by myself."

There's a "you go girl," from the other side of the door, and it's obvious his friends have crowded around outside to continue the show.

"I left before you could tell me to leave."

"That doesn't even make sense."

He drags a hand over his pained face. "You were with your hoity-toity fancy parents, Talia. You really think after they've spent years trying to get you to marry Harry, they'd so much as let you date someone like me? A black, sexual deviant, mechanic? No. I did what I had to do to protect both of us from a painful ending."

"Ha." Is this guy for real? "Is that what you think you did?"

His brow twitches as he falls silent.

"Because all I saw was a coward run away in the snow leaving me to figure out what the heck happened between us and process everything all by myself." I stride toward him. "And isn't that something you should have been around for? Or at the very least, made yourself available for?"

His shoulders sag at my unspoken accusation.

"What happened to aftercare?" I wave my arms wide in question. "You heard me when I told my parents I wasn't marrying Harry. The end. Forever. No take backsies. I'm done with him. I also told them I'd date who I want, and your race isn't a reason for me not to date you, being a douche canoe, however, is." Point to Talia.

His nostrils flare. "I'm sorry."

"You should be. Do you have any idea how upset I've been over the past week?"

He grunts. I really need to get a better read on those grunts. Is it a yes-grunt? A no-grunt? An I-don't-care grunt? Where are we with the grunt?

It's my shoulders that sag now, I'm tired of being confrontational and yelling at him even if it's all justified anger. It's exhausting. My jaw trembles as I blink back tears. "The only reason I came here was because your hoodie stopped smelling of you. And it's stupid. I bet you haven't even thought about me since you walked out the hotel door last week."

I lift my hand. "I'm not looking for compliments or affirmation." I'm totally looking for affirmation, but I don't want to seem any more needy or desperate by saying it out loud.

"Look. I get it, we barely know each other. But those few days together actually meant something to me, and seeing you walk away like that, without so much as a look back—Jagger, you didn't even look back." I sniff. Now mad with myself that I'm crying instead of swinging my finger at him in a rage. "I know that's what you do, play with people and leave. I knew going in. But I thought..." Another sniff.

"I don't know what I thought. But it felt like more than the play scenes I read about in my books. Was I wrong? Did I misread everything? Was I seeing things that weren't there? What about in the bathtub? Was that all a lie?"

Someone outside the door sniffs too.

"No, baby girl. You didn't." He steps toward me, brushing my hair out of my face. I've never missed the caress of another human being as much as I've missed the way his fingertips tickle the side of my face.

"You can't call me that." More tears. Why do I cry when I'm mad? I'm not weak. I just have feelings. "You can't make me feel things and then take it away, Jagger it's not fair."

I sound whiny, I can hear it, but I don't care.

He brushes his thumb over my lips, making me fall silent. "I didn't forget about you. I thought about you every second of every day, and the reason I didn't look back at the hotel was because if I did I wouldn't have been strong enough to leave."

"You're right." His thumb stays on my lips. "I got scared. I got scared you'd fall back into your old life, Harry, your parents... I was afraid they'd influence your opinion of me."

"That's not true." I shake my head. "That's bullpoop."

"Bullpoop?" His lips twitch.

"You're not making me swear just because I'm upset with you." At least that's what I try to say but his thumb makes it sound mumbled.

"You're right again. That's an excuse. It's easy to say I was scared you'd run. But I know better. I see your new found strength, and it's amazing. I'm scared because I'm scared. The last time I let a woman into my heart beyond playing downstairs, she ripped it out of my chest." His voice breaks. "And if I'm honest with myself." He clears his throat.

"I don't know. I don't want to say it wasn't really love, because it was. I loved my wife. But things with her were different. I was different."

Someone outside the door says "Wife?" and someone else clearly smacks them because there's a thump, an "ow," and a "shut up," all in quick succession.

Jagger shakes his head. "I hadn't explored this side of myself before. So I guess the best way for me to describe it is to say the love I had for my wife was incomplete, because I was incomplete. You know? It's like there was a piece of myself I didn't know about yet. And she passed away before we could explore that space together."

"She died?" Mackenzie's voice is laden with pain. There's another thump, an "ow," and a "Stop fucking doing that," on the other side of the door.

Jagger sighs. "But with you, I know who I am. And the possibility of there being more between us means there's a chance for more pain, too. I didn't know what to do with that. So I ran from it. Literally. I bolted from the hotel, and then fell flat on my ass. How's that for karma?"

He shows me his elbow where there's a scabby cut still-healing.

I'm not sure what to say, or how I'm feeling. I'm cranky with him for fleeing the scene of our fledgling... whatever it was. But his declaration makes me think. I know I don't have one hundred percent of him, but will I ever? Is he capable of giving his entire self over to someone again? How long will I have to wait for him to finally give up those last layers of protection around his heart?

"Look." He hooks his finger under my chin, and my body melts. They do it all the time in books, and I can see why. That subtle touch, the tiniest act of control, holding eye contact, it makes me warm inside. "You didn't overthink things. There is something between us. Something I'm scared to pursue, and have probably lost my chance to, but if you're open to it, I'd like to."

I can't fight the smile making my lips flicker. This grumpy, grunty man can be eloquent and adorable when he wants to be.

"I'm sorry." He plants the gentlest kiss on my forehead, making my eyes close and my heart squeeze. "Really, I am. I should know better. I *do* know better. Can we try again? But without the stupidity and freaking out?"

The giggle is quiet, but he hears it.

"Laughing at me in my hour of need, Half-Pint?"

"I can't help it. You're just so big and surly, and you're talking about being afraid. I can't imagine you afraid of anything. You're always so stoic and strong."

He shakes his head. "And by always, you mean those couple days where we were in close proximity?"

He's got me there. Always can't be a couple days.

"Fine. But I feel like there's not much you're afraid of."

"Kids." He nods, soberly. "Frogs. I have an irrational fear of frogs."

My chest tightens. I'm not sure what cause he has to go near frogs, but that sounds kinda awful. "Frogs? Is there a name for that?"

He nods again, his face grave. "Rrrrrribbitphobia."

I burst out laughing, smacking his bicep with my fingers. "You had me."

He's chuckling, too. "I really am afraid of frogs."

"I don't believe you anymore. You've lost my trust with your rrrrribbitphobia."

"My what?"

"Your rrrr—"

He's all-out laughing now.

"Never mind. You're awful."

"I am, but apparently you're into that kind of thing, so you're stuck with me."

"Can we go back to your silent smolder? Is that an option?"

He shrugs. "No take backsies."

"What if I prefer you grumpy and grunty?"

He slides his hands onto my waist, pulling me toward him. "You'll have to silence me in other ways."

When his lips move to touch mine, I stick my hand up to cover his face. "Wait!"

He groans, dropping his forehead to what would be mine if there wasn't a hand in the way.

"Please, Talia? Can we try to navigate this together please? I know kink is daunting for you, and I know you're scared I'm going to ask you to do whatever twisted concoctions are brewing in your mind that you read about in those books. But I'd like to think I've proved in our time together that we can find space to work together to see what we both like, right?"

I nod, but he can't see me. "Right." My voice is quiet, I'm not sure what I want to say, and yet there's a thousand words brewing on the back of my tongue.

"And I'm scared of a relationship, not because I don't want to commit to you, or us, but because I've been hurt so deeply before, and I need to work through that. Please? Can we try?"

I don't answer right away.

"Not to be manipulative or anything but you have to say yes."

I stay quiet.

"Half-Pint if you don't agree to give me another shot at this thing between us, and you go out that door to play with Archer, I will straight up kill my friend and colleague in front of people. Prevent a murder, say yes."

"Wow. Because that's not at all manipulative." I maneuver myself around in his grasp. "And they say romance is dead."

"I dunno who you're talking to, but from what I've heard, those books you read glorify those... What are they called? Touch-her-and-die-vibes?" He winks up at me like he knows something he shouldn't, his eyes glittering. "Bet you're soaking those pretty cotton panties of yours right now with all my caveman talk."

"You didn't."

He nods. "I did. I read the one you had on your eReader in the hotel. And let me tell you, we need to expand that bucket list of yours."

My jaw is hanging open when he gets to his feet. He sweeps my hair back behind my ear and cups my face. When his lips touch mine, the heaviness that has been pressing my chest down for a week lifts, lightening my whole body.

It's a simple, chaste sweep of his lips across mine, but the way he backs me up toward the door, the way he cages me in with his entire presence, the way he caresses my face as he kisses me, it all feels right.

"No sex in my office, Jagger." Slade's voice carries through the door.

Jagger gives me that wolfish grin as he picks me up by my booty and wraps my legs around his waist. He's not gentle as we crash into the door.

"Ow!" Slade's pained voice is super loud. "I said no sex, Jagger. Don't make me come in there."

The temptation to make fake-sexy noises is almost overwhelming. Heck, from the way Jagger is looking at me, I might make real ones.

He sighs. "Fine." He slides me to the floor, and my whole body screams out in disappointment. "Tuesdays are quiet nights here at the club. What about a non-alcoholic drink with some of my friends?"

There's a crack of skin-on-skin on the other side of the door, like someone's high-fiving someone else. "Please say yes, Talia." Mackenzie's pleading is adorable. She's as much of a people person as I am, and it's so nice to meet one of Jagger's friends who are open to including me right off the bat.

"Okay, but on one condition." I point at Jagger. "You need to wear your hoodie so it smells like you again."

"He will." Addison answers for him. "And if he doesn't I'll make Thor put it on him."

I dunno who Thor is, but he sounds formidable. I'd pay to see that happen. "Okay."

When we open the door, Slade and the three women take a step back. Mackenzie squeezes my arm. "You did great." Her smile is warm and friendly.

A guy walks up behind her, and Jagger places a possessive hand on my waist with a growl.

The new guy holds out a hoodie, it's pastel blue. "Paige asked me to bring this up."

Paige accepts the hoodie from the man, who seems to sense something's off and nods, turning to leave without another word. "Thanks, Archer!" Paige calls to his retreating back.

Everyone laughs, except Jagger, whose hand tightens around my waist. "I hate my friends."

"I don't. I like them all already. Maybe even more than I like you, Grandmaster Thunderpants. Let's go sit with them so I can hear all the dirt on you."

CHAPTER 23
Jagger

THE URGE TO FOLLOW ARCHER DOWN TO THE dungeon, and rip his arms off his body is strong. I know he has nothing to do with any of this, from how quickly his face paled it was clear it was Paige's idea of a joke. But still.

Talia slips into the hoodie as she walks, which somehow, she pulls off. Why an accident-prone woman would compromise her vision by putting a sweater on while in movement is anyone's guess, but I supposed that's just Talia.

We all sit around a table, except Slade who disappears behind the bar and comes back with non-alcoholic champagne. As far as I know the girls all plan to play downstairs later, so we're sticking to the safe stuff.

Half-Pint pulls her legs up under the hoodie on the chair. She looks like she's ready for a movie and chill, not to sit and sip expensive non-alcoholic champagne in a kink club, but she makes it work. Though the strain on her face, and how she keeps flicking her eyes around the space suggests she's not comfortable.

It's probably less to do with what she's wearing and more to do with the fact she's in an open kink club.

Taking the spare seat next to Paige, Slade offers Talia a glass. "You want to share where you two met?"

Paige gets up from her chair, circles the table, and grabs a seat from another table to sit as far away from Slade as she can.

"Don't mind her," He says to Talia with a charming smile. "She loves me, she just won't admit it to herself."

Talia glances at Paige's eat-glass-and-die facial expression and giggles. "I can totally see that. That's how I look at people I love all the time." She tips her glass to him before she takes a sip, her nose wrinkling at the bubbles. "The girls already know how we met. It'll be boring for them to hear it a second time."

Addison, Paige, and Kenzie object and encourage her to share our story with Slade. She recalls it in vivid detail and her hands move expressively as she speaks. The bar only has a couple of people dotted around, downstairs is probably busier, but we've been talking about bringing in some demonstrations for Tuesday nights to liven the place up a little.

I can't take my eyes off my girl, though. She has captivated my friends. They're leaning forward, asking probing questions, and laughing like she's been here for years. Fuck, she fits in with my social circle even better than I do.

I shouldn't be surprised, she is clearly a witch. She manages to bring people under her spell before they even realize she's trying.

Slade being Slade, asks Talia about her kink experience. If the lighting wasn't bar-dim level, they'd see the blush I know is creeping up her neck and into her cheeks.

Paige attempts to kick him under the table even though she moved. "Don't." She holds up her hand. "You don't have to answer that, Talia. He should know better."

If dirty looks could light shit on fire, we'd need the fire extinguisher in here.

Slade holds his hands up, palms facing Talia. "She's right, you don't have to. I was just making conversation."

Paige tuts. "Being a nosy fucker you mean."

Slade leans forward. "If you wanted to share though, we're a safe space." He gestures to the women around the table.

"*We* are a safe space." Paige points to Addison and Kenzie. "You're a dick."

"I could be your dick if you stopped fighting me, Paige."

Talia's head bounces between Paige and Slade as they throw shade at each other. I'd forgotten this is her first rodeo with them because of how comfortable she is here.

Deciding she's too far away, I pick her up and plant her on my lap. I expected a fight, and warmth blossoms in my chest when she snuggles in.

"I feel like you need context here, Half-Pint."

Paige and Slade are spitting venom at each other across the table. Addison and Kenzie are sipping their drinks and chattering like nothing's happening.

"They love to hate each other."

She nods. "I can see that. Am I also the only one in the world to see their chemistry is combustible?"

Kenzie leans over to refill Talia's glass. "You're not. But they're in denial."

"Or at least one of them is." Addison drains her glass. A giant Jason Momoa look-alike appears behind her, bending to kiss her cheek.

"Hey, Kitten. Are you ready?"

Addison gets to her feet, the wide smile of a woman in love across her face. "Yes, Sir. But first I'd like you to meet Jagger's new girlfriend, and our newest Sub Club member, Talia." She turns to me, gesturing at Jason mark II. "Talia, this is my dominant, Thor."

His smile is kind as he reaches out to shake my hand. "It's a pleasure." He jerks his chin to Jagger. "If he gives you any trouble, let me know, okay?"

Talia wiggles on my lap. "Oh, he's given me *plenty* of trouble. But I can handle him."

Thor laughs. "I bet you can. I look forward to getting to know you better." He ushers Addison toward the staircase leading down to the dungeon.

"They seem so nice." Talia's wistful voice doesn't seem to be directed toward anyone. "Isn't it intimidating down there? Am I the only one who was scared to go down there?" She laughs. "And we were the only two people in here. I can't imagine going down there while other people are... You know."

Her cheeks seem to have caught fire by this point. She's fidgeting and moving on my lap, and while I know it's because she's uncomfortable, my dick says it's time to go.

"I was terrified. Actually." Kenzie taps her chin. "I was blindsided about coming here for the first time. The girls took me here to get me to let my hair down."

"And you had fun?"

Kenzie lights up at Talia's question. "I met Austin on my first night here. He was Prince Charming. I slipped going down the stairs, and he caught me. It took us a while to get where we are now. I was very vanilla when we met."

Slade clears his throat. "If I recall correctly, he left a butt plug on your desk at work."

I brush a kiss against Half-Pint's cheek. "You might like those, baby girl, they're cold and metal."

When she tenses in my arms I kiss her again. "They come in all manner of shapes and sizes so you don't need to panic."

She softens again.

"He did." Kenzie nods. "And I wore it to work."

Talia gasps. "You didn't."

Kenzie is giggling so hard we can barely make out what she's saying. "I did. With Ben-Wa balls inside me. At the same time. Talia it was awful, I almost died while massaging one of

Austin's teammates." She pauses, tilts her head like what she said sounded weird. "I'm one of the trainers for the college hockey team Austin used to play for. The Snow Pirates."

Half-Pint's eyes are wide. "I don't even know what those things are, never mind how you kept them inside you while working." The awe in her voice is adorable.

I lower my voice to her ear again. "We can certainly try those things you know."

Talia casts me some side eye. "My romance novels tell me we'll need to negotiate. And even if they didn't, I've seen Fifty Shades. We'll need a boardroom desk, some pages with intimidating sexual things on them, and some mood lighting." She sounds so serious as she lists her demands.

Slade claps his hands. "She's right." He nods. "You'll need to negotiate."

"And a pen," Talia adds very seriously.

"Can't forget the pen." My voice rumbles in my chest.

Talia grins at Slade, Paige, and Kenzie. "In case you can't tell, I'm very vanilla."

Kenzie nods. "I got that." She claps, making Talia jump on my lap, brushing against my nearing painful boner. "That should be a shirt. Or a sticker. Or a shirt, *and* a sticker."

"We're working on a kink merchandise line." Slade gestures to Half-Pint's hoodie. "You're wearing one of our brand new ventures."

"I love it." I'm not sure she'd say otherwise, even if she hated it, but her enthusiasm is well received by Slade and Kenzie.

"It's so soft, and I love the color. It matches my blue hair."

"I love your blue hair."

These women are so sweet they could melt my teeth.

Slade's looking at my woman like she's growing horns in front of his face.

"What?"

He shakes his head. "She must be special. You don't do vanilla. You don't do relationships. And turns out, you had a wife. Who the fuck are you, man?" He slaps his calf, resting his hands on the ankle of his crossed leg.

"I don't know how you didn't know that about him, Slade. He's such a chatty Cathy, I can't ever get him to shut up." Talia's sass is dialed up to three hundred right now.

Kenzie bursts into another fit of giggles as Slade wags his finger. "Yeah. I really like her. Well, Ms. Vanilla, let's talk Protocol. It's a semi-casual space for people to come and express and explore themselves."

He holds up a hand. "And by semi-casual I don't mean hoodies and sneakers. I mean we don't have a membership, we're not exclusive, we're a kink club for everyday people who like to get their kink on. We're a safe, inclusive space, and we value education. So if there's ever something you'd like to see, or learn about, please don't be afraid to speak up. Or tell Jagger, he'll let us know."

Talia's eyes are sparkling. It's like Slade found her curiosity switches and hit all of them at once, like the buttons on an elevator panel. "I don't know much about anything, but I do like to learn."

Slade nods. "You don't have to talk to me about it. A lot of newbies can be intimidated, especially by dominant men. The girls are only too happy to talk openly about things as I'm sure you've noticed. We have a full dungeon master's team that work here, we have house submissives and dominants who do demonstrations, even our bar staff are at the very least kink-aware and sex positive if you feel more comfortable talking to one of them."

"I read a lot of romance novels." Talia's voice is slow as she speaks, like she's searching for the right words.

Kenzie pours another round of champagne, as two regulars filter in through the front door and head over to Nyx at the bar to order.

"So I know more than I *know*, you know?"

Slade smirks. "I know. But how much do you want to *know*? Are you simply curious to see some of those things from the pages come to life? Are there some things you'd like to try? Have you thought about exploring a dynamic with Jagger?"

If anyone else was throwing these questions at Talia I might say something. But there's no one in this world I'd trust to help a newcomer to the lifestyle more than Slade.

"You don't need to answer these questions to me now, nor ever. But they're something to think about."

My titanium-spined girlfriend doesn't fumble the pass, though. "I'd like to try some things. I mean, I have a list of things I'd like to try." She wiggles again, and I grip her hips before I make her grind against me until her butt is sticky with cum seeping through both our clothes.

"I started the list with Jagger last week."

The flutter of surprise that makes Slade's eyebrows twitch is almost imperceptible, but I've known him long enough to know he's pleasantly surprised she dipped her toe into kink, and that she's sharing about it.

"And how did you find it?"

She leans back against my chest like she's looking for support, so I curl my arms around her again. "Intense is probably the best word. I've never experienced anything like it in my life."

I'm so proud of her. This is a difficult, and probably embarrassing conversation to be having with a near stranger, and she's doing so well. I glide my thumbs up and down the outside of her thighs as she talks, as silent support and encouragement.

"Did you enjoy it?" Slade's questions aren't pressing, it's like he's having a conversation with an old friend.

Talia squirms again. "A lot. I've missed Jagger this past week. I wanted to do more with him."

Slade's hand twitches; from experience I know he wants to reach out and touch her cheek, to comfort her somehow. She may not be his submissive, or his responsibility, but despite the bravado, he's pretty empathetic.

I nuzzle into her hair. "I missed you too, baby girl."

She reaches around to cup my jaw, holding me to her. "I've missed you calling me that too, you know."

"I've missed you calling me things too." I don't want to out her preferences in front of people without her permission.

We're all quiet for a beat before Talia shivers in my lap. She looks around, I'm not sure if she's looking for an open door or to see if there's anyone close to us. "I called Jagger Daddy."

I'm not sure if she's saying it to both of them, or more to Kenzie because she's a woman, or if she's just saying it out loud because the burden of holding it is heavy, and she needs to share.

"Did you like it?" Slade's voice makes her head snap up. Was she expecting ridicule? Judgment? Shame? Those vibes don't belong between these walls.

She nods.

"Use your words, baby girl. You're safe here."

Her body softens in my arms. "I did like it."

"Did you?" He turns his attention to put me on the spot. "You don't have a Daddy kink."

"Didn't."

Talia threads her fingers into mine at my answer, squeezing my hand with her tiny one.

Slade's face breaks into a genuine smile. There's not a trace of wisecrack on his face. "I'm super happy for you both."

Talia melts into my arms, I can tell without seeing her face she's smiling back at Slade.

"Also here if you need any help or guidance. Or even if you simply need someone to talk to. Always." His voice is firm, assuring. I already know all of this, I know the man, and I know there's no one better suited to be a coach or mentor than Slade. "I'm totally curious what's on your bucket list, too."

Talia giggles. Kenzie smacks Slade. "Leave them alone, that's over the line."

"It's okay." Talia waves her off. "It's probably beginner stuff for y'all anyway."

Kenzie shakes her head. "And so what if it is? We all started somewhere, didn't we?"

From the way Kenzie leans into my woman, holding her hand as she assures her there's no shame in being a newbie, I find myself curious about her sexuality. From her bucket list, I know my little Half-Pint is curious about kissing another woman, and of all the women I know, Kenzie would be a perfect first-time, same-sex kiss.

Slade takes a slug of his drink right at the same time Talia finds her voice. "I'd like to be double penetrated."

Slade sprays his drink, coughing and spluttering having seemingly breathed the bubbly liquid in. Kenzie raises her hand to hi-five Talia, and when he's done recovering the ability to breathe, he raises his hand too. "I volunteer as tribute."

CHAPTER 24

Jagger

It's been two days since Talia announced she wanted to be double penetrated at the club in front of Slade. Have to admit, I wasn't expecting my little Half-Pint to come out of her shell as quickly as she did.

But at the same time, Protocol does that to people. Slade's built such a comfortable space that we lean into it across the board.

After the club, I followed her home, kissed her at the door, and gave her some space. Overcrowding someone, or kink-bombing them can be overwhelming, but in truth, she's all I can think about.

"Jagger?"

"Huh?" I jump, hitting my head on the underside of the hood of the 2020 Camry I'm working on, sending a sharp jolt of pain through my brain. "Fuck. Shit. Ow. What?" I snarl at one of the other mechanics who work at my shop.

"Visitor, Boss." Devin jerks a thumb over his shoulder pointing to the prettiest sight I've ever seen.

"Wow. You're a sight for sore eyes, Half-Pint."

Devin watches me curiously from under the hood of a

Mustang, but he doesn't matter right now. Nothing matters but Talia.

She's wrapped up in a beanie with a puffball on top, a scarf, an oversized coat, snow boots, and two wild eyes peek out at me from between the top of her scarf and the bottom of her hat. She's adorable. She's dressed like she's going to take on Everest.

I can't help chuckling. "You wanna explain why you're wearing your whole wardrobe?"

"Bessie's heat is broken."

I shake my head, clicking my tongue as I stride toward her. "If only you had a boyfriend who knew something about cars, hey?"

She laughs. "I don't want to abuse my position as your girlfriend and pull strings."

"For the love of God, Half-Pint, pull. Please? Let me fix her up for you. At least let me fix the trunk so you don't need rope." My voice is so whiny and filled with desperation I want to smack myself, but I really can't let her drive that piece of crap around, for her safety as much as anything else.

"How do you think that's going to impact my business? If people see you coming around here in that beat up old thing? Don't you think they're gonna believe I'm shit at my job?"

She's laughing now, Devin too, but she holds up her hands. "Fine, fine. Do what you want to her." She winks at me as she tugs off her hat.

"Can you give Devin the keys?" I hold up both hands, they're covered in oil. Knowing she's gonna give me what she calls a 'butt whoopin' I rub them on my pants.

"Jagger." Her low voice carries a warning I ignore by doing it again.

"Yes, Half-Pint? What can I do for you?"

"Stop gettin' oil all over your clothes for a start." The way she scolds me is hot.

"You'd have more chance of fixing your heat with a toothbrush than getting this man to listen." Devin slaps me on the back before offering a dirty hand to my girl.

"Devin."

"Talia." To her credit, she doesn't wrinkle her nose when she shakes his hand, nor does she wipe it on anything.

"And you're Jagger's new girlfriend?"

She nods, sinking her teeth into her lower lip.

"Nice to meet you."

"Nice to meet you, too, Devin. I've only heard nice things about you."

Devin snorts. "That's how I know you're lying."

I grunt, Devin takes a step back, and Talia takes a step forward. Fuck, I love that she's got such a strong confidence with me. It's gorgeous, watching her come out from under the weight of all those crushing expectations.

"Ready for lunch?" It wasn't planned, but considering I couldn't get her off my mind, I can't say no.

"I'll close up." Devin waves Talia's keys at me. "And I'll start cataloging what's wrong with... Bessie was it?"

Talia beams, and Devin smiles back at her. "That's her, my Bessie." She puffs out her already well puffed out chest. "Talk nicely to her, and she'll treat you well." She throws a glare my way. "Come on, Grumpasaurus. I'm hungry."

I am too, but not for food. I don't say that out loud, though. Devin doesn't need to know I wanna do dirty things to my woman.

A few minutes later, we're in the front seat of my car with the heat switched on and blasting my icicle girlfriend. "Where to?"

"Can we pick something up and go back to your house?" She won't meet my eyes. She's looking out the window, her ears a familiar color of pink that tells me she's self-conscious about asking.

"Of course, baby girl." I push her hair behind her ear. "What's up?"

She digs into her purse and pulls out a Manilla envelope. "I brought documents."

"I see this. To what end?"

"Negotiations." She waggles her eyebrows.

"Sex negotiations?"

"Yes, sir. Sex negotiations."

Would you look at that? My Half-Pint's growing up. She said sex, out loud, without stuttering or her face going the shade of a tomato. The newly familiar tingle of pride sweeps through my body.

"Sounds good to me. But food first. We don't negotiate on an empty belly."

She laughs. Will I ever get sick of that tinkling sound? It's hard to believe that not even two weeks ago her whole aura was like nails on a chalkboard on that damn plane, and now I want her around me all the time.

She's sunshine, and I'm chasing a hit of heat.

"No hangry sex negotiations. Got it. That's a good rule for life." She points her finger at me. "Thai?"

"You read my mind."

It takes about thirty minutes to pick up food and make our way back to my place. She's never been here before, but from the way her jaw drops, I'd guess she's surprised.

Her head snaps to me, and back to the front of the house. Then back to me.

"You live in the suburbs? Like a grownup?" She points to the house as she walks up the driveway. "A rich grownup." She mumbles, tilting her head at me. Her wicked side-eye game is one of my favorite things about her.

"You made assumptions about me based on my career."

She nods, pressing her bottom lip against her teeth with her index finger as I unlock the door. "You're right. I did. Your oil covered, grumpy butt self, came across like you didn't have your life together. I admit, I completely misread you."

She steps into the house, spreads her arm and twirls in a circle. "Jeez. How many bedrooms does this place have?"

I close the door behind me, carrying the food past Talia and into the dining room. "We'll talk about that later."

"I bet you have four bedrooms, don't you? Four rooms for just you. How do you clean it all? Is there a thick layer of dust over everything?" She feigns a dramatic gasp, clutching her chest. "Is this where you buried the bodies?"

"Plates, to the right of the stove. Silverware in the drawer next to the sink. Glasses in the cabinet next to the sink. And I have a selection of drinks in the fridge, if it's okay with you, I'll have a beer."

"So bossy." She plants her hands on her hips, and for a moment I wonder if she's going to sass me, but she grabs everything I ask as I take the food out of the bags.

"Holy granola, did you order one of everything on the menu?"

"Maybe. What can I say?" I shrug. "I like eating with you."

She sets the table, grabs drinks, then pulls out a chair and slides onto it. "So, how does this work? Do we eat and talk? Do we chit chat then get down to business? I've never negotiated a relationship before. In hindsight, probably should have." She laughs at herself.

"That depends."

"On what?" She's heaping rice onto her plate.

"On what it is you feel the need to negotiate."

"Oh." Her shoulders roll forward.

"I'm happy to take it day by day, scene by scene and figure our dynamic out between us as we go. But if you feel like you need more structure and boundaries, then we'll need to look at it for sure."

She straightens her back. "I need a more structured plan."

Fucking hell. Her assertiveness speaks straight to my dick, and while she's pouring food out, my dick's trying to pierce a hole in my pants. Visions of sweeping the food on the floor and fucking her senseless on the table flicker across my mind. It'd be way too far, too fast, but it'll happen at some point, and I can't wait to fuck her when the mood strikes.

I nod, trying to hiss a slow breath out between my teeth. "Okay, and have you given much thought to what that might look like?"

She swallows her bite. "I have." She nods. "And I think... Well, I think I want sex."

CHAPTER 25
Talia

Jagger drops his fork with a clang on his plate, and his mouth hangs open like a gaping fish. "You want sex?" The words are slow like he's rolling them around in his mouth and they taste funny.

Nodding, I don't back down. "I do. I feel like waiting for this big thing to happen is making me anxious. I want to get it over with so it's no big deal. I've done it before. I mean, it's been a while, but I have. It's hanging over me, and I'm getting more and more nervous about it."

He's quiet for a long moment before he returns my nod. "Okay. We can do that. What else you got?"

Huh. I was not expecting that.

I pull out the piece of paper I put together from the internet. It's got a section for definitions, safewords, boundaries, punishments and rewards, and responsibilities.

If I'm honest with myself, it's terrifying.

"Half-Pint?"

My head jerks up toward the sound of his voice. "Yeah?"

"We don't need that." He gestures at the papers in my hand. "Not right now, anyway. We can start super slow. If we decide we want to formalize our relationship we can fill in all of those pages. But for now, let's say we're going to date each other, try new things together. We have a safeword. We'll work on limits together because you don't really know what you like and don't like yet, so you probably have no idea where your limits are yourself. We'll figure it out as we go. Together."

What he says makes sense, but it sounds like he's making a lot of allowances for the fact I'm so vanilla. "But won't you get, I don't know, bored? Impatient? What about you? And your needs? Surely that's in here." I rustle the pages.

He puts his fork down on the table. "Talia, I don't have a preconceived list of things I need or want from a relationship. It's about give and take, exploring together. This." He points between us. "Is very new for me, too. So it makes sense to me that we just figure it out as we go. I don't need a contract. I don't need a list of things I absolutely need to do with you or to you. I want to please you. If you don't like something I like, then I won't like it, because you don't. And we won't know what those things are until we try them."

What he says makes a lot of sense, and soothes the unease swirling in my stomach.

"Would I prefer to know you're eating right, sleeping right, and drinking enough water? Absolutely. Kink scenes are draining mentally and physically and if you don't start off in the right space, it could be dangerous, or lead to injury. But it's not from a place of bossing around, it's because I care about you and your wellbeing."

"Same reason I really wanted you to let me fix up Bessie. I don't want to expel energy worrying about the fact your car isn't going to get you to where you need to be, when a simple tune up in my garage would put my mind at ease. It's not about controlling you, it's about making sure you're safe, healthy, and happy. Those are my primary concerns in a relationship with you."

He cups my chin, stroking my face with his thumb. "If you're not happy, I'm not happy. If you're not healthy, I'm not healthy. And if you're not safe, I'm not safe. It's just that simple."

I'm pretty sure that dreamy sigh I heard came from inside my body. This man isn't at all what I expected him to be. When he leans in to kiss me, his breath tickles my face. "Jagger." There's an ache in my chest I can't identify or define. Like I need to be closer to him, I need him to feel these emotions welling up inside me.

I can't articulate these feelings, it's a surge of warmth consuming my whole body. "That's beautiful." I don't know why my voice is trembling, or why my eyes are brimming with tears.

His face softens as he smiles. "I think a lot of people assume kink is dark and dangerous and brutal and full of pain. But kink is whatever you want it to be, baby girl. And as your Daddy it's my job to take care of you and protect you, even from yourself. You won't always like what I ask you to do, but it will always come from a space of wanting what's best for you."

"This feels even scarier than feeling pain and being controlled and told what to do."

He nods. "I've found the depths of emotion, for me, not necessarily for everyone else, are more amplified in a kink space. The level of trust, the layers of interaction between people, the vulnerability. It's all... more."

He slides his hand down the front of my throat. "Anyone can have sex. Dick in pussy. It's a tale as old as time." He adds pressure to the side of my neck. "But how many people can you name that you trust with your very breath?"

He doesn't linger. We haven't talked about choking, but he's made his point and let's go of my throat. Or at least I thought he had made his point. He pushes up from his chair and moves to stand behind me. He covers my eyes, but when he speaks, his voice is so close to my ear goosebumps spread across my skin.

"And how many people can you trust to be your eyes when yours are covered?"

I hadn't thought about that when he had me blindfolded on the bed, but it makes a lot of sense. Giving that level of trust to another person, especially when you combine it, for example with restraints, is a heavy weight to carry. And far more complex than simply sleeping with someone.

My breathing quickens as he stands there, covering my eyes. Not because I'm anxious or afraid, but the memories of being restrained, of the spreader bar, and of him touching me flood my body in waves of ferocious heat.

"Sex itself is vulnerable, but adding in elements that require unwavering faith in the other person makes it more so. At least in my opinion." He blows air across my neck. "When you meet someone new, you should work up to trusting them." His lips sweep across the sensitive skin under my ear. "You handed it to me on a platter, tied up with a pretty bow as soon as we met." Another kiss. A pained groan like he's fighting the urge to ravage me right there on the table. The building ache between my thighs wouldn't be angry about it if he did.

"It made me mad, Half-Pint. I'm not going to lie." His teeth sink into the skin, making me whimper, sending a shiver skating all over my body, his touch heightened by my temporary loss of sight.

He never mentioned being mad at the club, though. He didn't seem at all angry.

"The idea you'd hand over something as precious as your trust to some grumpy fucker you met on a random plane was incomprehensible to me." Another nip, another whine slips out from between my lips.

"Your trust is a valuable asset, baby girl. We don't give it out to just anyone." When he punctuates his sentence by licking the side of my neck, I'm clenching my thighs together so hard the muscles hurt.

He trails his finger from where my jaw hinges under my ear, to my chin, down the front of my throat, and down my sternum. Each gliding movement makes me hotter, wetter, the desperate need swelling inside my body becomes more demanding.

"Do you understand why?"

"Wh-why, what?"

His low chuckle is almost too quiet to hear. "Why we don't give our trust out to just anyone?"

I don't care about trust. I don't care about words. My clothes are on fire, making my body too hot for me to exist in. I need out. I need him to touch me, to take care of me, to take away this scorching fire burning my skin.

"Talia?"

I'm rolling my hips on the chair. "Please, Jagger. Touch me."

"Not yet, Half-Pint. This is an important lesson you need to learn in case we ever expand our relationship and have someone else play with us."

That sentence makes my breath stutter, words catching at the back of my throat. At least two of my bucket list items involve other people, and he knows it.

"Don't give your trust away. Make them earn it."

"M-make them earn it. Yes, sir." At some point, I closed my eyes, but when he jerks my hair so my head tilts all the way back, they snap open.

His brown eyes pierce into mine. "Good girl. It's important to me. Okay? We only play with people Daddy trusts to take care of his baby girl."

What is it about a man being so viscerally protective of his partner that drives me wild? My nipples are painfully hard, pressing against the inside of my bra. "Yes, Daddy." The heaviness in my body is already starting to leave, and my eagerness for levity, the floating feeling of not having a care in the world comes over me.

"We aren't having sex today, Talia."

I might cry. Every single piece of my body is primed and ready for more. "B-b-but why?"

"It's not a small decision. We wait between deciding to do something and doing the something so we're sure of our decisions, okay?"

I nod, not breaking eye contact. "My body feels like it's on fire, Jagger."

"I know, baby girl. And you're wet for me, aren't you?"

I nod again.

"Such a good girl." He caresses my cheek with the back of his fingers. "All wet and desperate for me, just how Daddy needs you."

The more he praises me, the deeper his words sink into my whole being. "I'd like to have sex for the first time at your place if that's okay?" He slides his hand under my shirt, trailing his fingers over the edge of the cup of my bra. Taunting, teasing, dragging out my agony.

"Why not here?"

"I'd like you surrounded by familiarity. I don't want you to have to get up and drive home, even the next day."

He thinks of everything.

"It's my job to think of everything, Half-Pint."

I didn't speak out loud, but his words echo my thoughts. I feel so safe with this man, so adored, and taken care of. It's like everything that's been missing in my life was delivered to me on the plane to Chicago in a blizzard.

When he pinches my nipple, I jump in my chair, yelping. He then rolls it between his finger and thumb, drawing a rhythmic hum from me as he cups the back of my head. He's tall enough he could slide himself in my mouth from this angle. My head's still tilted back, almost upside down, and from the outline in his pants, he's definitely hard.

"Daddy?"

He draws his stare away from watching his fingers working my nipple under my shirt, to my face. "Yes, baby girl?"

"Can I suck you, please?"

A longer, harder squeeze of my breast takes the breath from my lungs. "Say the words, Talia."

The pulsing pain in my nipple is stronger than the discomfort over the word he wants me to say. "Please, Daddy. Let me suck your cock. Please?"

The need to serve him is urgent, incessant, and all I can think about.

"Such a good girl when you're using that dirty mouth."

My core flexes. I always wondered if I'd be the kind of woman who could use those words, and have them used toward me, and now, I know. I definitely am. He bends down, kissing me upside down, before he frees his cock and places it on my face. "You've earned it, baby girl. Daddy is so proud of you and how far you've come."

He slides his cock into my mouth, the different angle makes it instantly harder to breathe, and I gag against the cold metal on his tip. "Easy, Half-Pint. Take it slowly."

Relaxing into this angle is more complicated than I expected, but it doesn't take Jagger long to get close. He's brushing his hand along my exposed throat as he guides his cock back and forth into my wide-open mouth.

He leans over, jerks up my shirt, and frees my breasts from their cups. As he thrusts, he kneads my breasts, brushes his thumbs over my nipples, squeezes, twists, pinches, even scrapes his fingers across the sensitive skin.

The more he plays with my chest, the closer he seems to

drive himself to the edge. "So close, baby girl. You're taking Daddy's cock so nicely. You look so pretty with your tits out for me."

His words almost derail me from getting him to come for me, and when I attempt to suck in a deep breath, his cock is in the way so I cough. "Easy. You're doing so well, I'm almost there." His words are clipped, forced, like he's straining to concentrate on saying them.

Tears stream up my face as he removes his cock, pumps it a few times and spurts jets of thick, warm cum all over my face. "I love seeing you marked for me." He tucks himself away. "Don't move."

I'm not sure I can. My neck has seized into this position. I've gone past the point of aching from holding the angle, to not feeling anything at all. He leans over me, appearing in my line of sight with napkins.

"Wait!" I collect some of his cum from my cheek and sweep it into my mouth. It's just enough to taste his creamy release.

Tipping his head back, he sighs. "Fuck, baby girl that's so hot."

I let his cum sit in my mouth before I swallow, letting it slide slowly off the back of my tongue. It's not my favorite, but I don't hate it. It's not something I want to do all the time, but I wouldn't mind swallowing for him sometimes. We'll see.

He cleans me up, reheats my food in the microwave and pours me more water, even though my glass is practically full. "Come on, Half-Pint, eat up."

We eat in a contented silence for a while. Every now and then he reaches out to brush my hand, or touch my fingers with his. It's the little things, how tactile he is, how gentle, that make my heart sing as we share a meal.

"Would you rather live twice as long or win the lottery?"

He doesn't roll his eyes at my question. Instead, he purses

his lips, tilting his head like he's thinking about the answer. "Lottery. If I'm the only one outliving all my friends and family, I don't want to. I'd rather get a shit ton of money, blow it all on the people I love, and all die at the end of our lives like we're supposed to."

I can't remember if he's ever mentioned his family before, but he's cracked the door, and I'm itching to push it open.

"What is it?" His brows twitch, a line appearing between them.

"Can I ask about your family?"

He rolls his eyes at that. "Of course you can. How can we expect to get to know each other if we can't ask questions?"

"You like life a lot quieter than me. I don't want to be annoying."

He almost snorts at that. "I like it when you're annoying." He takes a bite, then swallows. "But only you. Anyone else gets in my space like this." He points his fork in the space between us. "And I'd probably lose my mind."

"Thanks, I think." At least he's being honest, right? "I feel like Elizabeth Bennet right now."

Jagger nods, a smile making his lips twitch at the corners. "I am definitely a Darcyesque grumpy bastard." He shrugs. "He's got way better hair, though."

I giggle as he drags his palm over his almost bare head.

"I'm an only child. I'm sure you'll be shocked to learn. My parents are happily married here in Minnesota. They know about my deviant proclivities." He uses air quotes around those last two words. "And they're cool with it. No drama. No arranged marriages. No trauma." He shrugs like that's all I'm going to get from him. "What about you, Half-Pint?

Guess that *is* all I'm going to get from him. I gulp down some water, my throat tender from being overworked. "I have an older brother, Isaac, he's a pastor."

To his credit, Jagger barely reacts, but from the way his eyes narrow a tiny bit, he's not surprised.

"That tracks."

"And I have it all." I wave my hand. "Drama, arranged marriage, trauma. Even sex rehab after I slept with Harry."

He flinches like I smacked him.

"Sorry."

His hand skims my cheek, brushing my hair back. "No, Half-Pint. We don't apologize for our past. It's what makes us who we are today."

Ugh. How is he so handsome and philosophical at the same time? Some people get all the good stuff.

When we're done with lunch, he hand washes the dishes, dry them, and put them away. Learning his kitchen is fun, learning about my guy is even better.

Turns out his father is a mechanic, and he's wanted to be a mechanic for as long as he can remember. He spent his childhood taking engines apart and fixing up old cars with his dad.

When I've finished putting away the clean dishes, and Jagger has wiped down the counters, he smacks my booty with the kitchen cloth. "Wanna watch a movie?"

I guess I thought once we'd eaten, he'd kick me out. "Don't you have to go back to the shop?"

He winks at me. "Joys of being my own boss. I set my own hours. That, and I have a great team around me. The guys are a well-oiled machine. Excuse the pun."

Guiding me to the couch, he stays a step behind me. When we're settled under a blanket, me the little spoon as always, I let myself sink into his arms.

"Have you thought any more about what you'd like to do with your life now that you're not tied to Harry the Asshole?"

"I think I want to write steamy books. A series about vanilla women who meet sexually more experienced men and fall in love while learning about themselves and what they like."

"Don't they say you should write what you know? That feels a bit off the wall."

His humor is so dry, I'm never really sure if he's being funny or not. "I mean, I could write about a tiny female dominant who manhandles her giant, grumpasaurus boyfriend."

"That'd be more true-to-life."

"Uh huh. Whatever you say."

The vibrations of him laughing as he turns the TV on is a comfort I'm getting used to feeling. There's something about having his arms around me, his body curled protectively, feeling his body rise and fall as he breathes, that makes me feel safe.

"We're watching "The Secretary," it's part of your kink education."

I'm sure he had great plans for us to watch the movie, but I wake up to the credits rolling up on the screen, and Jagger stroking my face. "You missed the movie, baby girl. And you snored so loud the neighbors came to complain."

"I did not." I bound up from the couch, indignation fueling my stiff and slow movements. I give him a playful shove. "But it was a nice nap. Thank you."

It's on the tip of my tongue to ask if I can stay over. We didn't actually discuss a date, but I know if I don't go home tonight, he won't have sex with me tomorrow. He'll say I'm too close and didn't take my time and space to think about it.

So, after the longest make-out session of my life, where we kiss and kiss and kiss some more, I head back home, a swarm of bees buzzing in my gut, to reflect on whether I want to sleep with my super-dom boyfriend tomorrow, or not.

CHAPTER 26
Talia

I do. I most definitely do want to sleep with my boyfriend today. I've been up since four in the morning. I've cleaned my house twice, right down to the baseboards. Who cleans their baseboards? Certainly not me, but today I've cleaned them, and emptied and cleaned the refrigerator twice.

It's like Mama's coming, but worse. The windows are sparkling, the couch is vacuumed, and I even vacuumed the spider-webs from the light fixtures and crown molding. I've taken two showers. One before the anxious cleaning, and one after, because while Jagger is totally fine with me being a sweaty hot mess, I'd rather he be the cause of it.

What does one wear to essentially lose her virginity all over again? When I slept with Harry, we were teenagers. I know your hymen doesn't regrow, but I'm not in any way experienced.

I want to do it, need to even. But I'm freaking all the way out, not just a little. He's going to be everything I need him to be, I have no doubt, but what do I wear? How do I wait around knowing I'm about to have a man's penis inside my body?

A literal scream rips from my body when someone knocks the door.

"It's only me, Half-Pint." There's humor in his voice.

When he steps inside, I'm wringing my hands in front of my body, wishing I'd gotten drunk before he came over. How I've managed not to climb the walls is anyone's guess. Well, actually, that's not true, the faint lingering scent of citrus in the air reminds me I spent hours today cleaning, and re-cleaning my whole space.

"Breathe." His voice is firm as he takes me in. He keeps his distance, probably so he doesn't crowd me. That, or he's afraid I'm going to lose my mind, or breakdown into tears. In truth, it could go either way.

I force out a breath.

"Good." He guides me to the couch. "You clean today?" His nose wrinkles.

"That obvious?"

He nods. "We don't have to do anything you'd rather not do. You know that, right?"

"I do. Know that, and want to, I mean."

He pulls me onto his lap, inhaling the scent from my hair and skin. "We didn't talk about birth control."

"I've been on birth control since I slept with Harry. Mama and Dad weren't going to take the chance I'd end up barefoot and pregnant if their lectures and sermons didn't do the trick."

He nods. "I prefer not using condoms. But it's not my decision to make. I have my recent STD-STI screening. I generally get it done quarterly, and again after I sleep with someone for the first time, just to be sure. It's been a while."

He pulls out his phone and forwards me his results. "But if you'd rather I use protection, I absolutely will. I brought some in case."

"Even though you don't like it?"

He nods. "But I'm not pressuring you either way. You want it, it'll happen."

I go quiet, listening to the repetitive rhythm of his heart thump-thumping in his chest. It takes a long moment but I trust him enough that if I change my mind in the moment, he'll do whatever I ask of him.

"I'm not ready." My shaky voice is barely a whisper. As much as I want to change, be different, stand tall as New Talia, it's still such a hard adjustment from the mindset that I should only have sex with someone I love. I guess that's what my younger self stitched into the fabric of my parents' teachings.

No sex before marriage, to me, has meant no sex with anyone you're not in love with.

"That's totally okay." He strokes my face. "I have a feeling you're more than worth the wait."

CHAPTER 27
Talia

I DON'T KNOW WHAT I'M MORE ANXIOUS ABOUT, having a double date with his friends, meeting his parents, or his parents and my parents having dinner together.

All of these things are on the calendar over the next couple weeks. It's tempting to get everything lined up one after the other and rip off the Band-Aid, but that would send my guy rocking in the corner.

As soon as his mom heard about me, she wanted to meet me. In fact, Jagger said she offered to drive over right then and there, but he had to assure her we weren't physically together when he called. We've spread out the social commitments so Jagger can build himself up to facing them one by one.

Despite being anxious about the new people, I live for hanging out with people and getting to know them. This is one hundred percent my jam. I even managed to find the Stitch 'n Bitch group of old ladies from the hotel, and they're going to teach me to knit at their weekly get together.

As much as I already love Kenzie, her other half, Austin, is intimidating. He's just so... serious.

In the past week Jagger fixed Bessie, though he offered no

fewer than twelve times to send her to the scrap heap and replace her for me, and I started writing my first ever novel.

I've also hung out with Kenzie and the girls once as well. They're so nice. I've never really been in a space where women champion women. They have this close-knit, readymade girl gang that's daunting as well. I never presumed to cram my way into their space, but I didn't have to.

I'm sure they have their own friendships outside of the group, but they launched me into the Sub-Club group chat like I've always been a part of their world. It's nice, and reassuring. I have a lot of questions bubbling inside about the lifestyle I'm dipping my toes into, and they provide a no-judgment space for me to do that.

We're going for dinner with Kenzie and Austin, to some fancy steak place in town. Jagger's on his way to pick me up, and I've managed to stab myself in the eye with the eye liner stick. You'd think having done something since I was a teenager would make me proficient at it, however, you'd be wrong.

When the doorbell rings, I look like I've had a fight with someone, but only on half my face. My eye is red and watering, and when Jagger sees me holding a Kleenex against my face, concern flickers in his eyes.

"You okay?"

"I had an incident with my eye liner. Gimme a sec?"

He nods, a small smile playing on his lips as he watches me disappear to fix my makeup. I don't have time to procrastinate, he's here, and he hates being late. If I don't get my shit together he'd probably come pick me up and haul me away half-dressed.

Okay, he wouldn't do that, would he?

"Five minutes." His announcement rings around the house, and the passing thought turns into a legit fear.

My hair looks like I stuck my finger in a socket, but I'm

ready to go with thirty seconds to spare. When he sees me appear in the doorway, he holds up his hand to stop me, then spins his index finger in a circle like he wants me to turn around.

The low whistle he makes as I rotate, makes me beam. My bedroom floor might be covered with every dress I've ever owned, but I made the right selection in the forty five seconds I had left to choose.

"Ready?" He holds his hand out to me.

"Austin is scary." The words are out of my mouth before my hand glides into Jagger's palm.

"I don't think he's scary, but I can see why you do. He's seemingly cold and unapproachable, and my warm ball of emotions doesn't know how to handle that kind of person."

He's not wrong. And while usually I'd take it as a personal challenge to break his walls down, what if he just doesn't like me?

"Don't let your mind convince you he doesn't like you, Half-Pint." Jagger's stern voice draws my attention to his face from the floor. "I can see your brain working. He likes you just fine, but he hasn't known you long. I know you like and imprint onto people when you first meet them, but for some people it takes longer, like weeks, months, heck even years."

He cups my face before sweeping his lips against mine. "Austin likes you. Give him more than a week to get to know you, and you'll find he's not scary at all. Some people take longer than a finger-snap to make friends. We don't all have your super powers you know." He smiles like it's the most obvious thing in the world. I've never thought about the fact I can talk to people easily as being a strength, but I guess when he puts it like that, it makes sense.

I have flurries of nerves in my stomach as I approach the table in the restaurant. Austin stands up, stiff and formal, but smiling. And Kenzie, seemingly not at all concerned with the gentle ambiance of the restaurant, bounds up off her seat and launches herself at me with a squeal as we approach.

It's a quiet place, mood lighting, white linens, and exceptionally well-dressed, discreet servers who seem to know exactly when to step into our space. The food is to die for. Kenzie and I draw stares from around the room as we make yummy noises during our meal, and the guys take a back seat to our inane prattling.

By the time dessert rolls around, even Austin's asking me questions about myself. It's not bestie territory yet by any means, but my gut says I'll win him over eventually, I need to see where I can go buy some patience.

"Do you have to leave? Can we go somewhere to hang out?" Kenzie loops her arm through mine.

I glance at Jagger to see if I can get a read for his all-peopled-out meter, but he seems okay. I'm not sure I'd know to look at him yet if he wasn't though, so I nibble my lip and stare at him. "Jagger?"

"I'm good with whatever you'd like to do, Half-Pint." His answer seems genuine. He doesn't strike me as the kind of person to do something to please a crowd, especially when it comes to having his precious peace disrupted for any length of time.

Kenzie leans close to my ear. "Do you want to go to the club? Thor and Adi are there. We could go to the bar for a drink, or..." She squeezes my arm. "We could go downstairs and see what's going on in the dungeon."

Jagger must see something on my face in reaction to that suggestion because he nods. "We can head to the club."

It takes less than twenty minutes for us to get to Protocol. We stop to get our wrist-bands from the attendant at the door.

"Should I get a green one, Jagger?" Green means I'm available to do whatever I'd like with whoever I'd like. I give him wide, clueless doe eyes as I look up at him while Kenzie giggles to my left. While the place isn't too crowded, there's a healthy stream of people coming.

Jagger simply grunts at me like the question is too dumb to warrant a response, but I want one. I need one. There's a steady thrum of electricity in the air, the pulse matches the throbbing between my thighs. I haven't had time to get myself worked up and anxious about watching people downstairs, or what people might think of me.

Addison strides toward us, she's wearing a sparkly silver shirt. I mean, I think it's a shirt, it's a collection of strings of chain dangling one under another to form a shirt. It's gorgeous, but I don't know how she got into it, how she's getting out of it, or how it hides everything it needs to.

It's a halter-style top, there's a chain that leads up around the back of her neck and down the other side to connect the shirt. If that was my top I'd end up tangled in it. They'd need to cut even my short hair off to be able to get my shirt off, or I'd have to figure out a way to live in it forever.

Addison pulls it off, though. It's stunning. The bright silver shine contrasting against her long, auburn hair is breathtaking. She's pulling me into a hug before I can say anything. "You might want to close your mouth." She giggles. "But thank you."

"It's... I can't figure out how the dang thing works, but you look amazing Addison."

Her pale, freckled cheeks deepen with a blush. "It's not what I'd usually wear, but I couldn't resist it when I saw it." She shimmies her shoulders, making the couple dozen chains tinkle against each other. Pretty sure I saw a nipple, but considering what I'm about to see downstairs, I'm trying to act normal.

What 'normal' is when you're looking at your new friend's breast is anyone's guess, but I at least try not to make eye contact with it.

"You're adorable." Addison pulls me into a one armed hug, and I guess I wasn't as subtle as I'd intended to be. "It gets easier. It's so weird at first, seeing people's body bits on display, but it's all good. You get used to it. Soon you won't even blink when you see meat whistles on display downstairs."

I can't imagine that at all. Even when she says the words 'meat whistle' my body shrivels. The idea I'm going to see multiple peens downstairs is overwhelming, but also exciting.

This myriad of emotions swirling inside my chest is becoming familiar, but I'm looking forward to being able to step downstairs without the noose of anxiety gripping me in its hold.

"You can leave at any time." Jagger wraps the red wrist band around my arm. "Just say the word, okay? If it's too much we'll leave and come back when it's quieter. I don't want to push you too hard, too fast."

It's cute he thinks he's pushing me. I'm pushing myself. My curiosity at what goes on downstairs burns like the sunlight in my bones.

Mackenzie leans over my shoulder from behind. "If you want to watch someone you know, Austin is always game to demonstrate. He's not one of the house doms, but he'll never pass up an opportunity to play with me in the dungeon." She gives me a squish. "Might be easier than watching strangers, might not. You may find yourself weirded out even more at the sight of my girl parts."

"Thor's working, but if you want to watch your friends, I can convince him to take an early break." Addison winks at me.

I'd kill for even a fraction of their confidence.

They sandwich me together in a girl hug and their warmth heats my fraying nerves. "We've got you." One of them mumbles into my hair.

"And if you never get comfortable enough to play downstairs, that's okay too. You know that, right?" Kenzie is the sweetest person I've ever met. "You don't have to do anything you don't want to."

Rationally, I know that. I'm more afraid of my lifetime of conditioning to think those acts are deviant showing on my face. Hopefully it's dark, so if I do get resting-judgy-face, no one will see it. I'll ease myself in slowly, we'll pick a quiet part of the club and start with, I dunno, like, the mild petting section or something.

We head downstairs, in the main area, a woman Jagger calls Phoenix is doing a demonstration of what seems to be butt stuff. She's got a table full of things that seem to be, uh, insert-able, and there's a naked man bent over a bench in front of her. There's a, oh my, it's a hook, a giant metal hook attached to a rope that's mounted on the ceiling.

Doesn't that hurt?

Wow. There's no easing in to the dungeon, they meet you right as you come in with a bare butt and a giant hook.

Baptism by fire, or what?

Someone's hand slips into mine as I'm tugged away from the group of people watching the bare butt on the end of the giant fishing line. "Let's start a little less intensely than Phoenix's demonstration, sweets."

"Kenzie, you are so sweet."

She winks at me. "Just a bitch at heart, boo."

I don't believe her for a second, and from the way she's grinning at me, she doesn't either. Her heart is pure gold, I've known her for a few short weeks, and even I know that. She's precious.

"She is. Wait till you try to steal her French fries. She'd cut a bitch." Addison bumps me with her hip.

"She's not wrong." Kenzie wags a finger at me. "Don't ever take my fries."

Holding my hands up, I shake my head. "I'd never come between a woman and her fries."

They each link an arm in mine and guide me away from the commotion. I assume the boys are picking up the rear. We get to a corridor, the one Jagger and I were in when we got snowed in.

My friends turn to face me. Addison claps her hands. "What's it going to be? You wanna watch your friends fucking, or you wanna go with strangers?" She's nothing if not direct.

Jagger's hand finds its way to my lower back, the familiar warmth radiating through my dress. I turn to face him, and he takes my breath away. He's so handsome.

"What do you think, Jagger?" I'm practically bouncing on the balls of my feet with nervous energy coursing through my body.

He grazes my cheek with his fingertips. "This isn't something I can answer for you, baby girl. It's a decision you need to make for yourself."

I glance behind him to Austin, stoic and silent, his eyes fixed firmly on Mackenzie.

Thor appears by his side. "He's right, Talia. No one can make the decision for you. Some people find comfort in knowing the person they're watching is someone they know. Others don't ever want to see their friend's naked body. It's person specific."

It takes a long moment of surveying my friends before I make my decision. "Addison, could you—?"

She grabs Thor by the collar and drags him toward one of the doors like someone pulled the trigger of the starting pistol.

"Easy, Kitten." Thor tugs her to a stop. "Talia didn't even finish her sentence. She might want you to pick a good room for her to start in, not get your tits out for her."

Addison rolls her eyes but relents. "Okay, fine. Talia, am I getting my tits out?"

I'm giggling so hard I can't really answer, but I nod and Addison resumes dragging her poor boyfriend into the room.

Austin steps forward. "If you would like to be the only person watching, that could be arranged as well."

Kenzie nods. "We can make it private so it's only you and Jagger."

It's a sweet offer, but I'd at least want Kenzie and Austin in with me. If I get turned on watching my friend doing things with her boyfriend, I'd like to know I'm not the only one. And something about how expressive Kenzie is tells me she'll be easy to read in that situation.

Plus, I've got to start somewhere, right?

"That's okay." I shake my head. "If I do that, I'll never get comfortable with being around people and feeling... things."

Kenzie nods, giving me a warm smile. "Atta girl. You've got this. They're so hot together you won't be able to help yourself."

By the time we filter into the room, Addison is on her knees in front of Thor. Her hands are palm up on her thighs, but instead of head dipped low, Thor has her red curls clutched in his hand, head tipped back, and he's leaning over her. She's grinning up at him like she just said something she shouldn't, and if I'm not mistaken, she's giving him an eye roll.

Even I know that's not a smart thing to do to your dominant. It takes Thor no time at all to pull his dick free of his pants and press it in her mouth, hands gripping the back of her head so she can't move an inch. She clasps his thighs as he thrusts in and out of her mouth.

I'm not sure how long it takes me to realize Kenzie is on her knees next to me, mirroring what's happening behind the glass. Austin's peen glints in the dim light. He's pierced as well, but he has a line of piercings along his dick as opposed to the cross at the top like Jagger.

Huh. How do those metal ridges feel against your insides? I bet they feel pretty good.

Kenzie doesn't hesitate before she's sucking off a thrusting Austin. He mutters praise at her in a low and steady voice as sounds of her efforts echo around the space.

"How are you?" Jagger's hands curl around my middle from behind. "You doing okay?"

It's an interesting question. My body feels alive, like all my cells have been switched on at once, eagerness, curiosity creeping through my bloodstream.

Tuning into my body for a beat, I realize I'm more turned on than I expected to be. My nipples are throbbing, my breath coming faster and faster, my skin hot. I press his hand downward, shuffling my feet apart enough that hopefully he'll get my meaning without me having to tell him what I want him to do.

"Such a dirty girl." He hums against my neck as his fingers walk painfully slowly down my dress, hesitating at the hem. "Is this what you want, baby girl?"

Nodding, I can't help the moan that slips from my lips. "Please, Daddy. Please."

Kenzie hums on her knees to our right. In front of us, tears stream down Addison's face as Thor's hips piston back and forth.

When Jagger's fingers finally sink between my lips, my body sags against his chest. I'm soaked, so wet, in fact, it's not quiet when he glides his fingers back and forth. My head snaps to Austin, who's watching me curiously, probably waiting to see how I react to the fact my arousal is noticeable.

His intensity, his dominance is strong, radiating from him as he stands tall. He nods at me, like he's quietly encouraging me. Is the silent reassurance something they learn at dominant school?

"Do not fight it, Talia." His voice is low and steady as he addresses me.

Jagger's fingers move more quickly, skimming across my clit. "He's right, baby girl. Don't fight it, it's okay to be turned on right now. Look how hot your friends look on their knees. Look how Addison is enjoying sucking Thor's cock."

Oh, boy. His words speak straight to my core, resonating at a fever pitch that has me riding against his fingers chasing the orgasm that's brewing deep inside my body. My muscles tighten as I charge closer and closer to release.

Thor pulls out of Addison's mouth and jets of thick, creamy cum spray all over her face.

"She's doing so well, isn't she, baby girl? So pretty all covered in Thor's cum."

Something in his words entwine themselves around my clit, and I burst into butterflies and bright light before I know what's hit me. My legs buckle, but Jagger catches me, supporting my weight as I writhe through my orgasm in his arms.

I have no idea how long it takes for me to recover enough to see something other than stars and colors but Jagger's holding on to me as my trembling body comes back to the present.

In the room ahead, Thor's cleaning up Addison's face, and next to me, Austin's cradling Kenzie's head as he kisses her deeply.

"You doing okay, baby girl?"

Breathless, I can't form words, so I have to nod. As though he senses it was a powerful orgasm, he slides to the floor, pulling me onto his lap and curling me into his chest. "Easy, Half-Pint, just take some deep breaths for me, okay? You did so well, letting go like such a good girl." He strokes my face as he holds me.

It takes me a while to settle, when I finally return to my body, Thor has Addison bent over, and he's drilling her pretty hard. At some point between my orgasm and recovery, her shirt has been removed—which suggests to me it's been some time considering how complex that top was—and her breasts bounce with every thrust.

Kenzie crawls across the floor to sit next to me. "You okay? It wasn't too much?" Her concern is so touching. She's done her own sexual act, and she's worried about me.

"It was a big one." I barely get the sentence out before a yawn hits.

She smiles, nodding. "It was. I'm so glad you felt comfortable enough to share it, though."

I'd love to say I'm sated, finished, ready to go home and to bed, but something about the experience has awoken my need to be closer to Jagger. I want him inside me.

Kenzie and Austin leave the room, and Jagger helps me to my feet. "You doing okay, Half-Pint? You're very quiet."

Clearing my throat is louder in the quiet room than I expected. "I need..." I drop my voice.

Jagger leans toward me, sweeping my hair behind my ear, his face softening. "What do you need, baby girl?"

CHAPTER 28

Jagger

"More." The word falls from Talia's lips, a soft plea in the silence.

Thor is balls deep in a blissed-out Addison through the glass. It's currently two-way, they could see us if they felt like looking. So I switch it to one-way glass before turning back to my woman.

"Here? Now?"

She shifts her weight from foot to foot. Her cheeks are flushed, and if I were to guess, I'd say the tops of her thighs are slick with her arousal. She was wetter than I've felt her so far. Seems my baby girl might have a voyeurism kink we need to explore.

She nods, tugging at the low-cut neckline of her dress. "Please, Daddy. I can't." She pulls at the fabric like it's restricting her from breathing, like her need for something, for touch, for my cock consumes her whole body.

"I need you." Her wail is so desperate, my cock's already hard and throbbing.

Picking her up, I press her against the wall, her legs curling around my waist. Her desperation claws at my body, driving me to satisfy her, to take care of her, to fill her. But this isn't the time, nor the place. I'll make her feel good, but I won't do anything to her she's not ready to do, or something that she is caught up in the moment and convincing herself she's ready to try.

I rip her pantyhose with ease as her teeth skim the sensitive skin of my neck, making me shiver as I shift her panties to one side. "Not here, baby girl. But soon."

She tips her head back against the wall, her eyes wild with desire. "Jagger, please. Just... please." She sinks her nails into my collarbone, unleashing something deep inside me. One-handed, I pull my cock from its prison before gliding it through her soaking wet pussy a couple of times. She's so warm, so slick, so fucking hungry it's hard not to slam into her.

From the way her hips roll, the way she moans and purrs, she's aching to have me inside her. And when I pause to enjoy her for a heavy moment, she thrusts her hips at me. "Daddy..."

Fuck. I've never heard something so hot as my baby girl begging for my cock. I want to give her what she needs, but it can't be here, not like this, not right now, so against every cell screaming in my body, I ignore the tightness building in my balls and tuck myself back into my briefs.

"If you still feel like this tomorrow, we can do it, okay?"

Her lips purse, brows tent, and her eyes flicker like she wasn't expecting me to have any form of self-control. If I'm honest, I wasn't really expecting it either, but I'm responsible for this woman. Fuck. It's more than that, the warmth in my chest that flickers every time she looks at me, the way I want to spend time with her, see a future with her, want to protect her...

"I love you, Talia." The confession takes us both by surprise, but as soon as the words are in the space between us, the last piece of my heart clicks into place.

"You do?"

Nodding, I brush my lips across her temple. "I'm not saying that to make you rush your decision. More to explain why I'm not splitting you in two with my cock right now. It has to be right, baby girl." I kiss her again. "It has to be right."

Her eyes well with unshed tears as she nibbles her lip. She nods. "I love you, too, Jagger." Her voice is quiet and shaky, but the genuine love that sparkles in her eyes is undeniable.

I kiss her, slowly, deeply, like it's the first time we're really kissing each other, and when we finally pull our lips apart, she's panting.

"Thank you for being such a good Daddy and taking care of me." She doesn't wait before she's bouncing on me, her back sliding up and down the wall with jerky movements. "More. Please. I know we can't... do that, but... please?" She's panting, clearly trying to land on me with more and more force. I'm tempted to sit and let her bounce away, but right now, I need to take care of her. I need to make her come apart on me.

I need to feed her hunger.

Gripping her hips, I support her weight, driving against her pussy with each hard thrust, getting faster and faster. She's so wet she's dripping down my fucking dick like she's marking her territory.

She's holding me tight, letting me lead, letting me protect her from falling, carrying her weight, and drilling against her just the way she needs me too.

With every bounce her tits jiggle, her breathing gets heavier and heavier, and her nails bite into my skin even deeper. My only purpose for being on this earth right now is to make this woman come.

The tighter she grips me, the harder it gets to stay focused. She's dragging me along with her, straight into the gates of blissful release, whether I want to or not. I need to hang on for her to go first.

Gritting my teeth, I plow against her harder, she's screaming my name alternating it with Daddy over and over with reckless abandon, pleading with me not to stop. When she comes, everything goes black for a beat before every goddamn drop of cum from my body covers us both.

I need her to come again, to feel her walls around my fingers, imagining they're gripping my cock, so I spear two fingers inside her and press against her g-spot. The aftershocks ripple through her pussy, fluttering muscles tightening even more around me as she heaves out deep breath after deep breath to try to come back to zero, but I shove her over the edge once again, on a long, guttural scream.

When she eventually opens her eyes, they're softer, not as manic, not as wild and full of desire. She grins up at me, a wide and warm smile that makes me want to give her the world. "Thank you, Daddy." Then she bursts into giggles.

"What is it, baby girl?"

She laughs harder. "You're dripping." She crams her head against my shoulder.

"I think you'll find it's *you* who is dripping, Half-Pint. Let's get you cleaned up so we can get home for round two."

"I'D LIKE TO FEEL YOUR PIERCINGS WITHOUT anything between us."

He brought a tote bag with him. When he presents me with a bottle of Tylenol, I look at him.

"It's not going to be comfortable, Half-Pint. You're quite small, I'm, well, I'm not. I have piercings, it's been a while since you've had anyone down there, I'd rather get ahead of the pain."

I'm ready for the pain. I've read so many romance novels that go from one momentary sting to the most blissful experience of their lives that it made me curious for factual information. After searching for that on the internet, I regretted my life choices pretty darn fast.

He hands me a bottle of water from the bag, and my curiosity is off the chart. What else is in there? What did he bring? Is it like a Mary Poppins's bag? Will he pull out a lamp next?

He jerks his chin at the water. "Take the meds, baby girl."

"Mmmm. Okay." I do, and he nods appreciatively when I hand him back the bottles.

"Good."

"You want a drink? Something to eat?" All the moisture has left my body. Tension holds my muscles hostage, tangled in tight knots all over, and I'm sticky enough to need a third shower.

"Shhhh." He grabs me, picks me up, and plops me facing him in his lap, my knees resting either side of his hips. "Take a breath please."

It's hard to do that, my chest is tight with anxiety and nerves have my stomach twisting.

"You're going to make yourself sick if you don't cool down, Half-Pint. At some point I'm going to determine you're not ready and just call it. You're way too worked up about this. That's not me diminishing your feelings, I'm just saying, I need you conscious to consent to doing things with me. Fucking an unconscious woman isn't my kink."

How can he chuck those words around so easily? Every time he cusses it's like my body is torn between cringing and melting. I can't see myself ever throwing around the F-bomb, but maybe I'll come to be more familiar and less flinch-y when it's spoken around me. It's conditioning, the words themselves aren't a problem, but in my head...

Jagger's mouth has tugged into a smirk.

"What?"

"Your mind is racing so fast I can almost see tiny legs in your eyeballs."

He sure is romantic, isn't he?

"Can you kiss me already please? I'm in my head, and I don't know how to get out of my head. I've got questions and thoughts on repeat, and I want to put it all down on a shelf somewhere and kiss my boyfriend."

His warm hands slip under the hem of my shirt, curling around my waist. His hands are big, possessive, strong. Safe. He's holding my weight so I can relax into his grip a little. When his nose brushes mine, lightning dances down my spine.

When his lower lip presses against mine, I sigh into his mouth. When his tongue teases mine, pulling me from my mental prison, I loop my arms around his neck and pull him to me.

It's been such a short space of time since we met, but I want to explore things with this man. There's potential here for a deep and meaningful relationship.

His hands tighten, like he's reminding me he's got me without using words. How long do we kiss? I have no idea, I get lost in the nipping and biting, the lip-tugging, and tongues dancing. When he stands up, loops my legs around his body, and picks up his bag of tricks, I hold him tighter. He doesn't miss a beat as he walks, carrying me to my bedroom.

Except he has no idea where that is, so he toes open doors one at a time until he finds it. He's kissing my neck, nibbling on my jaw, everywhere his body touches mine ignites, like my nerve endings have been supercharged.

He places me tenderly in the middle of the bed before climbing on top of me, caging me into the mattress with his body. I don't want him covered, I need him naked, so my fingers scramble to get him undressed.

His shirt gets caught over his head, and he snorts, grumbling into the fabric curled around his face. I can't help but throw my head back and laugh.

When he's shirtless, I'm drooling. The planes and ridges of his chest are like something from a storybook. His skin is flawless, the lines of his tattoos sharp and clear, calling to me to trace my fingers over. They wind their way back around his shoulder and up his neck, and his muscles loosen as he pulls his pants off, leaving him in briefs and me fully clothed.

It's reassuring, comforting even, he's almost entirely naked, and I'm not. But that means the sensations are muted when he touches me the fabric barrier between us absorbs it. Just like when I pulled his shirt off, I get tangled in my own, except, instead of helping me out of it, Jagger dots a line of kisses down my collar bone. I don't know how I got tangled, but I can't get myself unstuck. I'm sort of cuffed by the sleeves of my shirt.

His trail continues along the edge of my bra, down my stomach, and within seconds he has my pants and panties off and my legs over his shoulders.

He blows on my crotch. "Are you too nervous to be wet for me, baby girl?"

That wobbly feeling hits my chest every time he calls me baby girl, it takes an extra beat to steady myself to answer. "No Daddy. I'm wet for you."

He spreads my lips with delicate fingertips. "So perfectly pink and glistening for me. You're such a good girl, aren't you?"

I bite down on the shirt that's covering my face, strangling a moan.

"And you have a praise kink a mile wide. My beautiful good girl."

He slides his thumb over my clit, making me shiver and roll my hips. "Just relax, Half-Pint. It's going to take a while."

I finally get my shirt off, and look down. He's staring up at me with adoration and awe in his eyes. I'm expecting his tongue, but his thumb hits my clit, gliding across my slick skin, making my breath catch in the back of my throat.

When two of his fingers enter me, I can't help purring. He kisses his way back up my body, working his two fingers in and out of me, pressing my g-spot, making me wiggle and squirm as he finds my mouth again.

"We're going to work with my hand for a bit, okay? See if we can't get you to relax for me."

I'm already molten, putty in his hand, and when his fingers press that intimate spot it makes me shiver and pant. He adds a third finger and my body tenses, my lungs locking. "Shhhhh." He murmurs against my skin as his soft lips glide across my chest leaving a damp trail. "Just relax and let it happen, baby girl."

His voice chips at the anxiety gnawing my brain. He's in control, he knows what he's doing, and he's not going to intentionally hurt me. When his tongue hits my nipple, I'm grabbing the sheets at my side, clutching them in a tight grip. "Please, Jagger, more, please."

I'm not sure what I meant, but him sliding a fourth finger inside me wasn't it. When he does, a gush of liquid comes out of me. My embarrassed groan isn't lost on him, and he pumps a little harder, making me squelch all over again.

His patience is unending. His rhythm is slow, in and out, his fingers gliding through my arousal into my body and back out again, my muscles following his lead; my body is an instrument, and he's playing me with ease and skill.

He's licked and sucked my nipples so much, my breasts are hyper tingly.

"How's this pussy of mine, baby girl? Doing okay?"

"Mhmm."

"Use your words please, Talia." His hand pauses, and I can't let him stop. I can't. I need him to keep going. There's a faint tingle at the base of my spine, and I'm pretty sure it's an orgasm brewing.

"Your pussy is good, Daddy. I need more, please. More."

"More fingers? You what my whole hand?"

"Yes, Daddy. Please."

"Baby girl. I think that might be too much."

"No. I want more. Please."

He hums. And when he tucks his thumb in, all his fingers are inside me, and my muscles clench around him, holding his hand prisoner. "Breathe through it, baby girl, keep breathing. You're doing so, so well for me."

My head lolls back.

"Look how fucking sexy you are taking Daddy's hand like that. Does it feel good?"

A gravelly moan gathers in my throat. "Yes, Daddy."

"Good girl. You're about to queef baby girl. Do you know what that is?"

Before I can answer what sounds like a great big toot comes out of my body. "Oh my goodness." My distressed moan makes him chuckle.

"There it is. Think we can do that again?"

Why in the name of anything does he want to make me make that noise again? I have no idea, but the embarrassment sticks to the sweat coating my skin. "Here we go, Half-Pint, relax. It's going to happen again." The embarrassing parp of air escapes from my body.

"It's just air, baby girl. Nothing to be ashamed about. It'll probably happen when my cock is tucked tightly inside this pussy of mine, too, you know. So tight." He moves his hand, placing the fingers from his free hand over my clit. That tiny tingle isn't so tiny anymore, and it's not staying put in the base of my spine.

My nipples, my clit, my g-spot, they're all singing from the same hymn sheet, and I'm about to explode. My body jerks and twitches on the bed, involuntary spasms as I charge toward release, a powerless passenger to Jagger's skilled hands.

"There we go, baby girl. Almost there, right? You're going to come for Daddy, aren't you? Be a good girl for me, Half-Pint. Be a good girl for Daddy and come for me."

My body reacts before my brain, muscles seizing, gripping his hand, freezing tightly, my back bowing off the bed, head tipped back in a silent scream.

"So close. I can feel it. My pussy's getting all tight and hot, isn't it baby girl? Your body's going to give Daddy what he needs. I'm not stopping until I get what I need."

Sweat's trickling down my face as he nips at my nipples with his teeth, then sucks one into his mouth, flicking at it with his tongue. It's the tipping point.

"Come on, baby girl. Give me all you've got."

When I scream, my legs clench, gripping his whole arm between my thighs. Wave after wave of release crashes into me as his fingers somehow move despite my body holding him hostage.

"Keep going, sweet girl. Come on, you're not done. You have more than that to give your Daddy." His gentle cooing in my ear prolongs my orgasm. I've never felt like a surfer riding the wave of an orgasm until now, but I don't want it to end. Those undulating ripples through my body make me feel like they could last forever.

I smack my hand out toward his body. "Now, please, please get inside me. Please."

He grins at me but keeps his hand inside me until he's positioned between my legs. He strips off his briefs and places his head at my entrance, the cold metal balls of his piercing a relief from the burning inferno at the apex of my thighs.

He licks off his fingers before putting his hands on either side of my head. "Are you sure you're ready?"

"Yes, Daddy." I roll my hips like that might make him go faster, but consent is important to him.

"If I start moving inside you, and it hurts too much, or you change your mind just say stop, no, or use your safeword, okay? Anything to signal you're not okay progressing. Okay, baby girl?"

The way he protects me, even from him, curls around my heart like a warm blanket. "Yes, Daddy."

He nudges his head a bit inside me. A laugh bubbles up inside me. I guess this is what they mean when they say "just the tip."

He hooks his hands behind my knees and opens me to him, sinking further inside me. There's a pinch of pain, an ache, a burn, the feeling of being stretched by something, similar to his fingers being inside me, but his hand had more flexibility to it. His cock is unforgiving.

I wiggle, he pauses. "You okay, baby girl?"

"Yes, Daddy."

He hums, sweeping his lips against mine. "Don't be a martyr okay? If it hurts, we'll stop and try again." His eyes pierce mine with a deep intensity that makes my toes curl.

"I'm okay. Please, don't stop."

He nods, and when he eases himself inside me a little more, my breath snags. Wowsers. Despite him having stretched me out with his hand, it's still tight. I'm sure there's a joke in there somewhere, but right now I'm more focused on making sure I can breathe when he's all the way inside of me.

It takes a while. At one point he offers to get lubricant from his bag but we make it work, and when he's all the way inside of me, I'm freakin' exhausted. Who knew sex was so draining?

He pushes my matted hair out of my face. "Are you still doing okay?" The concern is heavy in his voice as he searches my eyes. "We can stop at any time, baby girl. Any time at all."

There's a foreign object in my body, and with every breath in and out, I feel it. The pressure in my core is almost overwhelming. Every time he moves or shifts his weight those piercings wiggle inside me, and while I wasn't sure I'd climax from my g-spot, I inched closer as he inched himself inside me.

We lie like this for a long moment, like the whole world has stopped, him laying over the top of me, caging me in, his cock nestled all the way inside my throbbing body and me staring up at him like he hung the moon.

If I need to sneeze or cough, will he shoot out of me or something?

That makes me giggle, and before long, the bed is shaking with the weight of my laughter.

"Please tell me you're not laughing at my performance in the bedroom." Jagger groans, dropping his forehead on to mine, which for some reason makes me laugh even harder.

I shake my head. "I had visions of me sneezing and, well, you know." I move my hand like a rocket or shooting star, adding sound effects for good measure.

Making Jagger laugh is one of my favorite things. "You're lucky I'm secure enough in the power of my cock, Half-Pint." He brushes his nose against mine before planting the sweetest kiss on my lips. "How are you feeling?"

"Like you put a Mentos inside a bottle of Coke."

"Did you just describe my cock as a mint candy?"

Nodding, my giggles return with force. "And my vagina as a bottle of Coke, yes, yes, I did." I can't help laughing, and every time I laugh I move, and he moves, and it's taking my breath away. "I don't mean it in a bad way, there's a lot of..."

I'm not sure I can adequately describe how it feels lying here with my guy's pretty big peen inside my body right now.

"It's achy, like pressure, and when you move it's kinda chafe-y."

He nods. "That's all normal, and expected." He shifts his weight down onto his forearms, drawing a feral moan from me as the piercings scrape against my inner walls. "You need a time out?"

A bead of sweat trickles down his temple. Both of us are moving so slowly, so cautiously it's taking an astronomical amount of self-restraint not to let it fly, and maybe that's what we both need.

"Please don't stop. Keep going."

His soft lips touch mine, making my mouth fall open to let his tongue in. As his tongue meets mine in a sensual dance, his hips move. It's painfully slow at first. He drags himself out of me, before pushing back in one inch at a time. The cold metal on his head isn't cold anymore, but I still feel it pressing against me as he moves.

"You're doing so well. So fucking well." He pushes himself up, looks down at where our bodies meet, and rolls his hips which makes my eyes roll back in my head. "Look at how perfectly you're taking Daddy's cock, baby girl. I'm so proud of you."

The sigh that leaves my slightly parted lips carries some of the tension from my body, and I relax as he picks up the pace. He's not drilling into me like I've read about, but he's not going slowly. And the faster he goes the closer he takes me to the edge.

It's not long before my fingers bite into his shoulder blades, and I'm panting his name into his neck. "Please, please don't stop."

The rough graze of his teeth down the column of my neck makes me shiver, he goes faster. It must be painful for him to hold back. I bet he wants to rut into me without having to think about it, but he's not, he's holding back, making sure I'm comfortable. He's such a good man.

I can't take my eyes off his glistening skin, his flexing muscles as he moves. He holds his body weight so he doesn't crush me. He doesn't take his eyes off my face, constantly searching for signs I'm not okay. The pressure building in my body is astronomical, a tightness, a heaviness as he pistons his hips and his rod-still cock commands my body to respond.

"I'm close, baby girl. I'm going to need to empty my balls here pretty soon."

"So romantic." I can't help laughing again.

"I'm giving you a heads up so you can choose for me to come on you rather than in you. I don't want to presume."

Okay, that's pretty sweet.

"I-I-oh, I'm close, too." Something about the way he shifted his hips brought a more intense pressure to the soft spot deep inside of me.

"There you go, sweet girl. Are you going to come for Daddy?"

I think I answer, but it may be abstract noises at this point.

"You're so tight and hot, so dripping wet for me. Feel how easy it is for Daddy to slide in and out of you, baby girl?"

He's flipped some base-switch inside my brain, the only thing that matters is reaching the edge of this cliff so I can jump off and into the blissful release of my orgasm.

"Come on. I can feel your muscles clenching and twitching around my cock. So good, so close, does it feel good?"

I can't answer him, there are no words, only a frantic need to let go. My body's trembling, my muscles convulsing around him and when I detonate, the edges of my vision blur as I shake underneath him.

He caresses my face with his fingertips, his hips start to

move jerkier, and less rhythmic, but he's not slowing or stopping.

"Please don't stop, Jagger. Please. Please." I guess he likes my pleading because it doesn't take much longer before he's clenching his muscles.

"I'm going to come, baby girl. Are you still okay?" His jaw flexes as a muscle feathers in his cheek. How can he hold back like this? When he made me come, it hit me like a firework.

"Please come inside me."

The noise he makes is something between a growl and a roar as he tips his head back, closes his eyes, and empties himself inside me. The serenity on his face is so beautiful, like he's having a religious experience, and before I know what's happening, tears are streaming down my face as my body shakes with emotion.

His eyes flick open, land on me, and he kisses me so deeply, so tenderly, it's like he's trying to caress my soul. He presses gentle kisses on my wet cheeks before moving his lips to be next to my ear. "It's okay, baby girl, let it all out."

I've gone from giggling to crying in the time we've been in this bed, and I admit, I'm feeling unhinged, and I can't stop this swell of emotions, the streaming tears that roll down my face.

But when I search my boyfriend's eyes, there's no judgment there, just affection and encouragement. I'm not sure how he does it, but before I realize what's even happening, I'm curled up in his arms, my head on his sweat-slicked chest, and my blanket being pulled up over me.

"Shhhh. You're safe. It's all okay. Keep breathing and don't fight it."

I don't know how long I lie in Jagger's arms. I don't know how many tears fall, or even what they're really falling for—the life I lost waiting to give myself to Harry. The pain and trauma of my experience with him. The fact I'm lying in bed with the most beautiful soul I've ever met who's making me feel like a treasure. Or the fact I finally found a piece of myself I had no idea was missing—Maybe it's a combination of everything.

Either way, Jagger's not making me feel stupid for crying, which adds to the cascading emotions ricocheting through my whole being. He holds me, telling me how beautiful I am, how amazing it was, and right before I slip into sleep, he tells me he loves me again.

CHAPTER 29

Talia

I don't remember a time when I've slept so soundly in all my life. It says more about me than Jagger that I expect a cold and empty bed next to me when I wake up, but he's coiled so tightly around me I'm afraid to even breathe in case I wake him.

"Good morning, baby girl."

"Mmmmm." A satisfied hum rolls through my tired muscles. "Good morning, Daddy."

"You sleep okay?" He's nuzzling into my hair, can't tell if it's for the smell of my shampoo, or simply to get closer to me.

"Like the dead. You?" I tentatively wiggle my toes. I expect to feel sticky, I didn't even pee before I passed out cold in bed, which means I'm covered in... Fluids.

That hardness growing against my leg has to be his peen, and if it wasn't so achy between my legs, I'd absolutely indulge us both in another round. I don't have it in me. "I want more, but I don't think I should." I know he won't get crabby with me, I know he's not going to force anything, but I'm afraid to say the words out loud.

He pulls me against his chest, kissing my forehead as he rolls me. "Maybe I'm not in the mood."

That simply can't be. Last night was amazing, and I can't imagine ever not wanting to do that with him all over again.

He kisses the wrinkles between my brows from my frown. "I am absolutely in the mood." Another gentle kiss. "But I also know when we need to rest and recharge. I'm sure you're achy."

Nodding, my cheeks sizzle.

"I cleaned you up as best I could. You were out cold. Can I run a bath for you? Let you soak for a bit while I head down to make brunch."

Brunch? How long have we been lying around in bed for? "Don't you have to work?"

"I do." He nods. "But I can go in after lunch, and I can come back to check on you later before I go home."

It's like he's thought of everything. "I like this not having to go to class, not having a job limbo."

He chuckles. "Didn't you graduate a couple months ago?"

Nodding, I nibble on my lip. "Went to the commencement ceremony and everything."

"And you've just been here in Minnesota doing... what... since you graduated?"

I shrug. "Hiding? Avoiding having to marry Harry? I told my parents I had a job here that I couldn't walk out of."

"Did you?" *Now* he has questions.

"Kinda." Another shrug. "Coffee shop server here, volunteered for an animal shelter there... nothing I couldn't have given up if I'd wanted to go back."

He shakes his head. "You're far too full of brilliance and energy to waste it lying here in this bed every day forever."

My frown reappears. "That sounds entirely too boring."

He sweeps his lips against mine. "My point exactly. I'll go run a bath for you."

I try to protest, but he has no intention of listening. “Let me take care of you, baby girl. I want to take care of you.” He pauses, kissing me again. “I need to. If I let you run your own bath and went down to make breakfast I’d feel like shit. It would be constantly on my mind that it should be me taking care of you instead of you doing it yourself.” He touches his chest. “It’s something in here.” The gentleness he uses to brush my hair off my face and drop another light kiss on my temple makes my chest squeeze.

It doesn’t take him long. He offers to climb into the tub with me and wash my hair but I’m so hungry, my growling stomach answers for me. Instead, he suggests he goes to go cook food while I soak in the tub. Before he goes, he brings me water, and the book from my bedside table, giving me a wiggle of his eyebrows when he flashes me the cover.

Sinking into the fragrant, bubbly water that’s almost-but-not-quite too hot to sit in is blissful for my aching muscles. The steam tickles my nose and prickles at my skin as I sink into the bubbles.

Washing my hair takes far less time now that it’s cut, and it’s not nearly as hard to maintain, and yet in some ways it’s even more complicated.

I take my time, exfoliating my skin, shaving my legs, giving my aching muscles some time to unwind in the water. I know I’d slept with someone before, but in many ways, it feels like I lost my virginity last night.

Or at least, it was the experience I’d always dreamed that moment would be.

Knowing Jagger needs to work later scratches at my skin like sand paper. I’m clingy and want him to stay, but I don’t want to ask him to give up his work time to spend time with his needy girlfriend.

End of the day, the guy has a job and responsibilities. Something I’m going to have to give more thought to in the coming weeks. Staying in Minnesota brings with it a world of opportunities, but it also means I need to pivot quickly. I need to figure out a way to support myself beyond my trust fund.

I'm not scared, though. Usually, I probably would be. My mind would find a way into an anxious hamster-wheel of self-doubt and wondering whether I should have left Harry at all. But I don't have that heavy feeling pressing on my chest. In fact, if I quiet down and listen to my feelings, I might even hear a sparkle of excitement at the prospect of choosing my own adventure for the first time in my whole life.

There it is again. A flash, a buzz of potential, what ifs, and the smell of new beginnings. What do I want my future to look like now that Harry isn't in my life, and the weight of my parent's expectations are off my shoulders? What do I want to do with my life?

Do I really want to be an author? Or was that a panicked answer to the question I was asked because I felt like I needed to know?

Again, the not knowing makes me excited, it fills me with hope, not terror. I finally want to move ahead into the future for the first time in as long as I can remember, and I'm ready to make my dreams happen. Whatever they happen to be.

I take my time rubbing lotion into my body, all the way to my toes. I don't remember the last time I indulged my skin in some quality TLC. Heels, knees, and elbows get extra time, and I'm feeling like a new woman.

A real one this time.

When I stepped on the plane, I *thought* I was a new woman, or at least I thought I could be one. A new haircut, pretending to have a new attitude, thinking I knew who I was —my "fake it till ya make it" mindset wasn't backed up by anything other than a wing and a prayer, the knowledge I didn't want Harry but feeling like I didn't know who I was without him pressing me into a corner.

I'm steadier in myself, even though it's very early days. I'm sure I'll feel wobbly going forward but right now, in this quiet space with myself, I'm more level than I have been in a while.

Maybe I'll learn a new skill, or take up a new hobby. The possibilities are endless and each moment I spend with myself in the bathroom, more and more options burst into my mind.

By the time I'm dressed, I'm fizzing with nervous energy. I practically skip downstairs. There's a gasp in the kitchen. Is my guy a fan of daytime TV? Wouldn't that be something? My enormous, tattooed, scowly faced grumpasaurus loves watching TV dramas? I can't wait to threaten to tell all his friends. They don't kink shame, sure, but they may judge his love of watching shows about fixing up houses.

I'm already halfway into the kitchen before there's a tingle at the base of my neck that something is wrong.

Jagger's standing in front of the stove, barefoot, in tight briefs leaving very little to the imagination. His expansive chest and shoulders displaying the intricate ink etched into his skin. He's holding a frying pan in one hand, and a spatula in the other. His scowly face looks particularly scowly. Like, scowlier than usual. More scowly? Either way, it's like, next level Jagger scowl.

I might need a fan for my girl garden cause the smolder's super hot.

Movement behind me makes my feet stutter to a stop. I close my eyes for the briefest of moments, picking up the faintest scent of Chanel no.5 in the air. My stomach hardens like someone's poured quick-drying cement on me as I freeze.

When I meet Jagger's stare, his nostrils flare. I expect panic, but his eyes are dancing with a bright twinkle of amusement, and not even rolling my lips between my teeth can make me fight the snort that bursts out of my body.

My mouth is dry, another glance at Jagger's junk confirms

that yeah, he's still standing in the kitchen in his very revealing underwear.

"Mama."

Thankfully I wore short shorts and a tank down to breakfast, and I even thought to put on a bra. Points for me. I mostly wasn't sure I was ready for Jagger to see me all hanging out, but clearly he had no such misconceptions.

"Talia." Mama's voice is tight.

Dad clears his throat too, it's awkward, forced, like he wants me to know he's here but doesn't want to actually speak.

They're standing close to the door, like they just walked in and found him cooking. They can't have been here for that long or Jagger would have put pants on... right? Or did he let them in and simply went back to cooking? Oh... lord. The thickening tension is suffocating. Talia, say something. Quickly.

"I see you've met Jagger again."

Mama splutters. "All of him." Mama cracking a joke about Jagger's visible junk wasn't on my bingo card for today, or, you know, ever. And it's all it takes for Jagger's melodic chuckle to make an appearance.

"Half-Pint, your parents are joining us for brunch."

I can't bring myself to turn around and face them.

"Could you set the table while I put some pants on please?" The lightness in his voice isn't something I'm used to either, but I like it. He doesn't seem bothered by the fact my very strict, serious, conservative parents are standing mere feet away while he's on display, but the hilarity of the situation isn't lost on me either.

"Why bother?" Mama's smirking, I can tell from the sound of her voice. "We've seen it all anyway."

Dad clears his throat again, but says nothing.

Jagger grunts. "I'll put pants on."

When he leaves, I suck in a slow breath, ready to turn and face the parents who are eternally disappointed in me, the parents I let down by not marrying the man they chose for me or following the dreams they had for me.

Instead of anger, disappointment, or horror, Mama is smiling. "Talia, honey?"

"Mm?"

"Is he...?" She casts a fleeting glance at the door. "Is he...? You know...?" She drops her voice. "Pierced?"

CHAPTER 30

Jagger

I'M NOT EMBARRASSED MY GIRLFRIEND'S PARENTS saw me in my Calvin Kleins. Not even a little bit. But as I spear at the pancakes Talia's mom made for breakfast, I swallow down the brewing anger, geared up for a fight.

They were very pleasant while Talia's mom stepped in to cook for everyone. I wasn't far in to making breakfast, and she was bouncing around with so much nervous energy, I was happy to step aside and let her make whatever she wanted to.

But if they say one thing, one fucking thing to my woman about, well, anything I don't like the sound of, I don't give a fuck how good her pancakes are, she's out on her ass.

No questions asked.

The air is tight with tension as we eat in silence. Awkwardness pools in the space around us, and I'm not sure I have anything in my bank of small talk to make this moment any less weird.

"So." Talia's mom dabs at her mouth with a napkin before dropping it into her lap. "You're clearly sleeping together now."

Talia's dad gags on a mouthful of chicken, Talia's face goes so red I'm not sure she has any blood left anywhere else in her body, and I'm not sure where this woman is going with this. Her tone isn't judgy, more curious I'd say.

"Mama." Talia's fork is paused on the way to her mouth, a thick glob of maple syrup drips off and onto her chest. I collect it with my thumb, then hold it out for her to lick off. She doesn't hesitate.

"What?" Her mom shrugs. "I'm just making conversation."

Is she really that clueless? I doubt it.

"Mrs. Uh." Oh fuck. I'm drawing a blank.

The Mother, who I now realize I know neither her first nor do I remember her last name, casts her attention across the table to me. "Barclay."

"Mrs. Barclay." I'm not easily intimidated. Plenty of uppity pricks come into my shop all the time. These rich people don't scare me. But things with Talia are new and scary in and of themselves, and I don't want to lose that. I don't want for us to kindle this special thing between us only to have it snuffed out by her douchey parents.

Except Talia doesn't look scared, she's not pale, or shrinking into herself. She sits tall, her shoulders relaxed and back, her head high as she dunks her waffle into the swimming pool of maple syrup on her plate. How her food hasn't started floating is anyone's guess.

"This isn't what I envisioned for you, Talia." Mrs. Barclay—since she hasn't given me her first name, or permission to call her anything other than what she said—picks up her coffee but doesn't drink from the cup. "I admit, I had hoped you and Harry would resolve your differences, but after learning the extent of his betrayal and personality flaws, I'm very glad you decided not to marry that low-life." She spits the last words like they taste rotten on her tongue before flicking her hard stare to me.

"I don't know you Jagger. I don't know your last name or anything about you. And I'll admit, my prejudices about your profession." She sweeps a hand at me. "And your tattoos gave me pause."

Talia gasps when Mrs. Barclay mentions she doesn't know my last name, like it just hit her like a lightning bolt that she doesn't know either. She does, but I guess she doesn't remember. "Coleman." My whisper is to reassure her, but the amused twitch on her mom's lips tells me she heard.

"I admit it. I saw a man of your size, covered in tattoos and grease stains, and I immediately jumped to you not being good enough for my daughter."

Talia opens her mouth to protest.

"Let me finish, honey. Then you can yell at me if you need to." She finally sips her coffee. "I was wrong. I should know by now not to judge a book by its cover. I was worried about Talia, and how her behavior had shifted, how she was lashing out, changing her hair, her life plan, her partner all in one go. But the more I talk to her, the more I see her, the more I see I missed how unhappy she had become, how different she was."

Talia's trembling beside me, so I take her hand and squeeze it. I'm right here, silently giving her whatever strength she needs.

"I'm a big enough woman to be able to say when I'm wrong. And I was wrong to judge you without so much as getting to know you. I'd like to start over." She turns her attention to Talia. "With both of you."

Talia's jaw is hanging wide open like the pantry door, tears slowly meandering down her cheeks.

"Seeing you here, honey, you've changed. And I don't mean the wild hair. The way you hold yourself, the color in your cheeks, the way your eyes sparkle. All small changes I didn't see happening over the years until I was faced with this daughter bursting with sunshine I didn't recognize. I'm sorry for letting you down."

Her dad shifts in his seat with a nod.

"I know we made mistakes when it came to Harry and how we wanted your future to go, but your father and I have been talking, and we're both ready to support you in your endeavors, wherever they may take you."

Talia's mouth is wide open, so I nudge her body with mine. "You're catching mosquitoes, baby girl."

Her dad laughs. "Kevin." He extends his hand to me, and after staring at it for a beat slightly too long, I accept it in a handshake.

"Jagger. And it's a pleasure sir. I'm sure it goes without saying but I'm somewhat smitten with your daughter."

A squeak falls from my chatterbox's open mouth. "Smitten?" She swings to me. "You don't use words like smitten."

She's right, it's not normally in my vocabulary, but I'm trying to make up for the fact I only put pants on, and her mom is still at eye-level with my nipples.

Talia's face breaks out into a soul-touching smile before she reaches out both hands and pinches my cheeks. "Wait." She gasps. "My grumpasaurus is smitten for lil ole me? Whoda'thunk it when just a couple weeks ago you wanted to throw me out of a plane from thirty thousand feet?"

I've barely started growling when Mr. Barclay pipes up. "Jagger, are you growling at the apple of my eye, my one and only daughter?"

"Yes, sir, I am."

She's got my cheeks in a death grip, like when your grandmother comes to visit and she hasn't seen you since last Christmas.

"I can't imagine he wanted to throw you out of a moving plane, honey." Mrs. Barclay slices into a juicy chicken tender and squirts Mr. Barclay with chicken juice. He rolls his eyes as he dabs his shirt with a napkin like this is par for the course for the two of them.

I swallow my mouthful of food. "No, I absolutely did. She was relentless. I got her whole life story in the first four minutes of her landing in my lap."

Both parents jump, slow blinking, their silverware paused in flight.

"Not *actually* in your lap, right?" Mrs. Barclay looks back and forth between us right as my baby girl erupts into laughter.

She spends the next hour recounting how we met and everything—outside of the fucking and fucking-adjacent things. While Mr. Bar—Kevin—and I clean up the dishes, Talia and her mom sit on the couch and chat. Talia's so animated, her words coming out so quickly as she tells her mom her idea to write dirty books.

I expect her mom to hit the roof, and while there's a momentary silence and she bristles, to her credit she doesn't do anything that I can see or hear, to dissuade her. Thank fuck, because I'm starting to like her dad. Turns out, he's a car guy. He might be a white collar guy by day, but he loves taking apart engines and tinkering under the hood of cars in his spare time.

Dad's gonna fucking love this guy. He's a golfer too. The two of them will be out doing, well, whatever golfers do with their balls and holes every weekend, shortly after we get them in the same room together.

Huh.

My wife was the last woman I brought home to meet my folks. It's easier not to let them get attached when I don't get attached myself.

Mom is gonna flip her shit when she hears I have a girlfriend. I'd better leave it for a couple weeks before I subject Half-Pint to Mom. She'll have planned our entire wedding, picked out grandkids names, and bought the empty house on my street before I could even get out Talia's fuckin' name.

If there was ever a more excitable person than Talia, it's my mother. I can only handle her in small doses, so our weekly meal—which I wangled my way out of for the past couple weeks because of my trip, my heartbreak, and this week because of the weather—is about it.

That said, Talia loves people, she could totally be my shield, or blocker, or beard, whatever the fuck it's called when someone runs interference for you. Talia would not only do that, but she'd love it. Like, love. She and Mom would talk for days and forget the rest of the world is even there—mark my words.

After we clean up, Talia pulls out a selection of ice cream and board games. Her dad lights up like Christmas came early, and though I expect her mother—Julie—to object, she simply sets up the table and takes her seat.

There's definite love around the table, it's nice to see they're finally in a space where Talia feels like she's being listened to for a change. You can tell from the way she actually has a neck and her shoulders aren't glued to her ears that she's much more at ease than she was.

It's probably not going to be problem-free. People don't simply change overnight, but the more I watch my warrior-strong Half-Pint kick her parent's butts at Monopoly, and then Scrabble, and then The Game of Life, the more I realize they're going to be okay.

I have no idea what her brother Isaac is like, but from the good natured ribbing between her and her parents, there's a levity that seems to have been missing with Harry the douchebag in the picture. Perhaps the idea she's strong enough to walk away from them for real gave them the kick in the ass they needed to realize they could lose her if they didn't meet her where she was.

Around nine, I give her a kiss right in front of her parents and excuse myself to go home. My ass is barely in the car when something drives me to make a call.

"Jagger? What's wrong?" The worry weighing down Mom's voice is touching.

"Nothing, Mom. I just wanted to chat."

"Who are you, and what have you done with my son?"

I know she doesn't mean it as a jab, she's laughing now, her voice lighter and airy, but her words press into my skin.

"It's still me, Mom. I felt like calling." I swallow, readying myself for the deafening squeal of excitement that's about to befall me. "I met someone."

I DON'T LIKE THE FACT WE SEEM TO BE GETTING INTO the habit of being interrupted by our parents. We're slated to have dinner with Mom and Dad next week, so when someone knocks at the door, and I peer out between the blinds to find Mom's car in my driveway the following morning, I'm not exactly thrilled.

I love my parents, but Half-Pint needs her rest after last night, and we had a plan. I don't want to overwhelm her with new people. She takes strangers in her stride, and I've seen with my own eyes that her energy feeds off others. But Mom's excitement coupled with Talia's exhaustion from a night of playing at the club could make her even more exhausted, or worse, send her into drop.

Despite the irritation, I need to shut up the knocking before they wake—

"Jagger? What's wrong? Who's at the door?"

Fuck.

"It looks like my parents are here, Half-Pint. I'm sorry. I didn't ask them to come, and if you're not up to it, I'll send them away."

She sits up, stretching and rubbing her bleary eyes. "No, it's okay. You go down and I'll be down in a sec, okay?"

I'm reluctant to leave her, but she shoos me out the door. "Go, before your mom calls the police." Her smile is assuring. "It's all good, I'm ready."

It's not her I'm worried about.

When I yank open the door, Mom thrusts a giant box of donuts at me as she pushes past. "I need more information Jagger. You can't drop on me that you have a girlfriend and expect me to go on about my life like this isn't a monumental event. I need details." She's already well on her way to the kitchen, the coffee's probably on and mugs out on the counter by the time Dad steps into the doorway with a shrug, holding his hands up.

"I tried to hold her back, son. I did my best." He pulls me into a tight hug. "Good to see you, you're looking great."

"Hi, Dad."

He jerks his chin toward the tornado that is my mother. "She hasn't taken a breath from speaking at me since you told her about Talia. She's also heavily caffeinated, and has already picked out your children's names." He pats my chest. "Doesn't matter if the two of you don't want any kids, she's planned your whole future, and she's eying that house on the corner. I had to pull her phone out of her hands so she didn't call the realtor."

Her excitement is sweet, but I'm concerned about Mom's caffeine-fueled energy being too much for my Half-Pint. Dad swings the door closed behind him, and we head into the kitchen. Mom's got mugs out, milk out, and she's already working on the expensive coffee machine she bought me two

Christmases ago—because she needed my house to have fancy coffee for her visits—working hard.

"Mom? I need you to take a breath, please." She rounds on me, eyes narrowing like a shark smelling blood in the water. It takes her all of a second of looking at my face before she shrieks and claps her hands together.

"Is she here? She's here, isn't she?"

Holding up my hand, I shake my head. "Mom, she's not prepared to meet you this morning, so unless you cool your jets, I'm kicking you both out, keeping the donuts, and drinking the coffee with my girl."

Her eyes widen. She knows I'm not kidding. I'll absolutely kick her out and keep her caffeine and sugar.

She heaves out a sigh. "I'm sorry. I know I'm over-excitable, honey. It's been so long since you've brought anyone home. She must be so special. I have no chill." She holds up her hands. "First to admit it." She tilts her head. "But you have to at least give me *something*. Then I'll eat my Boston cream donut, drink my frou-frou coffee, and go back to kicking your dad's ass at crossword puzzles and Sudoku."

Dad groans behind me. "Adding extra boxes and filling in squares is *cheating*, Mariam. Not winning."

She waves a dismissive hand. "Po-tay-to, po-tah-to."

A giggle from the doorway draws all of our attention to the fearsome, blue-haired terror standing in one of my shirts that comes all the way down to her knees, and a pair of my shorts that damn near reach the floor. "Sorry." She hugs her arms around her middle like a belt. "Unexpected sleepover. I offered to go home, but he's protective. And his clothes are way too big. I felt like my little black dress from last night was probably a bit *extra* for meeting the parents."

Not to mention it's covered in cum.

Her face gets pinker and pinker as she talks, and her words get faster. She steps forward. "Talia Barclay. It's lovely to meet you both." She shakes Dad's hand, but Mom's vibrating at an unnatural frequency reserved only for children on Christmas morning, moms meeting their son's girlfriends, and Black Friday sales.

She pauses, arms outstretched, like her brain caught up to her body. "Hugger?" She hooks her thumb at me. "He's not really much of a people person. How do we feel about people?"

Talia's giggling.

"Never mind people," Dad says. "How do we feel about cheating at the crossword?"

Talia points at Mom. "Love people, love hugs, and he's a people person for the right people." She flashes the smile that could make my knees buckle in a heartbeat, then points to Dad. "I feel like cheating is a strong word, Mr. Coleman. I prefer to call it, uh, creative interpretation of the suggested method of completing the activity."

Mom grins. "You can stay."

Talia approaches, arms outstretched. "I mean, thank you, but realistically the only guy who can make me leave is the surly looking grump with his Mom's eyes, his Dad's jaw, and a severe resting b-i-t-c-h face."

Dad steps forward to shake her hand. "Earl, nice to meet you, Talia. We haven't heard much about you at all, but I'm sure that won't surprise you. I hope you're ready to be sufficiently grilled because my wife is bursting at the seams to talk to you." He turns to Mom. "We didn't actually know you'd be here this morning. But, she brought donuts. Hopefully the trade-off of still-warm sugar will be enough for the rapid-fire question time that's about to befall you."

Dad shakes his head. "She's excited is all."

"We were starting to think he would scare everyone off with his prickly exterior."

Talia laughs, stepping forward to move one coffee cup out

of the machine and put another in. When she presses the button to start it, she hands the mug to Mom. "I mean, he gave it a pretty good shot. He was downright rude when we first met. But I'm stubborn." She plants her hands on her hips. "And I wasn't letting a little snow and a grumpy hulk of a man get the better of me in a confined space."

Chuckling, I pull out a chair for her, indicating she should sit and let me handle the drinks. A little snow, she says. Enough to shut down an airport in the Midwest.

Mom pulls out the seat across from Talia, and Dad sits down next to Mom. She shoves Dad. "Don't listen to Earl. I don't have *that* many questions. Just a few. Dozen. And if you'd like for us to leave so we can meet up for dinner as planned, that works too."

Mom's words say one thing, but the hope in her eyes says something else entirely. Thankfully, Talia speaks 'Mom', and she seems happy enough to let them stay. I'll pull her aside in a while, but for now, I let them have their time with her, watching and listening from the counter as I make drinks for everyone.

I'm handing Dad's coffee to him when Mom says, "So, tell me how you feel about marriage." She's leaning so far forward on her chair she's practically in Talia's face.

"Well, Mrs. Coleman."

"Mariam," Mom supplies.

"Mariam," Talia concedes. "Well, Mariam. I think conversations about marriage shouldn't happen within the first month of a relationship. Especially when one party lost his beloved wife, and the other party has gotten out of an arranged engagement to a toxic butthead."

Mom sits back in her chair, her eyes flexing at this new titbit of information. She nods. "You're right. Definitely none of my business but I can't deny you've now piqued my curiosity with that salacious detail. We'll wait until we get to know each other better. Favorite color?"

Talia points to her hair, and her eyes. "Blue. You?"

"Green." Mom and Dad answer together, it's cute he remembers those details about her.

"Would you rather be able to talk with animals or with plants?" Talia levels Mom with an intense stare.

"Animals. We have the bitchiest cat ever to walk the earth, I'd love to know what she's saying when she meows at us."

Talia nods like it makes total sense.

"Favorite food?" Mom volleys back.

"All of it." Talia pauses, sighs at Mom's arched eyebrow, and then purses her lips. "Chili. It's so versatile. Over rice, in a baked potato, on tortilla chips to make nachos..." She licks her lips. "Now I want chili."

Dad nods. "Me too."

"Would you rather have to keep a terrible haircut for a month or let your mother dress you for a month?"

Mom laughs. "Haircut. I can hide it under a hat."

Talia giggles. The barrage of getting to know you and would you rather questions continue between my girlfriend and my parents, we order chili from a local cafe for lunch—over fries, on a potato, and over tortilla chips, and by the afternoon Talia's napping in my arms on the couch while Mom knits her a scarf on the loveseat next to Dad.

If you'd told me a couple weeks ago I'd be sitting here right now, I'd have laughed in your face. I had no intention of letting my defenses down even a little. I wasn't so much as considering giving my heart to another woman in my lifetime. I was done.

I'd loved, I'd lost, and I'd built myself a fortress around my chest so I couldn't feel anything ever again.

But staring down at the force of nature lying in my arms, I can't help but think this one might be worth feeling for.

Epilogue

TALIA

(Six months later)

IT TURNS OUT, THE LOCAL STITCH AND BITCH MEETS twice a week. Once at the hotel where Jagger and I met them, and the other at the Sugar Bean cafe. Mama and I walk in, arms laden with a bunch of supplies I'll probably never use because Mama seems to have taken all the yarn skills in the family, and the whole group stops to assess us.

Betty, Gertie, and Philomena are sitting side by side, they pause, place their projects in their lap and raise their eyebrows together, like a synchronized event. If they were in the Olympics, they'd get full points.

"Talia! How did you find us? You're not one of those stalker kinds, are you?" Betty purses her lips as though she's really giving it consideration.

"Betty, if you don't want to be stalked, you probably shouldn't hang fliers up with the exact location and time of your meetings."

She approaches me with her arms outstretched. "I suppose

you have a point. Did you figure your shit out?" She eyes Mama like she knows there was something hinky going on, but doesn't say anything.

"Yes, ma'am."

"And you're still with that delicious drink of water, right?" Her eyes narrow like she'll kick me out of her knitting cult if I say I'm not with Jagger, and considering how some of the ladies behind her are already on the edge of their seats waiting for an answer, she probably has the votes.

My cheeks burn. "Yes, ma'am. I am still with Jagger."

Philomena fans herself. "Lucky bitch."

Mama introduces herself to the ladies and while they make space, I order three drinks. Mariam is on her way. I can't tell if Mama and Mariam schemed to quick-learn how to knit and crochet so we could do this activity together when Mama is in town, or if they've always been crafty and simply needed an excuse to get out and hang out.

The dads are watching sports together, and Jagger's doing some extra hours at the shop so we can get away early to go out for Addison's birthday dinner. Except, it's not at all her birthday dinner. It's her engagement dinner.

I found Thor staring at the ring last week in Protocol. Poor guy was pooping his pants. I assured him I wouldn't spill the beans, and she will absolutely, positively say yes to his proposal.

The ring is blindingly gorgeous. Like, a weapon-of-mass-destruction level huge. Way too big for me, but absolutely perfect for Adi. She's going to love it. I told him that, too.

By the time I sit down with our sloshing mugs of various hot drinks, Mariam has already crammed herself in between Betty and Philomena and is making new friends as she untangles two projects that were shoved in her bag.

"Stitch and Bitch with the mother in law, Talia." Betty clicks her tongue.

"Does this mean you and Jagger are going to tie the knot soon?" Philomena smirks over at me, expectation in her eyes.

I flap my hand at them, ignoring the stares of both Mama and Mariam. "It's barely been seven months you guys."

"When you know, you know." One of the other ladies pokes me in the arm. "And we all knew when we got snowed in. Get with the program, Talia, dear."

It's hard not to laugh, but she's also not wrong. I do love Jagger with all my heart, and if the last six months have taught me anything, it's that the more time that passes, the more I love him. There's no taking anything back at this point. We're end game. I know it, and he knows it, but I'm not going to rush or push him into anything.

"He'll be ready when he's ready, y'all." Leaning into my Southern roots makes Mama smile. "And if he's never ready, he's never ready. I don't need a piece of paper to tell me that he loves me. I feel that in here." I touch my chest.

"Okay, but y'all're gonna give me grandbabies, right?" The concern in Mama's voice makes me giggle, especially when Mariam puts down her coffee cup and levels me with a stare.

"Talia, baby, please don't tell me we're not getting grandbabies. I know it's your body, your choice and all, but... you'd make the most beautiful human beings this world has ever seen." She already knows we want kids, in fact, we want kids more than we want to get married.

I'm tempted to throw my skein of yarn at her. "Yes, Mama, yes Mariam, yes, Betty, Gertie and Philomena, we are hoping to have a whole army of little Jaggers and Talias running around tugging on all your yarn projects."

Mama claps her hands together, Mariam picks her coffee up and takes a long slurp before nodding. My suspicions that they've already picked out our kids' names are confirmed as I watch both our mothers interact with the women we met when fate brought us together and snowed us in at the hotel.

They've even picked out the flowers for the wedding, and one of the women in the group's grandson is in a band that would be "perfect" for my vibe.

I'm not sure what vibe that is, but it's making them happy to talk about a future for Jagger and I, and since that discussion also makes me happy, I can't bring myself to ask them to stop, even if it may never come to pass.

By six o'clock, I'm starving. I came so close to blurting out the surprise to Addison as we drove to the restaurant for her birthday meal. As much as my guy hates people, and groups of people, he's becoming more social for my benefit.

And my getting closer with the girls is giving him an excuse or permission to get closer to the guys, too. He may pretend he hates people, but his own people...? He really freakin' loves, and he's even getting better about showing it.

It's been enjoyable to watch. He hugged Thor last week, and the poor guy thought Jagger was dying or something.

Speaking of Thor, he's pale as a sheet. He's recently cut his hair, so he can't even hide behind the curtain of locks. Jagger knocks Thor's knee with his own shortly after we're seated.

I'm not sure Addison has noticed her guy is a bag of nervous energy, but I'm drowning in it, gulping it down as it rolls off him in waves. Hopefully he's not going to make us all wait until the end of the night before he pops the question.

Slade and Paige are the last of our party to be seated, and from the disheveled nature of Slade's tie and the lipstick marks on his cheek, they've been here for longer than we've known.

It's weird to me that they're together considering how much Paige loathed him when we first met, but it works. I guess all that chemistry meant it couldn't not work, right?

The server pours champagne for everyone, except Mackenzie who told us last week she and Austin are expecting. My heart is so full for my friends. I may not have known them for as long as they've known each other but each of them is family to me all the same.

Thor picks up a spoon and clinks his glass, bringing a hush to the table. "Can I have everyone's attention please?"

At this point, there's not a single person in the restaurant who isn't watching us.

"I know we're here tonight to belatedly celebrate Addison's birthday from last week, but that's not really why I asked you all to join us."

Addison's face morphs from elation to confusion. But when Thor slides off his chair onto one knee, her gasp is swallowed by the collective gasps around the room, and tears trickle down her face.

"You have brought more to my life than I knew was even missing, Kitten. And the way you love me and Matty with all your heart is special, you're special, and I want you to be mine for always." Tears trickle off the tip of his nose as he shakes his head. "I had better shit planned to say than that, but I feel like I'm gonna puke so could you please say yes so our friends can eat?"

His verbal vomit is adorable, and before anyone can breathe, or blink, Addison has launched herself off her seat and straight onto Thor. He lands on his back with a thud. "Is that a yes?"

She nods as she kisses him, and we've already ordered our appetizers before they come up off the floor for air. The others carry on like they see this all the time, but the amusement of the other patrons and staff is clear.

They say it comes in threes, Kenzie having a baby, Addison getting engaged, and from the way Slade is looking at Paige it won't be long before he pops the question, but I'm hoping the third thing will be Jagger saying yes when I ask him if we can live together, on our way home from dinner.

The Stich and Bitch crew were right about something, I love him wholeheartedly and want to spend all my free time with my favorite person. That would be easier if we lived under the same roof.

Hopefully, he agrees.

Epilogue

JAGGER

As we climb the steps into the plane taking us to Talia's childhood home in Louisville, Kentucky there's an easy calm over my whole body. Our friends got engaged over dinner last night, and on the way home my quiet and nervous Half-Pint asked me to move in with her.

After we talked through options for a couple hours, we decided to rent out her place and she'll move into mine. There's a shameful amount of space in my house, and I'd love for her to help me fill it. Plus, we stay there more often than not since it's closer to my garage.

When I get to our row, I take a step back to make space, pausing behind my seat. Talia's wild eyes meet mine. "I'll take the window." Her voice is breathy, her cheeks pink, and she's got the tiniest glimmer of concern in her features.

Probably because there's a toy inside her body, and I have the remote control to set it off at any time tucked safely in the front of my jeans. She's had it inside her from the moment we got through security. I haven't set it off yet, but the light sheen of sweat across her forehead tells me she's struggling.

I'm not sure if she's struggling with the ache building in

her body, or the fact if I set it off in public, she'll have to stay quiet, and I can say many things about my beautiful baby girl from our seven months together, but quiet, she is not.

She plops onto the chair with a whimper.

"Easy, baby girl. You can't go slapping that pussy of mine around. Forget what was inside you, did you?" I slide my fingers into the front pocket of my jeans. "Maybe I should remind you."

She smacks my hand, rolling her lips between her teeth and shaking her head so frantically her blue hair falls into her face. "No, please. Not while people are boarding." Her eyes leave mine, finding the line of people in the aisle waiting with their carry-ons and ready to find their seat so we can leave.

"Please?" The word is a plea, I'm not sure if she's pleading with me to turn it on, or not to, but either way my fingers are itching and twitching. The temptation to make her fall apart right here as people walk past is fucking intense.

By the time we're fully boarded, pre-flight checks are done, and we're up at cruising altitude, my girl is fast asleep. If it was quieter, I'm sure I'd hear those adorable little snores as she snoozes. Joke's on her, however, because things are about to get interesting.

The toy she's wearing can't be comfortable, it's C-shaped, with a piece sitting pretty on her clit, or probably near her clit given all the movement, and the other part is inside her, resting against her g-spot. Her face is still flushed. She's never worn something like this inside her for this long, and I know she's probably soaking through those yoga pants she's wearing.

If it wasn't a full flight, I'd haul her tiny ass to the bathroom and fuck her over the sink, but getting stuck in an airplane bathroom with my cock out isn't something I have planned for this trip.

Pulling out the small controller, I smile to myself. I'm so fucking excited to watch my baby girl struggle at thirty thousand feet. It's going to be glorious. I give the power button a squeeze turning it on to the first setting. The vibration seems to be so slight it doesn't impact Talia as she sleeps.

Leaving it for a while, I enjoy watching her sleep. After a few minutes, her lips part. When I push the button again, it takes another beat or two for anything to register, but while her eyes remain closed, her hand slips between her thighs.

It's a slow wake up into consciousness for my girl. I give her time, letting her come around and realize what's happening—even if all I want to do is go straight to the tenth and strongest setting and make her scream for everyone to hear.

The way her hand cups her pussy is so fucking hot. I still can't hear her, the plane is so loud her whimpers are being swallowed by the ambient noise, but she's panting, her chest is rising and falling in quick succession.

Another click of the remote makes her eyes fly open, and her teeth sink into her bottom lip. Another click and her knees press together, her head turning so her wild stare can find my gaze.

Her hips are grinding against the chair, her head tipped back, mouth parted in a silent scream as she tries to ride the toy crammed inside her dripping wet pussy. My cock's pressing at the seam of my jeans, rock-hard and ready to pound my girl into oblivion. But I don't touch it. The noise of the plane is drowned out by the hammering of my own heartbeat in my ears. My leg is pressed against my girl's thigh, and where our bodies touch, sparks ignite, the need burning through the fabric of my clothes.

The impulse to pick her up, rip off her pants, and shove my face in her aching cunt is raw, deep, and urgent. I'd encourage her to hold on tight to the headrest behind my head and ride my face like the uninhibited goddess she is.

Her hand clamps onto my thigh, eyes and lips squish

closed, and her free hand covers her face like that might silence her body into stillness. Another click of the remote and she's gone, her body shudders, her nails sink deeper into my thigh leaving a bite of pain despite the thick clothing, and her eyes now roll back into her head.

Her body jerks and spasms, convulsing and twitching for what feels like hours. I lose track of how many times she comes, but I don't turn off the toy for at least twenty minutes.

Talia progresses from gripping my thigh and covering her face to straight up biting her knuckles and clutching the chair so tight her knuckles turn white.

Leaning over to speak in her ear is a mistake, that waft of vanilla invades my nostrils and makes me want to do dirty, dirty things to my pretty little girl.

If she was wearing a skirt or dress, I'd consider plopping her on my lap and fucking her right here to take the edge off. The idea of her deplaning and walking into baggage claim with my cum rolling down the inside of her thighs has me biting the inside of my cheek.

I'm going to have to go into the bathroom and let off some steam. I'm not sure I can take the pressure of the plane and the pressure building in my pants.

"One more for me, baby girl. You can give me one more, can't you, beautiful?"

Her eyes flex wild, sweat trickling down her exhausted, flushed face. She shakes her head.

"What's your safeword, Half-Pint?"

She shakes her head, rolling her lips back between her teeth and biting down.

"Talia?" The growl that comes out of me is animalistic.

"Unicorn," she says loudly enough for me to hear.

"Are you using it?"

She shakes her head again. "Not using it."

"Okay. Can you be a good girl for your Daddy and come

again for me?" I cup her head with my palm, pulling her face toward mine. When I press a soft kiss to her forehead, her body sags. "Such a good girl for your Daddy, aren't you baby girl? Always ready to give him what he needs. And you know that right now, what Daddy needs is just one more orgasm from his baby girl, isn't that right?"

I push the button again as I pull her face to mine, our lips crashing together in a vicious kiss as I swallow the moans and cries of the orgasm that threatens to pull her apart at the seams.

When she reaches the apex of her release, she breaks the kiss, grabbing my body and spearing her teeth into my shoulder. I grunt, not flexing or moving away from her. Instead, I hold her against me, pressing her into my body as the last tremors and aftershocks leave her weary body.

As soon as the seatbelt signs are switched off, I pull her into my lap and hold her against my body as she sleeps for the remainder of the flight. This woman might be little but she's also fucking fierce.

I can't wait to ask her grandmother for the family engagement ring. She got it back a few months ago. Harry the halfwit handed it back to Talia's parents when we were all together in the hotel. And while I'm not sure when exactly I'm going to ask her granddaughter to marry me, I do know Talia loves that fucking ring.

And with any luck, she'll even say yes when I ask her.

If you're not ready to be done with Talia and Jagger, I've written up a spicy little bonus scene where Talia gets to tick off #14 on her list (kissing a girl):

https://dl.bookfunnel.com/nou9nozsnb

Author Note #1

Have you ever sat down to ~~write~~ read a book and the characters come out differently to how you imagined them when you were going in? That's what happened with Talia and Jagger for me.

I had planned the forced proximity, I'd planned the grumpy sunshine, but the nature of her complex history with Harry and her parents, and the epically slow burn were not on my 'Obey' bingo card.

It's weird how characters take shape throughout the crafting process, we start with a blank page and make a list. You sit down and say right, this character's going to be like this, and then when you get into their psyche, deep-dive into their past, their trauma, their personality you realize you were a little off the mark, and they guide you into fixing it so you tell their story the right way.

Let's address the elephant in the room because I can feel the cringe vibes from here. We're clearing one thing up from the get-go, okay?

Having a daddy kink is *not* about your actual dad.

I'm not one to kink shame, but the idea of a daddy kink being correlated in any way to my actual father gives me the ick. And a lot of people get ick-ed out because they don't understand the psychology behind the dynamic. It's most definitely not about biology (at least generally speaking.) If you're curious, there's a cosmic crap ton of reading you can do on the subject – be careful what you search on the internet or at least make sure your security settings are on so you don't end up with pages of porn!

Society is a fucker. It has conditioned us to think about one very niche and specific thing when the term is used, a single, familial definition, when in the kink sphere, it's another pet name in the list of things for people to call each other.

For some people it's about the dynamics, being taken care of, trust, vulnerability, and intimacy. And just because someone has a daddy kink doesn't mean they have issues with their own father figure. It's not because they're damaged or broken that they want to call their lover "daddy."

A Daddy Dom is a protector, providing guidance, affection, protection, safety, and sometimes discipline and decision making to his Little. "Daddy" is the brand of dominance that a dominant leans into—as opposed to say a sadist dominant, or a pleasure dominant.

Like I said, I didn't set out to incorporate a DDLG dynamic into this book, it was nowhere to be seen on my outline. But as the relationship between Jagger and Talia started to unfold, it evolved very naturally into that space. I think in the end it came out pretty damn beautifully. Jagger is the perfect Daddy Dom to his Little, and Talia, while she enjoys the role of a Little in the bedroom, spends much of the book reclaiming her strength and owning herself and that contrast, that counterpoint, is something a lot of people enjoy in their lives too.

So many of my strong, stoic, powerhouse friends who are boss bitches during the day, mom bitches at night, balancing school pick-ups and after school activities, and doing all.the.things ache to hand over control and submit to their partner. There's something freeing about handing over control to someone else.

It's not just about your dominant making the decision to order what's for dinner on any given night, it's deeper, it's more, and that responsibility is something that any dominant worth their salt will take incredibly seriously.

Anyway, this dynamic kind of blindsided me, I had plans to write a DDLG dynamic later in the series but these two owned it, and I have zero regrets.

I'd love to complain they took forever to write, or that they gave me deep and traumatic pain to work through like some of my other couples. But the truth of the matter is, Jagger and Talia flowed from my fingers with relative ease.

Once I let them lead me, they told me their story with eagerness (and adorableness). They also made me haul in some old familiar faces to help tell their story—which I have to admit, I love. Seeing Austin and Mackenzie from Two for Boarding in my Minnesota Snow Pirates series make such a strong reappearance in this series makes my heart happy as they were one of my favorite couples to write and one of my reader's favorites in my back list.

A drive-by Thor and Adi action never hurt anyone either, right? I'm loving watching this found family grow. Seeing Paige, Adi, and Kenzie bring Talia into their fold filled my heart with happiness. If there's one thing we all know I love, it's found family. And I can't *wait* for the Sub Club to grow over the rest of this series.

I feel like I've really pushed myself out of my comfort zone in some ways with embarking on this new pen name in this sub-genre, and yet in others, it kinda feels like I've found home.

Author Note # 2

Why are you writing about a black guy?

This question is one I've had enough times over the past couple of weeks—since I announced my cover model in my reader group—to warrant me answering the question right here for everyone to see.

For those of you new to my writing, this pen name is one of two. My original pen name is Lasairiona McMaster. And if this is the first book of mine that you've read, it's important for you to know that I write diverse and inclusive romance. I write my worlds and my characters in rainbows because the world is full of color, and it's one of the most beautiful parts of our existence.

I write LGBTQ+ characters, leaning into the bi-sexual characters because, as a bi-sexual author, those are my 'own voice.'

I write culturally diverse characters because while I'm an almost-40-year-old white woman, I've traveled the world, immersed myself in other cultures, and writing one culture, race, or color of skin just isn't my jam.

In my very first series (which has since been pulled from sale to get re-edited and re-worked) I had a black guy side character, he played hockey, was gay, and everyone absolutely fucking loved him. My readers begged me for his story, and I was too scared to even contemplate writing a gay black man's story.

But the more I grow as an author, the more I find my feet,

my voice, and my desire to write a diverse fictional world to reflect the diversity I'm surrounded by in the real world.

I'll also give you a heads up—this series will also have an F/F, Sapphic, lesbian romance as one of the books as well, because this world, these characters, they're every color of every rainbow, and I'm so blessed and honored to tell their stories.

Did you use black, male authenticity/sensitivity readers?

Yes. I did. I get outside input on culture, race, and even things I haven't experienced first-hand whether that's in hockey, or kink, I ask people who know more than I do about what I'm writing.

For this book my authenticity readers, EJ, G, Jenny, and Chris gave me input on my black male representation. And for that, I can't thank them enough.

Acknowledgments

Lewis—As always, my heart, my light, my little dictator who keeps me right and makes sure I get shit done so he can tick off my wall of Post-Its, you're amazing. These past few months have been hard, you've gone from being a little boy to a tween, and we're learning to navigate this awkward space of growing up. It's not easy, but I'm so epically fucking proud of you, and you have no idea. Stay brave, little man, stay brave, love big, and keep asking questions. I love you, always.

Tracie—We always manage to get out of sync. We'll say right, let's start a book at the same time, and we'll never finish together. You were plotting your big scary new series while I wrote this one, and some days the absence of a 6am kick in the cooter was profoundly felt. But you still kept me on task, you still ignored my whining, demanded greatness, and pushed me over the finish line with the sole of your shoe firmly stuck to my injured butt cheeks.

Your guidance and logic are so fucking frustrating—wait, I mean really annoying sometimes—kidding, while they're all those things, they're also things that center and ground me when my Enneagram 4 feelings get all kinds of messed up and overwhelming.

I'd be lost without you.

Karina—Despite the fact you refused to write the ending of this book for me when I got lazy and threw a tantrum at The Prom, and despite the fact you suggested putting dinosaurs or zombies at the end, I still love you. Mondays at The Prom with the asshat who vapes under his jacket, the best gravy chips in town, and copious amounts of procrastination and tea, break the back of my week for me and help set me up for success. But more than that, they've brought us closer together, and I am so proud of watching your authorling wings spreading a little more each week.

Andrew—How could I do what I do and write these books if you didn't listen to me whine about Phil at the gym, or shit being too hard, or my feelings overwhelming me, or Lewis hating me and losing his shit because I confiscated his Xbox controllers without you telling me to cool my heels and take a breath? I couldn't. Thank you for keeping me semi-cool under immeasurable pressure, and making me laugh through my many, many tears.

Shaun—The last stages of this book were sponsored by our long-distance white chocolate and macadamia nut cookies —which didn't help the waistline but helped the productivity —and your lectures about fitness, nourishing my body, hydrating, and not being a dick to myself when I was being a dick to myself. You'd think after twenty years of friendship I'd be used to your lectures, but you're still an ever present pain in my already sore ass.

Jenny—Thanks for stepping in at the 11th hour and giving this a run through for me. You recognized my panic and stepped up like the boss bitch you are. Thank you for making time for me, my book, and for helping me to make it better. I can't wait to smush you so hard with my boobage this fall.

Ivy—I'm not sure you know how much I love you to pieces, or how much I respect your knowledge and experience and ability to give feedback in a helpful (and pleasant) way. When I finished writing Jagger and Talia, I was convinced you wouldn't want to read them, just as I was convinced you wouldn't want to read Thor and Adi. You, my dear friend, are #KinkGoals, and I am so very grateful for your friendship over the past few years.

Melanie and Irene—Y'all put up with an inordinate amount of bullshit from me on the daily and you still love me all the same. I appreciate you all more than I can say, but I needed to mention it because you'd kick me off the island if I didn't. You're all amazing, and I'm eternally grateful for your patience and ability to repeat your advice over and over and over again when I get tunnel audio and need it given to me again.

My VIP Club Protocol Ream Subscribers—Ashley Lewis – my very first subscriber ever! And Erica a quick number two, Anne, Chann3rz, Schellie, Sandra, and Lyn. You guys took a chance on me when I started out doing something new. My subscription platform was new and scary, and I wasn't sure I was going to be 'enough' to inspire people to come and get early access of chapters. I can't thank you all enough for your support and encouragement of my work. And I can't wait to keep growing that platform and bringing y'all exclusive content and fun things in the coming months.

The Prom (Megan), Twilight (Kara, Paddy, Conor, Siobhan), Springsteens (Mariann and Laura)—Regardless of the stage of my process, whether it's plotting, drafting, editing, or staring into space and drinking tea to avoid actually working on my manuscript, you guys are always there with tea, good craic, and smiles to make the process a little less painful.

My Alpha readers—Amy R and Katie 'Violence' Wilks. Y'all are a part of the furniture by now. This one was a weird one, it came in fits and starts and took a while to find its feet, but you guys were there for each chapter asking for more and keeping me right. Thank you both, as always, for making sure I don't lose my shit and burn the manuscript to the ground.

Christiana—Real talk: I was absofuckinglutelyterrified of you getting access to my document, and I was 291% sure you'd hate it. Thank you for adding context where I was lacking, and for helping me out when I got tangled up and thought I was shit. You're the best.

Sheena Hensler - It's okay, Jesus Understands – Gerkins 8:69. That's it. That's the no context acknowledgement. I hope you laugh as hard as I do.

My Editor—Editor Jess at heaauthorservices.com—*flails in ugh.* I'm having a moment. I always do when I get to the end of the book and have to send it to you. Meeting you last year was pretty cool, getting to hang out with you for a whole week and pick your brain on things was even cooler, but the way you've helped course-correct certain things in my business and career has been life changing. Thank you for having my back, and my manuscript, especially when sometimes I have no fuckin' clue what I'm doing.

My cover designer—Lori Jackson—Another winner in the books (literally! Lol!) this series has been gorgeous from the get-go in so far as covers, and I appreciate your patience, attention to detail, and your hard work to make each cover beautiful.

And finally, my proofreader Corinne, my ARC readers, my Facebook reader group *Margaritas, Men, and Mischief with Lasairiona*, and to each and every one of you who pick up this book: a bazillion thank yous. I truly hope you loved it enough to pick up the next one. Tell your friends! And if you're not in my group—come join us, we don't bite (unless you ask us to!)

Resist

PROTOCOL: BOOK THREE

If you you're a glutton for punishment, then don't forget to preorder book three in the Protocol series... It's irresistible!

Preorder RESIST now :

books2read.com/protocolresist1

About the Author

Lasairiona Lewis writes sassy, classy and badassy women and strong, yet vulnerable men. She challenges reader's expectations by openly dealing with mental health issues, often exploring tough-to-handle topics and 'taboos' and books with a whole lotta heart.

She can either be found enjoying a gin and lemonade by the Irish sea, or baking sweet treats in her kitchen while singing at the top of her lungs. When she's 'home' in Texas, and isn't eating fresh-popped popcorn while buying things she has absolutely no need for in Target, she can be found at Chuys eating her body weight in chips and queso and washing it down with a margarita swirl. She loves to make friends out of strangers.

www.Lasairiona.com

Sign up to my newsletter:
https://sendfox.com/QueenOfFireLas

facebook.com/QueenofFireLas
instagram.com/queenoffirelas
bookbub.com/authors/lasairiona-e-mcmaster
amazon.com/author/lasairionamcmaster

Made in the USA
Monee, IL
22 April 2024

57070513R10184